Charles Royce was but thirteen years of age when his stepfather, the Earl of Weybridge, arranged for his kidnap and murder. But instead of burying his body in a shallow grave, as ordered by the earl, his kidnapper sells him to the Captain of a slave ship bound for Jamaica.

Eighteen years later, when Charles returns to London society to attain his revenge, it is as a very different person indeed.

For, whilst in Jamaica, Charles becomes Charlotte, a beautiful young debutante and wife to one of the richest plantation owners on the island. When her husband succumbs to yellow fever, the beautiful and fabulously rich Lady Charlotte returns to England with one ambition in mind — the complete and utter destruction of the Earl of Weybridge.

Lady Charlotte soon discovers, however, that revenge is not a dish best served cold, after all. Instead, she discovers revenge is a dish best tempered with love for her friends, with love for her family, and with her love for a very special man.

Lady Charlotte's Revenge
Copyright © 2019Charlotte Johnson
ISBN: 978-1-4874-2486-2
Cover art by Martine Jardin

Published by eXtasy Books Inc or
Devine Destinies, an imprint of eXtasy Books Inc

Look for us online at:
www.eXtasybooks.comorwww.devinedestinies.com

LADY CHARLOTTE'S REVENGE

BY

CHARLOTTE JOHNSON

CHAPTER ONE

James Beaufort, 8th Duke of Camberly, stood before the ornate silvered mirror on the wall of his study and smiled to his reflection benevolently. He had, as usual, spent an hour or so on his correspondence, just as he did most mornings. This had been followed by a visit from Mr Paul, his *Man of Business*, for the monthly inspection of the estate books, and James had been exceedingly pleased with the state of affairs. Why even the estate in Scotland was turning a profit, thanks in part to the changes in farming policy he had introduced when succeeding his father.

"A good thing, too, for Anne's gowns alone are costing a small fortune," he said to himself.

Carefully he poured himself a small glass of his favourite Scottish whiskey and then wandered over to the picture window to stare out into the garden of his London townhouse, his attention drawn by the laughter he could hear. It was a beautiful day, and James found himself smiling once more as he observed his daughter with her friend, Lady Jane Chalmers, the two of them engaged in some sort of feminine conversation that would surely baffle any gentleman listening in.

Unexpectedly, his heart and mind became suffused with a host of mixed emotions. At very nearly nineteen years of age, Lady Anne Beaufort had blossomed into an incredibly beautiful and accomplished young woman. Not only was she a talented musician, being proficient on both pianoforte and harp, but she had also taken responsibility for the efficient

1

management of the household of Grantly Manor, doing so with grace, humour, and sensitivity that endeared her to each and every servant.

But he knew time was fast approaching when he would be destined to lose her to another, and the thought saddened him intensely.

Three weeks before, the entire household had moved to the townhouse in Belgrave Square, so that preparations could be made for Lady Anne's first season in London. In two weeks' time she would be formally presented to the Prince Regent at court, and, a day later, would make her first appearance at the Duchess of Harrow's famous debutante's ball.

Yet again James wished, with all his heart, that his beloved wife still lived. Margaret would have shielded her daughter with the ferocity of a mama bulldog protecting her pups. She would have helped Anne to avoid the less scrupulous members of the *ton,* who would think nothing of compromising a naive young lady in order to get hold of a sizeable dowry. Margaret would have gently guided her daughter through the trials and tribulations of the marriage mart to make the best possible choice, only ever considering a love match to be good enough for her girl.

"Perhaps you should have remarried. At least then you would have had a suitable chaperon for Anne," he groaned, knowing that talking to himself this way was never a good sign.

James shook his head sadly as he turned from the window, relishing the burn of the whiskey in the back of his throat as he sipped his drink. At four and fifty years of age, whilst no longer in the bloom of youth, he was still a fit and active man, and was often told by his friends that he could easily attract a wife should he so wish. But when Margaret had died, part of his heart had died too, and he had no desire whatsoever to offer it once more, only to have it crushed yet again. Besides, he needed no wife, for he already had a wonderful daughter in Anne, and his son, Richard, Viscount Addington, was developing into a splendid young man. Currently on his grand tour after graduating from Cambridge University, he would undoubtedly be a credit to the title of duke when it became his turn to inherit.

"But the fact remains," he mumbled aloud, "that I still need to find Anne a suitable chaperon if she is to have her season. Perhaps I will have to ask Mother after all."

Inwardly, he groaned at that thought, for he had no doubt that, despite the affection Anne held for her grandmother, she would not relish the idea of the dowager duchess being appointed as her chaperon.

Suddenly, a polite yet firm knock on the closed study door interrupted his train of thought and, as James looked up, Stevens, his butler, entered, holding a small silver tray in one hand. Despite his advanced age, the man's back was ramrod straight and the uniform he wore as immaculate as ever.

"Yes, what is it, Stevens?"

"There is a lady caller, your grace, requesting a moment of your time. I told her that you were unavailable, but she was most insistent. She asked me to give you this." The man held out his silver tray.

On the tray was a calling card that was clearly of superior quality and, after picking it up, James viewed it carefully, noting that the name was beautifully embossed in real gold leaf.

Lady Charlotte Winters.

Instantly, James's interest was aroused. Lady Charlotte Winters! He had heard that name bandied around his club over the past couple of weeks, where speculation about the woman was rife. By all accounts, she was a widow recently returned from the West Indies and was said to be as rich as Croesus himself. She would have to be, if she was to rent Conway House for the whole of the season, the townhouse only four doors away from his own in Belgrave Square.

Looking up he smiled at the butler.

"You had better show her in, I suppose. Is she chaperoned?" he asked with a sudden afterthought.

"Yes, your grace. By the biggest African man I have ever seen. But she has requested that she speak to you alone."

"Oh, very well. Show her in, Stevens."

"In here, your grace?" Stevens gave him an incredulous look, his expression leaving no doubt in James' mind that his butler thought the study was a highly inappropriate place for such a meeting.

"Yes, in here," he snapped.

"Yes, your grace." Stevens sighed and gave a cursory bow before turning back to the door, leaving James in no doubt that his butler disapproved of his choice of room.

As he waited, James could not help but speculate as to who or what this woman was all about. Just the fact that she had requested to see him alone suggested she might be a woman of advanced years, for no respectable lady would risk her reputation by being un-chaperoned.

Yes, she's probably as old as the hills and as ugly as sin, too.

A few moments later there was another knock, and James watched as Stevens opened the study door, standing to one side to respectfully permit his visitor to enter.

"Lady Winters, your grace," Stevens announced, so as to facilitate some form of formal introduction. "His grace, the Duke of Camberley."

In preparation for meeting the woman, James had schooled his expression into one of benign indifference, and he suddenly found himself offering a silent prayer of thanks to the gods for doing so. For had he not, he knew, without any shadow of doubt, he most probably would have gasped aloud when he first glimpsed his visitor.

Old she was not. Nor ugly as sin.

James had always been an admirer of the feminine form, and the lady who stood before him matched, in every way, his ideal. She appeared to be around thirty years of age and was dressed in a beautiful cream coloured day dress that must have been expensively tailored to perfectly fit her slim, graceful body. She was tall for a lady, yet still a good head shorter than he. Her arms were slender and graceful, her breasts small yet pert, her waist trim, and her lovely auburn tresses had been expertly crafted into a very pretty chignon, a style that left little tendrils of hair framing her face to perfection.

And what a face it was.

Contrary to fashion, she wore cosmetics upon her skin. Unlike some women of his acquaintance, who seemed to plaster the stuff on with a trowel, Lady Winters wore but a subtle application of makeup. She was enhanced with a light dusting of powder on her perfect skin and a little rouge on her cheeks to emphasise her high and aristocratic cheekbones. She also wore kohl on her lashes, which only served to draw his gaze to her startlingly blue eyes, and a little ruby stain on her plump and very kissable lips.

In short, Lady Charlotte Winters was undeniably beautiful.

Suddenly, James felt the heat rise in his cheeks as he remembered his earlier uncharitable thoughts. So he bowed politely to allow a moment to compose himself, shaking his head a little to clear his mind of all the improper thoughts that seemed to be lodged there.

Graciously, he indicated an armchair to one side of the room. "Please, Lady Winters, please be seated. May I offer you some refreshment? Tea perhaps?"

"No, thank you, your grace," she replied.

Lady Winters took the offered chair, smoothing her skirts beneath her so she could sit demurely, and James moved to a second chair, deliberately maintaining a neutral expression as he contemplated the woman's speaking voice. From her appearance, he had expected a soft, high pitch to her words, but she had spoken with a deeper, huskier tone that, in his mind, only added to the woman's allure.

James was intrigued.

"So, of what service may I be to you, Lady Winters?" he asked, noting the growing nervousness in the expression on his visitor's face.

The woman sighed uneasily, her gaze, at first, cast nervously down to the floor. But then she lifted her head and looked back at him with a deep penetrating stare, her brilliant blue eyes searching his face in a way that instantly reminded him of someone he had once known. The memory of it was there, in the back of his mind, yet for some reason, he could not place it, could not recall who it was that Lady Winters reminded him of.

He stared back at her, suddenly feeling small. For there was something in her expression, an air of stubbornness perhaps, that suggested she was observing him in a manner that would allow her to judge the character of the man before her. Then she smiled, and James could not stop himself from smiling back, knowing, perhaps, that he had passed some unwritten test.

"I have something of great consequence I wish to discuss with you, your grace. But before I begin, I must ask . . . I must ask for your word as a gentleman that what we are to converse about remains between these four walls. Please, your grace, your word. It is of the greatest import to me."

James felt a surge of annoyance as he heard these words. After all, he considered himself a man of integrity, one of high office, and to have someone, especially a young woman, impugn that by actually asking for him to give her his word, irked him considerably.

But then he looked closely at the young woman once more. He noted how she had captured her bottom lip tentatively between her teeth and how her hands were clasped nervously in her lap, and something in him, perhaps an innate ability to judge someone's character, sensed there was no malice intended. Instead, it was quite apparent that the request had been made with but one thing in mind — an obvious desire to protect herself from some ill-conceived scandal, perhaps.

He did not hesitate. "Of course, madam, you have my word as a gentleman."

Lady Winters took a deep breath, and her gaze flickered anxiously away from his. Then her eyebrows furrowed for a moment as she looked back, her expression now one of purpose and resolve, giving James the feeling that he, somehow, had yet again passed some undisclosed test.

She sighed, and her eyes narrowed with fierce determination. "Your grace, I am here with news of Charles Royce, son of the late Sir Oliver Royce and the now Countess of Weybridge . . . and . . . I believe . . . your godson."

In shock, James gasped as all the air seemed to abruptly vacate the room as he registered her words. Then his pulse began to race.

Charles Royce, son of his lifelong friend, Sir Oliver Royce, had disappeared on his way to Eton school for his first term, never to be heard of again. At the time, it was thought he had been taken by a press gang, men who roamed the countryside looking for *willing volunteers* to crew the ever-growing number of ships needed in the war against France. Enquiries had been made, of course, but from that moment on there had simply been no trace of him, and after seven years, he had been presumed dead.

And now this chit of a woman was sitting before him, as bold as brass, saying she had news of him.

"What!" Instantly, James moved to the edge of his seat, closing the distance between them and stared intently into the woman's eyes. "Please, Lady Winters, tell me. Is he alive?"

"Alive and well, and here in London," Lady Winters replied.

"What? Where?" James demanded. "This is incredible news. If this is so, you must take me to him immediately." He jumped to his feet and glared at the woman, hardly daring to believe what he was hearing.

Lady Winters remained motionless on her chair, yet he could plainly see that she was desperately struggling to retain her composure. Apprehension and dread swept across her eyes, and for a moment, he even feared that she was going to rise, that she was going to flee. So with a conscious effort to control himself, he took a step back and breathed deeply in an effort to still his mind.

"Please, madam," he begged. "Can you not tell me where he is? Can you not take me to him?"

"I cannot." Her voice was now almost a whisper as she pointed back to his chair, her gesture beseeching him to sit once more. "I cannot take you to him."

"And, pray tell, why not?"James struggled to contain his anger, his impatience surely evident as he refused to sit. Yet Lady Winters was not to be intimidated, and, in total amazement, James could only glare as she stared back at him, her beautiful gaze holding his own, her small breasts heaving as she once more took a deep breath.

"I cannot take you to him," she whispered, "for he is already before you. You see, your grace, I *am*, or should I say I once *was* your godson, Charles Royce."

CHAPTER TWO

It was like waiting for a volcano to erupt.

As Charlotte uttered her words, she heard the duke take a deep rasping breath, only to hold it there like the calm before the storm. But then his mouth dropped open, his pupils dilating in surprise as what she had said registered upon his mind. Disbelief flooded his face, just as Charlotte had expected it would, his features quickly contorting into anger.

Then tempest broke.

"Well, young lady," he roared. "I am not sure what game you play, but you are certainly *not* Charles Royce. That much is plainly evident."

But Charlotte was prepared and ready to face his incredulity.

"Oh, but I am, Uncle GG," she whispered, using the name she had adopted for him when but three-years-old. "Do you remember how you used to let me ride on your back when I was a child, and how I gave you that name, Uncle GG? Do you remember the pony you bought me for my sixth birthday? I called him Hermes, for I fancied he would fly as fast as the winged god himself. Do you remember how, on the following day, I broke my arm when trying to jump Hermes over a fence that was way too high for the both of us? Do you remember how inconsolable I was when my father died, and how you held me and rocked me to sleep because my mother, in her grief, was incapable of giving me the comfort that I needed? Do you remember how you took me fishing one day, and how I managed, in my desperate enthusiasm to please you, to get a hook in my arm?" she added as she showed the duke the tiny scar on her left forearm. "It was on that day you promised me that you would be as a father to me, to always be there for me," she added as a single tear sprang to her eye. "Do you remember, Uncle GG?"

Slowly the duke sank down onto his chair, his mouth wide open with shock, and Charlotte began to hope, began to believe, that her words might have cut to the chase. Yet there was still anger there, disbelief and scepticism, too.

"No . . . no, it is not possible!" he said, unable to keep the incredulity from his voice. "Knowledge of these things does not justify your claim. You . . . you are plainly not Charles! How could you be? You are . . . you are . . . a . . . a . . . woman!"

"Yes, *plainly*," she echoed. "Yet I am who I claim to be."

"No! Despite what you say, I cannot believe you," the duke countered as he once more stood and glared at her.

"But it is true, and I can prove it. On my right shoulder blade, I have a birthmark. When I was little, my mother used to call it my *angel's kiss*. Do you remember, Uncle James?" Charlotte asked, daring to call him by his given name.

"Yes," he whispered.

"And what shape was the birthmark?"

"I will not say, for you must show me to prove your case."

Very slowly, knowing that the duke was still not ready to believe, Charlotte turned away from him and pulled the shoulder of her dress down over her arm, revealing the delicate outline of her back. There she exposed a small red birthmark in the shape of a perfect crescent moon, a mark that was as unique as any wax seal. For a moment, she sat with her back straight and her eyes closed as she waited for the duke's reaction, the silence between them almost palpable, a silence that was only broken as breath hissed from his mouth.

"Oh my God," he whispered.

"I have but one final proof, your grace." With a knowing smile, Charlotte pulled her dress back over her shoulders and then turned back to the duke. "Although that would require me to divest myself of all my clothes, something I would rather not have to do."

"No . . . no, that will not be necessary," the duke stuttered."But surely you can understand my scepticism. Before me I have a young woman, who claims to be my godson, and, whilst I admit to recognising your birthmark, I . . . I . . . I . . ."

As the duke seemed to lose the ability to speak, Charlotte once more captured his gaze, her mind more than a little troubled with the enormity of what she was about to reveal. However, she also knew that if she were going to be successful in her endeavours, the truth would need to be told to the man before her.

"If I was to tell you what befell me, would you then accept the truth in what I say?" she asked.

"Yes, yes, perhaps. Yes, of course," the duke replied. "Please . . . please do."

CHAPTER THREE

Charlotte took a deep breath and closed her eyes for a moment so as to order her thoughts. Despite an outward appearance of calm, her whole body was trembling and tense, and her heart was pounding so much like the pistons of Mr Stephenson's famous Rocket steam engine, she feared her legs would no longer support her weight should she try to leave.

The duke was just as she remembered him to be, albeit some 15 years older. He was tall, his physique still imposing and masculine, with little sign of the paunchiness that often afflicted most of the older members of the *ton*. Of course, he had more grey in his hair, and his face carried more lines than she recalled, but he remained the handsome man she remembered from her youth. Yes, this was the man she had once called *uncle* all those years before, the man she had trusted as a boy. But so many years had gone by since then, so many hardships and secrets untold that, even though she had repeatedly rehearsed what it was she wanted to reveal to him, she quailed at the prospect.

"As you no doubt remember, I was only eight years of age when my father died in a hunting accident," she croaked and then coughed. "He and my mother were, at that time, the centre of my whole world, a world that was, in an instant, turned upside down. For not only did I lose my father in that dreadful hunting accident, but my mother, too, as her grief overcame her."

"Yes. I remember her anguish and melancholy all too clearly, for even I, her husband's closest friend, could do nothing to console her," the duke replied, the distant look in his eyes giving testament to how much he had actually cared.

"If you recall, our estates bordered those of the Earl of Weybridge's. He played the part of the sympathetic neighbour well and even waited for a whole month after Mother officially came out of mourning before coming to call with nothing but courtship on his mind."

"I remember all too well, and believe me when I say I tried extremely hard to discourage the man."

"I know you did, your grace, and for that, I will be eternally grateful. But Mother was lost, unable to cope, and unable to manage Father's estates on her own. To her, George Hamilton was like a knight in shining armour. Not only did he blind her with his charm and good looks, but, in return for her hand, he also promised to relieve her of the burden of managing the Thorpe estate.

"So they married, and Mother moved to the earl's house at Haycock Abbey to take up her role as countess. I, of course, was required to go with her. This, in turn, meant that I was forced to leave behind everything and everyone I loved, even my pony, Hermes.

"For my part, I hated the earl from the very first moment, almost as much as I hated living at Haycock Abbey. And then there was Henry Hamilton, the earl's son from his first marriage, who, from the outset, seemed to go out of his way to make my life miserable. Mother did her best to shield me from any unpleasantness, but the earl would hear nothing of his son's cruelty and bullying ways.

"One day, after a very unpleasant incident with Henry, my mother took me to one side, and in an effort to bolster my spirits, she explained the terms of my father's will to me. She told me how Thorpe Hall and all of the estate, all three-thousand acres, had been left in trust for me for when I turned one and twenty. Even though I was still very young, when I learned of this I was overjoyed, and, in my childish naivety, I made up my mind to endure my stepfather's and my step-brother's cruelty until I came into my inheritance. Then I determined that when I reached my majority, I would take my mother away with me and we would live in happiness forever at Thorpe Hall."

"Yes, I am aware of the conditions of the will," the duke said, "just as I am aware of what happened after the earl had Charles declared legally dead. The estate, being un-entailed land, reverted to your mother's ownership, and thus, by marriage, to the earl himself. At present, whilst the earl retains tenure of the estate, Lord Henry Hamilton, Charles' step-brother, has Thorpe Hall as his residency. However, I do believe that the estate adds a considerable sum to the earl's coffers each year."

"And that, I believe, is the very reason for my disappearance in the first place," Charlotte muttered in a voice that was barely above a whisper.

"What! Do you mean that the earl was responsible for Charles' . . . er . . . er . . . your disappearance!"

"Yes, in fact, I know so, although, other than my own ears, I have no proof. If I may continue?"

"Yes, yes, by all means."

"I had barely turned thirteen years of age when the earl informed me that I would be starting at Eton. In truth, I was quite excited about the matter, for it would get me away from Henry, who, just the year before, had been sent down from Eton for some serious misdemeanour, and was, by then, attending Harrow instead.

"Mother had wanted to accompany me on my journey to school, but my stepfather would have none of that. He argued that I needed to start standing on my own two feet, and I have to admit that I felt quite *grown up* with the prospect of doing so.

"At first everything went well with the journey. That was until the carriage transporting me to school pulled into a coaching house to change horses, and, instead of staying in the coach, as I had been instructed, I alighted to stretch my legs.

"It was at that very moment my life descended into the very pits of Hell.

"All I really remember is a rough hand clamped around my mouth and a sharp blow on the back of my head. I think this blow must have rendered me unconscious, for the next thing I remember is finding myself bound, gagged, and blindfolded, and lying in the back of a cart underneath a pile of sacking that had been used to conceal me."

"Oh, the bastard . . . er . . . villain." Genuine anger flashed across the duke's eyes.

"We must have travelled for an hour or so before the cart stopped. So as to not reveal myself, I pretended to remain unconscious, but I could clearly hear two different voices discussing me. One, a rough, uncouth voice, clearly came from my abductor. The other unmistakably came from the Earl of Weybridge, my stepfather. I heard him, your grace, as clearly as I hear you now. I heard him pass a purse of coins to the man he had hired to make off with me and I heard him give the man instructions to find a quiet stretch of woodland before putting a bullet in my head and burying me deep. No, there is no doubt in my mind that it was the earl that orchestrated my kidnapping and that he wanted me dead."

"The blackguard. I will kill him for this," the duke growled with barely contained fury.

"Quite. Well, fortunately, or unfortunately, depending on how you look at it, my abductor saw this as an opportunity of making even more money out of the deal. Instead of following the earl's instructions, he took me to Liverpool, a journey of several days, and before I knew what was happening, I had been sold to the master of a slave ship, one Captain Thaddeus Jones, a truly evil man.

"What followed became a period of real despair for me. For you see, whilst the captain could have his pick of the slaves he carried, his sexual tastes lay in a very . . . in a very different direction. There is no polite or easy way of saying this, your grace . . .Jones was a buggerer of boys, and it was to be me on whom he would force his attentions when the desire took him.

"I was shackled like a slave, but in the captain's cabin instead of the hold, and I was repeatedly forced by him to perform whatever sexual perversion he could devise. He was a large man, too, and I but a boy, so his attentions often left me bruised, battered, and bleeding. I was even, on occasion, given to members of the crew. I suppose it was the fact that I was small and slender in stature, almost girlish, that made me appealing to the men. Believe me when I say, having suffered so much at the hands of these men, had I the chance, I would have gladly thrown myself overboard to end my life."

The duke gasped. "Oh, my God. I am so sorry you had to suffer this."

"At first, I tried to resist, but after the beatings I received, I soon learned to acquiesce to their demands, to even feign enthusiasm. I think, perhaps that is why the captain tired of me in the end, for to have me struggle just added to his enjoyment.

"It took nine long months to collect a shipment of slaves and to sail into Kingston in Jamaica. Nine long months of being repeatedly raped."

Once more Charlotte paused in order to compose herself, the horror of these memories almost overwhelming her. Even though it had been so long ago, uncontrollable tears began to form as she spoke aloud of her dreadful experiences. Quite deliberately, now needing a moment to compose herself,

Charlotte took a small handkerchief from her reticule and dabbed at the corner of her eye.

"I'm, sorry, your grace, but the memory of this is still quite distressing for me," she sniffed. "Anyway, shortly after arriving in Kingston, I made a futile attempt to escape, something that the captain did not take too kindly. Rather than beat me, as he had on many occasions before, he instead dragged me ashore by the scruff of the neck. Before I knew what was happening, I was once more sold, this time to the madame of a high-class brothel that catered to the entitled and wealthy of Jamaica."

"I cannot, for the life of me, imagine how you managed to endure," the duke murmured.

"But endure I did. For two more years, I was repeatedly *hired out* to anyone who fancied a boy for the night and had enough coin to pay for me. As you can imagine, I quickly learned to use my body to please those that had bought me, for fear of the punishments I would receive if I did not.

"In a strange sort of way, I also found a kind of family there, too. Like myself, many of the girls who worked in the brothel were just trying to survive, and I soon became like a surrogate *baby* brother to them, one who they tried their best to protect. In fact, at times, it was almost as if I were one of them in all respects.

"This became a very confusing time for me. Often, I would find myself fantasising about what it might be like to actually *be* one of the girls, and countless times, I found myself lying awake at night wishing, with all my heart, I had been born a woman. It got to the point where, more often than not, I would imagine myself as one of the girls when with a *client*, just so that I could forget who and what I actually was.

"Then, as time passed, this fantasy, this need I seemed to have inside me, became an obsession. It was for that very reason that, at the age of fifteen, one of the more experienced girls, Sally, caught me in her room trying on one of her dresses.

"I was mortified to be discovered this way and fully expected the flogging I deserved. But to my surprise, rather than getting angry, Sally took it upon herself to indulge me, to let me put on a dress, to paint my face and arrange my hair into a feminine style. It actually started as a jest, a little harmless fun on a quiet night, but to everyone's amazement, by the time she had finished dressing me, I was, without doubt, a far better-looking girl than boy. It appeared the madame thought so, too, as from that night on, I was required to dress as a girl each evening and was sold to customers as the *girl with something extra under her skirt*."

"That must have been awful for you."

"In part, yes, for no one in their right mind would choose the life of a prostitute. But in other ways, being forced to dress as a girl was something of a salvation for me. I was allowed, no, encouraged, to look like the young woman I had fantasised about becoming. I grew my hair and was taught how to use cosmetics to enhance my feminine persona. The other girls donated clothes for me to wear, too, and I soon became adept at making myself look feminine."

For a moment, Charlotte paused, as she once more collected her thoughts, for what she was about to reveal she had only ever spoken about once before.

"But for me, this soon became so much more than merely altering my physical appearance. It is difficult to put into words, but from the very first moment I was put into a gown, I felt, well, I felt complete. It was almost as if, for the first time in my life, I had become the person I should have been all along. I loved the makeup and the way having my hair dressed made me look feminine and pretty. I loved the feeling of stays compressing my waist, the sensation of a chemise around my legs. I also loved the way that being a girl changed the way customers viewed me. But, most of all, I discovered some form of inner peace when dressed as a girl, almost as if I was destined to remain that way forever.

"It was a few days before my sixteenth birthday that my life was to take a turn for the better."

"What happened?"

"I met Sir David Winters, one of the richest plantation owners in Jamaica. After my episode with Sally, he became one of my regular visitors and developed a great fondness for the feminine me. Then to my complete and utter amazement, in secret, he paid the madame a king's ransom to *purchase* me, and I was taken to his residency in the north of the island, where my life was to begin again, even if that life was to be the life of a woman."

"My God! I met Winters once, many years ago. He was about the same age as myself, was he not?"

"Yes, he was nine and thirty when I first met him. Anyway, the moment I entered David's home, any thought of becoming Charles once more evaporated like brandy left too long in the sun. From the very first, and to my growing delight, I was required to be Charlotte, the woman I am today. I was bought clothing and undergarments befitting a lady, and I was trained in all the womanly arts. I learned piano and how to sew, embroider, and paint. I was taught to dance and ride as a lady and was even instructed in the art of running a household.

"David also employed the services of a rather unique servant for me, a sort of a lady's maid but more — so much more — and one of only two in the household who came to know of my true gender. Phoebe, for that is her name, turned out to be a skilled practitioner of the healing arts, and three times a day she would bring me a potion to drink, a medicine so foul tasting that, even today, it makes me shudder as I take it. Each day she would also massage salves into my face and chest. At first, the potions made me sick, a little like a woman in the early stages of her confinement, but then, and to my great astonishment, my body began to change.

"As a boy, I had expected my body to grow and alter into that of a man. But for me, that did not happen. Quite the contrary, to be exact. I began to develop breasts and my hips widened. I grew no facial hair, my skin remained blemish free, and even my voice refused to deepen. I did not grow much more in height either, all of which I attribute to Phoebe's potions.

"For his part, David was quite remarkable. Whilst I was expected to share his bed, not once did he treat me as anything but the woman he wanted me to be. At all times, he treated me gently and with respect, and I came to care for him deeply . . . to love him even.

"Then, when I turned one and twenty, David deemed me ready, and for all intents and purposes, I became his wife. He introduced me to Jamaican society as such, where for the next eight years, I lived openly and was, remarkably, accepted as the woman I am now. Fortunately, my appearance had changed so much, had become so much more ladylike, that even Sally, when I passed her one day in the street, did not recognise me.

"Then, two years ago, my beloved David succumbed to yellow fever. For a while, I was devastated until other events dragged me from my despondency. You see, in his will, David left me everything—his vast fortune, his plantations, his houses in Jamaica, his workforce—and it soon became apparent to me that I could not remain melancholic if I were to honour my husband's legacy on the island."

CHAPTER FOUR

With his mind buzzing, James sat back in his chair and studied the person in front of him, a large part of him still not certain what to make of all this. The truth of the matter was that he was still not certain he could believe what he was being told, and he was still unsure how it could be possible that the boy he once knew was now the woman who sat before him. Yes, the evidence was compelling—the scar on the arm and the birthmark that he remembered so well almost impossible to forge. But how could it be? How could it be possible that a boy . . . a man . . . could look so perfectly female?

As a young man, he remembered attending a function at his club where *entertainers* had dressed as girls. It had been a ribald and bawdy evening, and he clearly recalled, with disgust, how vulgar and unconvincing the actors had been as women. However, the person sat before him could never be described in that way, for in truth, she looked every inch a perfect lady.

Then he studied her once more, his eyes fixed upon her beautiful face. Yes, at first, she had been understandably nervous, but now she sat in a confident manner, no subterfuge hidden behind her expression. And it was for the very reason that she appeared to have been totally honest with him, that his heart began to accept.

"So, if, as you say, you are now free of these horrors, why not go back to being Charles?"

"Then may it be said that you accept I am who I claim to be?" Charlotte retorted.

"Mm, it would appear that I am beginning to. So let me ask you my question again. If you are who you say, why not *be* Charles once more, now that you are free to do so? Your mother would be overjoyed to have her son return home safe, and I, for one, would love to see the look on the earl's face as you reclaim your inheritance."

"Which is one of the reasons I choose to remain Lady Charlotte! My current guise protects me from my stepfather. Whilst I no longer fear him, should he ever discover my true identity, I am certain he would make an attempt on my life just so he can keep control over my father's estates.

"But the real truth of the matter is that I will never return to being Charles, your grace, for this is who I now *choose* to be. Long ago, I accepted that I should have been born with the feminine gender. I am now and will always remain, until the day I draw my last breath, Lady Charlotte Winters."

"Remarkable, truly remarkable. So what is it you want of me?" he asked, now coming to the crux of the matter. "Why come to me at all?"

For a few moments, they sat in silence until, much to James's surprise, Lady Charlotte stood in a rustle of silk and walked over to his desk. Carefully she poured out two small glasses of brandy, one of which she handed to him, tossing the other one back in a single swallow.

"Before I answer that question, would you tell me of my mother?" she asked as she returned to her chair.

"I will tell what little I know, for she is seldom seen in polite society these days. In truth, whilst I have tried, on numerous occasions, to see the countess, I have always been rebuffed by the earl, with whom I have never seen eye to eye. However, on the rare occasion our paths have crossed, she seemed but a shadow of the woman I once knew. She never really recovered from your father's death and then your disappearance sent her into a spiral of melancholy that was only alleviated by the birth of her daughter."

"Ah yes, her daughter." Charlotte smiled. "My sister."

"Your halfsister, to be exact. Lady Amelia. A delightful child, and an innocent, too. In fact, Lady Amelia and my own daughter, Anne, are close friends, despite my own personal animosity towards the earl. She is the same age as my Anne and will be making her *come out* this season as well."

"And therein lies my dilemma. You see, my one ambition in this life is to be able to reconnect with my mother, and at the same time, get to know my sister. I long to see my mother, to find out how she fares, and to ensure that she is happy in life. It means so much to me, your grace, to know that she is safe and content. I would say the same for my halfsister, too. However, in order to do this without raising suspicion, I must do so as Lady Charlotte Winters."

Then, for James, the penny dropped.

"Ah! So now I see of what value I can be to you. You wish for me to engineer an introduction to your mother and sister. 'Tis a dangerous game you play, especially knowing to whom your mother is married."

"Yet one in which I must participate. It has, I must admit, occurred to me that I might come to know my mother and my sister by attending some of the same functions during the season. But alas, Lady Charlotte is a lady by marriage only, the *widow* of a mere knight of the realm, a *tradesman* to boot. So for me to be accepted by the *ton*, for me to get close to my mother and sister, I need someone of status, someone above reproach, to sponsor me. A duke, perhaps," Charlotte said with a wry smile.

James rubbed his hand over his face as he peered intently at his visitor. There was now little doubt in his mind that this person was — or had once been — his godson, Charles, just as he had little doubt that he would never truly understand the horrors of what he . . . she . . . had been through.

But how could he help? After all, should anyone discover that the Duke of Camberly's godson now dressed as a woman, even if that woman was truly ravishing, the scandal would ruin him, would destroy the chances of Anne ever making a good match, whatever the size of her dowry.

But then again, as he stared at the woman before him, his mind slipped back to the simple Christening ceremony all those years ago. Before God, he had made a promise to cherish and protect his godson, whatever might befall him, and it had been a promise that he had always intended to keep. As he felt the guilt of failure in that task wash over him, he knew what his answer must be.

Decisively, he made up his mind as to what to do, knowing that honour dictated he at least attempt something to help.

"Lady Charlotte," he addressed her formally, "you must understand my position and the difficulty of what you ask. Should anyone associate me with someone such as yourself, a . . . erm . . . a . . . well . . . a man dressed in women's clothing, if the truth were ever to come out, the scandal would be the talk of the *ton* for years."

"But—"

"No, let me finish," he interrupted. "Many years ago, I made a promise to your parents, and to God, that I would protect you, that I would always be there for you, and I did so again after your father died. Until now, I have failed in that obligation. Therefore, if I can, I will help you, but with one unbreakable condition. My first responsibility will always be to protect the good names and reputations of my own family, and despite my promises to your parents and to you, whatever happens, I will do whatever I need to do to ensure this."

"As will I," Charlotte replied. "You have my word on that. Should anyone suspect my true gender, I will make it perfectly clear that I pulled the wool over your eyes, too. But, in truth, since making my own *come out* in Kingston society, there has not been a single occasion where anyone has demonstrated the slightest suspicion about my true gender. So I, for one, do not fear discovery, as I have absolute confidence in who I am today."

"Now that I can believe." James chuckled. "So how do you propose we proceed?"

It was at that very moment that there was a swift knock on the study door, and before James could utter another word, his daughter, Anne, came rushing into the room unannounced. She was simply attired in a white muslin day dress, and her golden hair was arranged in an uncomplicated twist. Despite the abruptness of her entrance, James could not help but look at her fondly.

"Papa," Anne gushed. "I wanted to remind you that I have an appointment with my modiste this afternoon and that I will require the carriage . . . Oh!" As abruptly as she had entered the room, she stopped completely in her tracks as she saw Charlotte stand, obviously expecting her father to be alone in his study. "Oh, I do beg your pardon. I did not know you had a guest, Papa."

James stood as well, smiling indulgently at his daughter, knowing that she probably felt mortified at having disturbed him this way. Just the way her cheeks were flaring told him that. But there was something else on his mind too, a fierce protectiveness, an instinct that told him that he was not ready to introduce his godson, goddaughter, whatever, to his own daughter. But what choice did he have if he were to not look like a cad? After all, his *guest* was standing right there in front of them and could hardly be ignored. Decisively, he made up his mind.

"Anne, let me introduce our new neighbour, Lady Charlotte Winters. Lady Winters, may I present Lady Anne Beaufort, my daughter," he said formally as he watched both dip a knee respectfully each other.

"Lady Winters!" Anne obviously recognised the name, for her eyes lit up with astonishment. "It is a real pleasure to meet you. But please, let me beg your forgiveness for bursting in on you like this."

"There is nothing to forgive, Lady Anne," Charlotte said in return, "for your father and I have concluded our business."

"Papa, how could you!" she admonished. "How could you entertain an un-chaperoned lady in your study when we have a perfectly nice sitting room right next door? Why, I suspect from the lack of a tea tray, that you have not even offered her any refreshment."

"Lady Anne," Charlotte interjected, "let me put your mind at rest. Your father and I were alone at my request so that I could discuss a somewhat delicate matter with him. Fortunately, being a widow of one and thirty years of age means I do not have to be so guarded of my reputation as might you. So, being found alone with your father is of little consequence to me. As for tea, please do not berate him for his lack of hospitality, for refreshment was offered by your father but declined by myself."

"Then you are forgiven, Papa," Anne replied with a mischievous smirk. "So, may I use the carriage this afternoon? I will take Alice with me, and Bates will accompany us both."

"Which modiste do you use?" Charlotte asked. "For I too have an appointment this afternoon, with Madame LeClerc."

"Madame LeClerc!" Anne shrieked. "An appointment with her is as difficult to get as catching a moonbeam. I would love to have a gown made by her. Mrs Pennyweather's establishment makes my gowns for me. She is an excellent modiste but not in the same league as Madame LeClerc."

"Then perhaps you would like to come with me this afternoon, and I will see if I can persuade her to take you as a client?" Charlotte asked.

Somewhat astounded, James stood and watched Charlotte

and Anne as they interacted, instantly recognising that his daughter had not the slightest suspicion of who Charlotte really was. Like he had, when he had first met *Lady Winters*, Anne had simply taken her at face value, had accepted her for the lady she appeared to be. Despite this, he was guarded too, for he did not like the way the conversation between them was going, nor the way that Charles . . . Lady Charlotte . . . had inveigled her way instantly into Anne's confidence. It was quite obvious that she had suggested the invitation without giving one moment's thought as to the consequences of her proposition.

"Please, Papa, may I?" Anne begged.

For a moment, James paused, his mind undecided as to what to do. Whilst he was now certain of the true identity of the person who stood before him, what did he really know about her . . . him . . . her? What did he really know about her motives behind making such a suggestion? For all he knew, this *Lady Charlotte* might want nothing more than to do harm to him and his family. Accordingly, how could he possibly entrust his daughter to this . . . this . . . person . . . this man, who now dressed as a woman.

But then he looked again at the person who had bared her soul to him, just moments before. There was no doubt his godchild presented himself as an incredibly beautiful young woman, a woman with poise and confidence — and incredible eyes — just as there was no doubt in his mind that her eyes held no subterfuge or malice.

"Please, Father," his daughter begged. "I have always wanted to go to Madame LeClerc's dress shop. Please, may I go with Lady Winters?"

James smiled fondly. As always, he found it so difficult to say no to Anne, and her entreaty could not go unanswered, especially as a refusal might draw suspicion. A compromise was the answer, one that would do nothing but protect his daughter.

"I will permit it on one condition and that is you take my coach instead. Your lady's maid, Alice, can accompany you both, and Bates will drive, with Jones to help."

"With your permission, that would be eminently acceptable, your grace," replied Charlotte. "Perhaps you would also like to come along to give us the benefit of your wisdom when Anne chooses a gown?"

"Oh yes, Papa," gushed Anne, completely missing this little byplay as it passed between her father and Lady Charlotte. "Do!"

James stared at Charlotte, for her words had so obviously been chosen to let James know she would accept any conditions he chose to impose on her. For a fraction of a second, he even considered that option, especially as Lady Charlotte's reasons for extending an invitation had been so patently obvious. But then, he could not keep a straight face for a moment longer and he splurted out an uncontrollable guffaw.

"Whilst I am certain that I would enjoy accompanying you, my sweet, I am equally certain that I can occupy my time much more profitably, say by watching paint dry."

CHAPTER FIVE

As she had done so many times before, Charlotte stood in front of her looking glass and stared back at herself, yet again looking for any little imperfections that might give her away. It was a nervous habit she had fought hard to overcome, yet in moments of stress, it was something she always seemed to do.

"Come away from there, Lady Charlotte, for you know, as well as I do, that you look perfect," Phoebe admonished, her African accent so thick it could be cut it with a blunt butter knife. "Now tell me, have you taken your medicine today?"

Charlotte turned around to her friend, wrinkled her nose, then smiled guiltily as she stripped out of the dress she had been wearing for her visit to the duke.

Phoebe, who was of a similar age to Charlotte, had been her companion from the moment Charles had entered David's household in Jamaica. A little taller than Charlotte, Phoebe was undeniably attractive for one of her race, with a figure that, whilst athletic in build, was indisputably curvaceous. Her long thick jet-black hair hung loosely down her back and framed a beautiful face with plump lips and a pert little nose.

Unlike most of the slaves on the island, Phoebe had actually been born in Jamaica. Her mother, a highly respected medicine woman within her own tribe, had been taken into slavery whilst pregnant and had given birth to Phoebe shortly after being sold to the estate of Sir David Winters. David, never slow to recognise ability, had given Phoebe's mother a privileged position, one of *doctor* to the estate's workers, where she had not only ministered to the sick but had become midwife, too. It was only natural for Phoebe to follow in her mother's footsteps, and at the tender age of eight, she had begun her apprenticeship in the healing arts.

But that had all changed for Phoebe when Charlotte had arrived in the household, for David, in his infinite wisdom, had somehow recognised that Phoebe would make the perfect companion for a very frightened and vulnerable boy.

"What am I going to do with you?" Phoebe asked as she went to a side table and retrieved a brown bottle and a silver spoon. Carefully she poured out a spoonful of the medicine and held it up to Charlotte, almost as if she were a child. Charlotte pinched her nose, closed her eyes and opened her mouth and felt the spoon deliver the foul-tasting potion.

"Ugh." Charlotte shivered as she swallowed. "I will never get used to that taste."

"But you know it is worth the discomfort, for it is Phoebe's medicine that makes you such a beautiful woman." Phoebe smiled as she replaced the cork in the bottle.

"Are you ever going to tell me what it contains?"

"Like I have said so many times before, you would never take it again if you knew what it contained. Then you would have to go back to living like a boy! Now, which gown would you like?" she asked as she skipped over to Charlotte's wardrobe.

"The cream one with the big buttons at the front, I think, and the lavender bonnet with the matching shawl. That should be perfect for this afternoon."

"Yes'm," Phoebe said with a small curtsy.

Charlotte sighed theatrically as she heard the deference in Phoebe's voice. "Phoebe, how many times have I told you that, whilst you still act as my lady's maid, I consider you to be, first and foremost, my friend. You are a free woman now, no longer a slave, and I would much prefer it if you would call me Charlotte, especially when we are alone together."

Phoebe grinned, showing a set of white teeth that contrasted starkly with the darkness of her skin. "I will try, Lady Charlotte, but it is hard for me to forget. Now let us get you dressed, shall we?"

It took but a few minutes for Charlotte to slip into the dress she had selected. As the weather looked likely to be a little cooler that afternoon, the cream coloured gown would be perfect, for it was a little heavier, with long full sleeves and some lovely brocade detailing. Then, after slipping on her bonnet and tying the ribbon beneath her chin, she once more turned to Phoebe.

"So how do I look?" she asked, wanting, needing, confirmation of her appearance from her oldest friend.

For a few seconds, Phoebe fussed a little with the curls of hair that peeped from the edges of the bonnet. Then she stood back and smiled.

"As pretty as a picture. You will soon be fightin' the men off with your parasol, if you asks me," Phoebe replied.

"Talking of men and parasols. What of Samson?"

Samson was her *man*, her servant, her bodyguard, and was the only other person in the world who knew of Charlotte's true identity. Like Phoebe, he was a freed slave, and she had brought Samson with her when she had returned to England from Jamaica. Charlotte knew full well that the two of them had skirted around each other, hiding their true feelings for so long and realised the time was long overdue when she should do something about the situation.

"That man," Phoebe sighed. "He moves at the speed of a garden snail. I will be an old maid before he speaks."

"Then perhaps it is time you speak for him, for I long to dance at your wedding."

"You an' me both, Lady Charlotte, you an' me both. Now

down them stairs with you. The lady will be here soon."

"Yes'm," Charlotte teased as she picked up her reticule.

****

"Do you think that Lady Charlotte will mind you accompanying us, Papa?" Anne asked as she settled herself into a seat of the Landau.

"I should think not," James replied as he clambered in after her. "After all, was it not she who suggested it? Besides, it is not my intention to stay long with you. Like I said before, I will probably have Bates drop me off at my club and then get a hack home later this evening."

James turned his head away from his daughter so that she might not see the lie in his eyes. He rarely went to his club during the week, and never without his carriage to get him home. And then there was the way he had dressed, too—a waistcoat and jacket accompanied by a perfectly tied cravat, new buckskin breeches, which he wore with his favourite boots that had been polished to a mirror finish by his valet. He even, for pity's sake, had a top hat and cane. If he was not careful, Anne would surely suspect something was amiss, especially as he intended not to let her be alone with Lady Charlotte for even a second.

The Landau, pulled by two magnificent bay horses, lurched forward, moved a hundred yards down the cobbled street and then stopped once more outside Conway House, the home that had been rented by Lady Charlotte. James stepped down from the carriage and was about to walk to the front door to announce himself when the door was opened by a huge black man dressed in livery uniform.

The man was a giant, well over two yards tall, and had shoulders that were almost as wide as the door itself. In awe, James stood and stared as the man took a step to the side to allow Lady Charlotte to pass by. She paused to say something softly to him, but judging by the scowl on the man's face, her words had done little to alleviate his concerns. Lady Charlotte, for her part, smiled reassuringly and patted him on the arm before walking down the steps towards the carriage.

"Your grace. This is a pleasant surprise, for I did not think that you would be accompanying Lady Anne and myself. Instead, I thought you might be gainfully occupied elsewhere, say in watching some paint dry."

The faint smile tugging at her lips, as she dipped a little curtsey, proved her tease, and James, in a moment of pique, had to suppress a cynical retort.

"I . . . er . . . thought it prudent, in the circumstances," James replied instead. "That is some man you have there," he added as he looked around to see the giant scowling at him.

"Yes," she agreed. "That is Samson, and he takes his role of my protector very seriously. He is not at all happy at being left behind."

James smiled ruefully, his keen eye not missing for one second that she had probably guessed the reason he had decided to accompany them to the modiste. After all, he had made it abundantly clear that he would do anything to protect his daughter's reputation. However, he had another reason for accompanying them, too. At the end of the day, if he were to decide to help her, he had to see what she claimed was true — to see for himself that society would truly accept her for the woman she appeared to be. Whilst there was every indication that his godson could fulfil the role of *Lady*, he had every intention to put him . . . her . . . to the test. Then there was the little matter of trust as well, and that would have to be earned. After all, Samson might be *her* protector, but James was determined to protect his own daughter, not from danger but from scandal instead, and this was a message he clearly intended to send.

Silently, they walked the few steps towards the Landau, where, being lost in thought, James automatically offered his un-gloved hand to help his godchild mount the steps of the Landau, just as he would have done for any other lady.

But what happened as she took his hand astounded even him.

Like James, Charlotte was not wearing gloves, and as she clasped her naked hand over his own, something totally strange and unexpected occurred.

The very second their hands met, James felt a charge of energy leap between them. An intense and uncontrollable shiver of pleasure leapt up his arm, a bolt that instantly cascaded deep down into his groin, making it fizz like the finest champagne. It was like nothing he had ever experienced before, and as he fought to suppress an audible groan, he also had to fight the instinct to snatch away his hand, just as he would have done had he accidentally placed it within a fire.

And, judging by the way Lady Charlotte had also given out an involuntary little gasp, she had felt it, too.

So as to not appear to be ill-mannered, James carefully handed Lady Charlotte into the Landau, now desperate to be rid of her touch. It was then that James experienced his next surprise. For the moment she released his hand, the sense of loss he suffered was almost tangible, and a sudden and completely irrational desire to take hold of it once again swept through him.

Not daring to look at her for fear of embarrassing himself, James climbed the step of the carriage, feeling the springs of the carriage dip for a moment as he pulled aside the tails of his coat so he could sit opposite the ladies. From the corner of his eye, however, he keenly observed his godchild as she settled herself elegantly into the seat next to Anne. Suddenly, to James, the whole situation seemed farcical, for as he pretended to pay no attention to her, she appeared to take no notice of him, turning to face his daughter instead.

"Where would you like to go first, Lady Anne?" she asked in a voice that sounded somewhat shaky and thick with emotion. "Shall we go to Mrs Pennyweather's establishment or to Madame LeClerc's?"

Lady Anne grinned sheepishly. "I hope you don't think me presumptuous, Lady Charlotte, but I . . . er . . . sent a message to Mrs Pennyweather to rearrange my appointment for another day. So if it pleases you, I would like to go to Madame LeClerc's."

"Madame LeClerc's it is then. Driver, Bond Street if you please," Charlotte called, which was followed by a respectful *Yes ma'am*, from the groom.

As the carriage made its way sedately through the streets of London, James took a few moments to take stock of the situation, still reeling a little from the shock he had experienced when grasping Lady Charlotte's hand. So, whilst he maintained a practised expression of diffidence, he carefully observed the occupants of his carriage from the corner of his eye.

There was a part of him, quite a large part, he had to admit, that hoped he might find some reason, some flaw he could use to distance himself and his family from this person. But the harder he looked, the more difficult it became for him to see Charles as anything but the woman she appeared to be.

His daughter, he noted with pride, was undeniably beautiful, her golden blonde hair contained delightfully in a pretty bonnet. She was an accomplished young woman too, and he had no doubt that once she had made her come out, she might even be dubbed an incomparable.

However, even he had to admit that the *woman* who sat next to Anne, whilst different in look, was equally beautiful, her features giving not even the slightest indication that she had not been born that way. But it was more than his . . . her outward beauty that amazed him. Charles appeared to have absolutely no qualms about dressing in feminine clothes, and as Lady Charlotte, oozed the self-confidence of a more mature woman. Just the way she spoke, the way she walked and held her body, the way she interacted with those around her, would leave no doubt to the casual observer that she was anything but the lady she appeared to be. In fact, his late wife would probably have dubbed her a *woman of quality*, and the more he saw of Charlotte, the more he reluctantly seemed to agree.

Inwardly, he groaned.

It took but twenty minutes for the carriage to arrive in front of Madame LeClerc's establishment, a beautifully appointed modiste's shop. Much to the amusement of James, the wheels of the carriage had barely come to a halt before his daughter was jumping out of her seat with undisguised enthusiasm. Sooner than anyone could say *jackrabbit*, Jones, the second groomsman, had also jumped down onto the pavement and was already handing an excited Lady Anne, and a more sedate Lady Charlotte, respectfully out of the carriage. Unable to suppress a smile at his daughter's anticipated shopping experience, James also alighted from the carriage and followed behind, cringing slightly as he, for the first time in many an age, entered the land of silks, crinolines, and ribbons.

"Lady Winters, a pleasure as always," a soft feminine voice called as they entered, a voice with the merest hint of a genuine French accent. "But who is this beautiful young woman you have with you, and why have you not brought her to my establishment before now?" she scolded with mock severity.

Charlotte turned to the woman and smiled in return. "Madame LeClerc, may I present Lady Anne Beaufort and her father, his grace, the Duke of Camberly."

If the woman was surprised at the status of her customers, she did not show it. Instead, she smiled politely, curtsied respectfully to James and Anne, and then turned back to

Charlotte.

"Madame LeClerc, I have a great favour to ask you," Charlotte began. "Lady Beaufort is to be presented to the Prince Regent at the beginning of the season, and whilst I know how inordinately busy you are, I was hoping you might find time to create something really special for her to wear. I would deem it a great personal favour if you could do so."

For a moment, the woman looked grave as she walked over to Lady Anne, viewing her with a professional eye, whilst Anne mimicked a petrified tree. But then Madame LeClerc clapped her hands sharply, and another young woman suddenly appeared from behind a set of drapes, dropping a simple curtsey to the customers in the store.

"Sarah, would you please take Lady Beaufort into the fitting room and take her measurements," she ordered. "Madame LeClerc is going to take great pleasure in making her look like a princess."

From his vantage point on an uncomfortable armchair at the back of the shop, James was able to discretely observe the proceedings. Anne, of course, on hearing that the Madam would make her gown, had been unable to hide her excitement and had flapped her hands together, as she had so often done as a child.

Lady Winters, on the other hand, was a completely different kettle of fish, and James could not help but look on with something akin to awe and fascination as he watched his godchild intently.

Charlotte was deep in conversation with the dressmaker, and it was quite obvious that Madame LeClerc, a professional and experienced modiste, had absolutely no idea that the woman she was talking to was, in fact, a boy. Instead of the disgust and ridicule that might have been expected, the modiste's demeanour was one of respect and admiration for the woman who stood before her, and again he marvelled at just how easy it was for his godchild to be accepted for who he appeared to be.

When, earlier, he had decided to accompany his daughter, he had reasoned that he was doing so for her own safety and had always intended to stay in the shop, to make sure that Anne was not going to be compromised in anyway by whom Lady Charlotte really was. But now, simply judging by the way the modiste had accepted her as a customer, it was patently obvious that Lady Charlotte was in absolutely no danger of being revealed for who she was. Of that, he was now certain.

But could he actually trust this person? Of that, he was *not* certain.

Moments later, however, as Anne reappeared from behind a curtain, James groaned, knowing, from bitter experience, the personal hell in which he now found himself. This was going to take hours, hours of mindless torture, hours and hours of fabrics and patterns and ribbons and lace, and again, in his mind, he moaned as if he were in pain.

But what to do? Could he leave his daughter? Could he trust his godchild? Once more he stared at Charlotte, almost as if he was trying to divine her very thoughts, and yet again, he saw no malice there, no ill will or wickedness. Instead, all he saw was the serene and calm features of a lady, a lady who was so obviously engrossed in the most feminine of pastimes. Then he had a sudden thought. Could he not leave Jones, the footman, to watch over Anne? He was a very capable man who would surely watch out for her wellbeing. His mind made up, James stood.

"Anne" — he called out before the shop girl managed to whisk her away once more — "Lady Winters. I fear that I must leave you to your patterns and fabrics." He turned to the modiste. "Madame, please spare no expense with this gown. My daughter *is* to look like a princess. Lady Charlotte, you have my thanks." With a quick nod, he turned to his daughter. "Anne . . . Jones will wait outside whilst I have Bates take me to my club. He will then return for you within the hour."

Charlotte once more dropped a respectful curtsey, and yet again, she smiled that enigmatic little smile.

James, having returned from his club at a much earlier hour than anyone had expected, was sat with his daughter in their small dining room where, as usual, they shared their evening meal.

"Papa? What do you think of Lady Charlotte?" Anne asked with mock innocence as she sipped delicately at a spoonful of cook's famous vegetable soup.

James sighed, having expected that very question. He looked at his daughter more severely than he had intended and then coughed to hide his mounting discomfiture.

"She seems pleasant enough," he replied, keeping his voice as neutral as he could in an effort to disguise his true feeling upon the matter.

"Well, I think she is simply marvellous," Anne gushed. "She has wonderful taste in clothes, and I cannot believe how easy it was for her to persuade Madame LeClerc to make my coming out gown. Have I told you of the wonderful gold silk that we have chosen?"

He smiled, for how could he not? "Only about four times, my darling."

"And did you know she owns three sugar plantations in Jamaica? She inherited them from her husband after he passed away. She must be terribly rich, for she ordered no less than four gowns from Madame LeClerc and has plans for even more."

"Yes, I know. I knew her late husband, Sir David Winters, a long time ago."

"Is that why she came to see you today?"

"Yes," he lied. "Having just returned to England, she wanted to introduce herself."

For a few moments, the conversation ceased, allowing him to concentrate on his soup, whilst all the time expecting more from his daughter. He knew her so well it was almost as if he could see the gears and cogs in her mind whirring around and around, like those of his clock on the mantle.

"Father" — she started softly, her voice almost sing-song like — "has anything yet been settled about a chaperon for my coming out, for my season?"

"I had thought to ask your grandmama."

With a wry smile, James watched his only daughter shudder at the thought. Whilst Anne loved her grandmother to distraction, it was obvious that she had no desire whatsoever to spend her whole season under the scrutiny of a woman whose idea of fun was for a young lady to sit for hours with a piece of embroidery.

"Might I suggest an alternative?" Anne asked timidly.

"Who? Lady Charlotte, I suppose."

"Yes! Don't you think she would be perfect? A respectable widow. A lady much closer in age to my own. Who could more perfect to act as my chaperon?" The words tumbled from Anne so quickly they almost seemed to merge together, and once more James had to fight back a smile as he listened to Anne's natural exuberance. "Please, Father."

Slowly and deliberately, James placed his spoon into his now empty soup dish and turned to look his daughter square in the eyes. He could see the excitement there, and yet again, his heart wanted nothing more than to give her the world. But how could he, knowing what he knew about *Lady Charlotte*? Then his mind suddenly leapt to another thought, the conclusion that *Lady Charlotte* was deliberately and calculatingly using this as another way to inveigle herself into his life.

"Did she put you up to this?" he growled.

"No, Papa." Anne was adamant in her response, the honesty in her eyes enough to for James to know she was telling the truth. "It was completely my idea. I suggested it to *her*, if you must know. I like her. I enjoy her company and think she would be the perfect person to be my chaperon. But for some reason, Lady Charlotte flatly refused to entertain my suggestion, not even for a second. Please, Father, would you speak to her for me? Please?" Anne begged.

"No, I will not."

****

That evening, as Charlotte lay back in her bath, she allowed her eyes to close and then sighed deeply to still her mind. Breathing in the relaxing scent of the lavender oil that Phoebe had added to the bathwater, she dipped her hands beneath the surface of the water, and for the thousandth time, allowed herself to caress her skin, relishing how silky smooth it felt. Smiling to herself, she then let her hands drift upwards to her chest to caress the small yet perfectly formed breasts she now possessed, loving the tingle that coursed through her body as she fondled her nipples.

From the very beginning of her journey into womanhood, David had relished the gradual changes to her body elicited by Phoebe's medicines, and he had loved her breasts almost as much as he had loved the flesh between her legs.

Yes, there were times when he would allow her to be in control of their lovemaking, and Charlotte remembered how she had adored his body, how she loved nothing more than to take his manhood in her mouth before straddling his legs with her own, to make love to him with her body.

But more often than not, it was David who would take the lead, and she had soon come to realise that, for him, her pleasure was paramount. For hours upon end he would caress her with both hand and mouth, the ecstasy he induced merely an erotic prelude to the beauty of their lovemaking.

Fondly, she remembered an occasion when David had lovingly stripped her of every item of clothing before laying her naked body down upon the bed. With her long auburn hair pooled around her on the pillow, Charlotte remembered posing for him, playfully cupping her then tiny breasts as he gazed down at her. Eventually, he had covered her body with his own, his hands and lips softly caressing her, sucking her, wherever he thought he could bring forth the most pleasure. And then he had entered her body, both reaching a most glorious release as he did so.

That was the first day that David had proclaimed his love for her, and a sudden tear dripped from her eye at the memory.

"Stop this, Lotte," she growled to herself. "David is gone. Focus on what is now important!"

She allowed the events of the day to play over her mind once more, knowing that the wheels of her great plan had finally been set in motion. It had required every ounce of her courage to face the duke, but the risk she had taken appeared to have been successful. Not only had he confidentially accepted who she was, but had also introduced her to his daughter, Lady Anne, a close friend of her halfsister no less.

Charlotte smiled to herself, knowing she had played the opening movements of her scheme to perfection, not caring that she had deliberately failed to tell the duke the whole truth about her return to London. How could she? For had she told him everything there would be little chance of him ever speaking to her again, let alone offering his help.

The truth of the matter was simple. No one would ever know the depths of despair Charles had endured before he had been *rescued*. Because of it, in Charlotte's heart, there now lived a hatred so pure that it threatened to consume her, a desire for revenge so strong that she would readily destroy the reputations of the entire *ton* to achieve it.

There was one person who, without any shadow of doubt, was responsible for this misery and pain. No one, not even the duke or Lady Anne or Lady Amelia or even her mother would be allowed to stand in her way as she took great pleasure in destroying the Earl of Weybridge.

CHAPTER SIX

It had been three days since her encounter with the duke and his daughter, and still, there had been no indication that he was attempting to help Charlotte in her cause. Not that she blamed him, for as a duke, and second cousin to the Prince Regent, he had a great deal to lose, especially as Lady Anne was to be a debutante this season. But now she needed to know, for if he had decided to not to help, she would have to consider other ways of infiltrating the earl's family so she could exact her revenge.

So it was that she found herself sat at a writing slope, quill pen in hand, as she composed a short missive to the duke, requesting that he find time in his busy schedule to see her once more. Then reaching for a silver shaker, she carefully dusted the ink with fine sand.

"There," she declared, "if he deigns not to reply, I shall have my answer, will I not?"

Just then, there was a knock on the door and a very nervous looking maid poked her head into the parlour.

"Begging your pardon, milady, but I couldn't find Mr Samson, so I brought this myself." She handed Charlotte the calling card that she was carefully holding in her hand. "There is a lady here asking to see you."

Quickly Charlotte looked down at the card and grinned broadly as she saw the name printed there.

Lady Anne Beaufort

"You did quite right, Millie. Would you please show her in? Then, if you would, go and ask cook if she could provide tea and some of those delicious cakes of hers."

Charlotte smiled as the young girl scurried away, only to smile once more as Lady Anne came bustling into the room. Charlotte stood, and as convention dictated, the two ladies curtsied to each other before Charlotte surprised Anne by kissing her lightly on the cheek in greeting.

Anne was attired in a lovely pale yellow day dress with a contrasting gold spencer and matching bonnet, and yet again, Charlotte thought what a beautiful young woman she was turning out to be.

"This is a pleasant surprise, Lady Anne," Charlotte said. "I had begun to think you no longer wanted to be acquaintances after I turned down your request to be the chaperon for your season."

"No, far from it." Anne grinned as she took the seat that Charlotte had indicated, her smile lighting up her beautiful face. "In fact, I have still not given up hope of persuading both you and Father to allow it. However, I am here on an entirely different matter. You see, it is to be my nineteenth birthday in two days' time, and Papa has said I may host a small dinner party in celebration. I am here with your invitation." She reached into her reticule and pulled out a white envelope which she handed to Charlotte.

Again Charlotte smiled. "That is wonderful, Lady Anne, and I am delighted to accept your invitation."

"Oh, do you think we could dispense with the *Lady*. We are both *Ladies*, so perhaps I may be so bold as to call you Charlotte. You may, of course, call me Anne."

"Or you may call me Lotte, as did my friends in Jamaica. Now, pray tell, who else will you be inviting to your dinner party?"

"Papa and Grandmama will be there, of course. My friend Lady Jane and her parents, Lord and Lady Chalmers. My Uncle Johnny, Viscount Holmes, brother to my late mother, and his wife, Viscountess Elena. I have also invited my friend Lady Amelia, who will be coming out with me this season. Unfortunately, this means I have also had to invite her parents, Earl and Countess Weybridge, and her brother Lord Henry Hamilton as well."

As those words were spoken, Charlotte felt her heart threaten to stop, and she had to fight with her mind to prevent her face betraying all the emotions she was suddenly feeling. The first was jubilation, for the duke, in allowing Anne to extend her an invitation, had clearly indicated his willingness to help. But it went much further than acceptance, for it was quite clear to Charlotte that the duke intended to use this social occasion as a safe way to *introduce* her to her family. The prospect of that happening had her shivering with trepidation, and with anticipation too.

Fortunately, at that moment, there was a knock on the door, and this time it was Phoebe who entered, carrying the tea tray. It was just the diversion Charlotte needed. Anne, much to Charlotte's amusement, had obviously not been prepared for someone such as Phoebe and she watched as surprise flashed across Anne's face when she caught sight of the colour of her skin.

"Tea, my ladies?" Phoebe asked as she placed the tray onto a small tea table. Once more Charlotte smiled, for if Phoebe had seen Anne's reaction, she had quite obviously chosen to politely ignore it.

"What? Oh, no, thank you," Anne blustered, the colour of her cheeks displaying the awkwardness of the moment. "I do not have time today. I'm afraid I have so many errands to run and my carriage is waiting outside, but I am so much looking forward to seeing you at dinner, *Lotte*."

"Till then." Charlotte smiled as she once more kissed Anne on the cheek.

"Let me show you out, Lady Beaufort," Phoebe offered.

Charlotte watched the two of them bustle out of the room only to have Phoebe return a few moments later so that she could sit and have tea with her mistress.

"Oh, I likes that gal," Phoebe said as she sat next to Charlotte and reached for the silver teapot. "You know she 'pologised for reacting the way she did when she saw my colour."

"Yes, I like her, too, Phoebe. But more importantly, the duke has come through for me. He is inviting the earl to Anne's dinner party, my mother, sister, and stepbrother, too."

As the moment to depart for the dinner party approached, Charlotte found herself getting more and more nervous. She and Phoebe had been secreted in Charlotte's bedchamber all afternoon so Phoebe could work her magic on her mistress. Charlotte had been bathed and Phoebe had used a gentleman's straight edge razor to ensure that Charlotte's skin was entirely smooth and hair free. Then Phoebe had applied her cosmetics to Charlotte's face, not too much, but just enough to enhance her feminine features without anyone being able to suggest she might be a *painted lady*.

Likewise, her chosen gown was elegant yet demure, the neckline high enough as to not show even the merest hint of bosom. Yet, despite this, the gown was luxurious in form, a rich ruby red silk interwoven with real gold thread, with a matching golden sash at the waist and a matching shawl for her shoulders. Even Charlotte's headdress was made from the same golden ribbon, her hair pinned up with delicate tendrils framing her face in the most delightful way.

No, the last thing anyone would accuse her of being was anything remotely like the demimondes of society, for her appearance was one of sophistication and elegance.

But, despite her appearance in the looking glass, despite her confidence in her ability to easily pass as the woman she had become so many years before, Charlotte was undeniably nervous.

"Phoebe," she whispered as she perched lightly on the edge of her bed, being careful not to wrinkle the delicate material of her dress. "Do you think me idiotic for going through with this?"

Phoebe took one look at her and then came to sit next to her, picking up her hand to hold it between her own, sighing a little as she gave Charlotte a knowing glance.

"Do you remember the first time Master David took you into Kingston? You were barely twenty-one years of age, and Phoebe's medicines had not really had enough time to work. Yet, even then, despite the fact that your transformation was not quite complete, everyone who made your acquaintance accepted you for the lady you had become. Tonight will be no different, you'll see."

"But . . ." Charlotte moaned as she rested her head lightly on Phoebe's shoulder.

"You know that I love you like you was my own sister, Miss Charlotte. Do you really think I would let you risk everything you have achieved if I thought there was even the littlest chance of your secret being discovered?"

Charlotte sighed heavily. "No, I suppose not, my darling girl. And I must stay true to my plan as well. So I will go and be Lady Charlotte Winters, the perfect, demure, feminine, and might I add, incredibly wealthy widow from Jamaica. I will seek out the lay of the land, and tonight Lady Charlotte will once more come into the lives of her mother and her sister. I will find out where the weaknesses lay for my stepfather and stepbrother, and when the lives of my mother and my halfsister, Amelia, are secure, then and only then will I silently unleash the hounds of hell."

"That's my girl," Phoebe said.

"Oh my, it all sounds so simple, does it not?" Charlotte groaned.

"When is anything in your life ever simple, my lady? Now come, for Samson is waiting to escort you to the duke's home."

Samson was indeed waiting at the bottom of the stairs, dressed in the livery that had been made specially to fit his massive frame. As the two of them descended the stairs, he looked up from where he was standing, and once more Charlotte's heart went out to him. For it was not she that Samson was watching, but Phoebe, and the painful longing in his expression said much more than any words. Instantly, despite her own growing nervousness, Charlotte resolved, yet again, to do something about the situation.

As it was only a short distance to the Beaufort residence and was also a beautiful clear evening, Charlotte had decided to walk. Regrettably, her evening slippers were much too fine to be spoiled by walking on a dirty pathway so, before leaving the house, she slipped her stocking covered feet into her outdoor shoes and gave her satin slippers to Samson to carry. Then they walked, side by side, in silence, until Charlotte deemed it safe to speak, out of earshot of Phoebe.

"Samson," she asked softly, "why is it that you have not spoken for Phoebe yet? You clearly love her, and she loves you, too, you know."

Instantly, Samson stopped in the street, his back ramrod straight, his gaze fixed on anything but her.

"Please, Missy Charlotte, do not ask me that question," he replied in his deep bass voice.

"No, Samson, I would like to know. In fact, I will go so far as to order you to tell me."

Samson stood like a statue. This was a man who, rightly so, had been named for his namesake in the Bible. This was a man who, when her husband had one day been attacked, had beaten down six armed robbers without blinking an eye, the two knife wounds inflicted upon him during the struggle hardly slowing him down for a second. This was a man who feared no physical danger and who, Charlotte was certain, would gladly lay down his life for her. Yet now his whole body shook, a look of pure fear appearing on his face as Charlotte tilted her head upwards to look him square in the eye.

"Please, Samson," she murmured. "I would like to help if I may. Tell me why."

"Samson is not good enough for Miss Phoebe," he muttered. His head dropped, his gaze on the pavement as if trying to cover the obvious embarrassment he was feeling. "Miss Phoebe has had schooling from you. She is a princess of her tribe, a healer. I can barely read and write. No, Samson is . . . I am not good enough for her." He looked back up, his misery showing in his eyes. "Besides, if Miss Phoebe and me . . . if we were to marry, you would send us away. I heard one of the other servants say so. Then what would I . . . we do? What would become of us then?"

Charlotte stared at Samson incredulously as the truth of the matter hit her squarely between the eyes. As one of only three people in London who knew her true identity, she trusted this man with her life, and his loyalty and strength were things she had come to count on every single day. But the reality of the situation was that, when she had decided to return to England, she had not even asked if he, or Phoebe for that matter, actually wanted to accompany her. Time and time again, she had made it clear to both of them that they were free, that they had the right to choose their own path in life. Yet still, she had treated them as slaves, had assumed that the two of them would want nothing more than to accompany her to a far away and entirely foreign land.

Ashamedly, Charlotte suddenly realised just how much for granted she had taken his support, with little consideration for his feelings. After all, it had been she who had dragged both him and Phoebe away from the only true home they had ever known ir. Jamaica. Now he must be feeling more than a little insecure and out of place in London, especially if he thought there was a possibility that he may be sent away.

It was then that Charlotte felt a sudden surge of anger as for the first time she acknowledged to herself how selfish her decision had been. The shame of it hit her hard, and she knew, without any shadow of doubt, she needed to set matters aright.

"Samson," she implored. "I would like to apologise to you, for I have been a terrible person."

"But for what, Missy Charlotte?"

"For dragging you away from Jamaica, from your home. Like I have tried to explain to Phoebe on many an occasion, you are no longer a slave but a free man. Nor are you merely a servant to me. You are my trusted friend. When I decided to return to London, I should have given you the option to stay behind."

"But I would not have done so, Missy Charlotte."

Charlotte could do nothing but sigh with relief at his reply, for she suddenly realised she would not know how to endure without him and Phoebe at her side. A fierce determination gripped her.

"So then listen to me, *Mr* Samson, and listen good. Other than Master David, you are, without doubt, the best man that I have ever known. For Phoebe, you are the *only* man, and if anything, she does not think herself good enough for you! Your reading and writing have much improved in the last six months, but what you lack in education, you make up for in many other ways. Not only on numerous occasions have you demonstrated your willingness to be my strong right arm, you have, as well, taught me that I am more than capable of defending myself. You are also, I must say, the finest man with a horse that I have ever seen.

"So, I make you a promise. If you ever choose to leave my

service, I will permit it and give you sufficient funds to last you a lifetime. I will even arrange passage back to Jamaica, if that is what you want. But understand this. If you do venture to leave me, I will fight with every breath in my body to keep you by my side.

"As for Phoebe, I will make you another promise. On the day that you two marry, I will dance at your wedding with pride and love in my heart. And when the hundreds of little Samsons and little Phoebes come along, I will love them all as my own. That is how much I value your friendship, Samson."

Samson grinned, his back ramrod straight. Yet he did not utter a single word in reply. Instead, he turned and once more continued the walk towards the Beaufort house with Charlotte trailing along behind, almost as if he were the master and she the servant. In a matter of moments, they stood outside the steps leading up the huge townhouse where two elegantly dressed footmen attended the doors. It was only then Samson turned back to her deferentially.

"I will think on it, mistress," he said. "You have my word. Now, do you wish for me to wait for you, Missy Charlotte, to escort you home?"

Charlotte sighed. "No, thank you. I will have one of the duke's footmen accompany me, and as it is not far, I will be perfectly safe." Samson scowled, but she stood her ground. "Besides, you know perfectly well what I would like you to do instead of waiting for me."

Without waiting for his reply, Charlotte turned and took hold of her skirts so she could walk up the stairs without tripping over the hem of her dress.

When she was announced by the butler, Charlotte was pleased to see that she was neither the first nor the last to arrive. Anne jumped up with glee as she had entered the room, her steps bringing her quickly to Charlotte's side. Despite her nerves, Charlotte could not help but admire Anne, a slight twinge of jealousy flitting across her mind when she saw the beautiful gown she was wearing. It was simple in design, the midnight blue material contrasting perfectly with her golden hair and with the black velvet choker she wore around her neck. The neckline, however, was cut a little on the low side, and Charlotte could not help but feel a little envious when observing her friend's ample womanly assets.

"Lady Charlotte, welcome." Anne smiled with genuine pleasure as she curtsied politely. "And may I say, Lotte, how beautiful you look this evening. Doesn't she, Papa?" Anne asked as James moved to her side.

"Yes, indeed. Welcome, Lady Winters."

James offered her a slight bow.

Charlotte curtsied deeply, hoping the simple gesture of respect would convey the gratitude she felt. Only then did she smile nervously in return.

"Thank you, your grace. It pleased me greatly to be able to accept your invitation this evening."

The duke smiled, and for some reason, Charlotte felt a shiver go down her spine from an entirely unexpected surge of attraction she felt.

"Perhaps, Anne, you would like to take Lady Winters around the room and introduce her to everyone?"

"My pleasure, Papa."

Within a matter of moments, Charlotte had been escorted around the room. She was first introduced to the Dowager Duchess of Camberly, Anne's grandmother, then to Lord and Lady Chalmers, and also Anne's friend Lady Jane—who turned out to be yet another pretty young debutante of similar age to Anne. By then the duke was standing to one side of the room, conversing with another couple, who Charlotte soon discovered, after Anne had made yet more introductions, were Anne's uncle and aunt, Viscount and Viscountess

Holmes. However, much to Charlotte's relief, and perhaps disappointment, there seemed, as yet, to be no sign of the Earl and Countess of Weybridge, Lord Henry Hamilton, nor Lady Amelia.

Soon Charlotte found herself a sandwich, seated between a very excitable Anne and her friend Lady Jane.

"Oh, I am so pleased you could make this evening, Lady Charlotte," Anne gushed.

Charlotte smiled. "I would not have missed this for anything, Lady Anne. May I wish you a very happy birthday."

Unable to resist the moment, Charlotte reached into her reticule for a small box wrapped in a square of silk and tied with a little ribbon and handed it to Anne.

"What is this?"

"A birthday gift from me." Charlotte grinned.

Anne gave out a little squeal and her hungry fingers scrabbled at the ribbon, pulling away the silk square to reveal a small velvet box. Charlotte was pleased to see her new friend's fingers tremble a little as she lifted the lid and then smiled knowingly as both Anne and Jane gasped when they saw what the box contained. For inside was a perfectly matched pair of diamond eardrops, the large stones of which glistened eagerly in the candlelight that illuminated the room.

Anne gasped as she turned to the lady who now sat on the other side of her. "Oh, Lotte, they are beautiful. Look, Grandmama. Look what Lady Charlotte has gifted me."

The duchess was a much older yet striking version of Anne herself. She was dressed in a modest yet beautifully crafted gown that contrasted perfectly with her twinkling and intelligent eyes. Yet, whilst Anne's face had lit up with pleasure, her grandmother's face could have been set in stone as she returned Charlotte's gaze.

"I thought they might compliment your coming out gown, Lady Anne," Charlotte murmured.

"Hmpph! She has all of the family jewels for that," the duchess grumbled.

At first, she thought the duchess was going to be difficult, but as Anne took out one of the eardrops to hold it against her ear, Charlotte saw the dowager's eyes soften with love for her grandchild.

"And now my choice will be doubly difficult, will it not, Grandmama," Anne beamed. "Thank you, Lady Charlotte, for a most generous gift. I must show Papa."

It was at that very moment that Charlotte felt her heart stop, as Stevens announced the final guests for the evening.

"His Lordship, the Earl of Weybridge, Lord Henry Hamilton, and Lady Amelia Hamilton," the butler droned.

Unable to move, Charlotte sat motionless on her chair and felt her face drain of all colour, for this was the moment that she had dreamed about for so many years. It was also the moment she had dreaded with every fibre of her being.

She recognised the earl immediately, although he was now considerably older and more portly than the last time she had seen him. He was immaculately dressed in tailcoat, golden waistcoat, and breeches, and wore a perfectly tied cravat, fixed in place with a small ruby pin. Yet despite his finery, Charlotte felt a shiver of fear ripple down her spine, for his face was exactly as she remembered it to be — smug, superior, his ice-cold eyes like two pieces of coal from the deepest mine.

Swallowing hard, Charlotte suddenly found herself fighting the urge to vomit as a host of mixed emotions assaulted her in a matter of seconds. This was the man who had ordered Charles' death for the sole reason of acquiring his bequeathed estate. This was the man who was indirectly responsible for the years of pain and misery and rape that Charles had been forced to endure.

For that, she would never forgive, never forget.

Yet he was also, ultimately, the cause of her existence

today, for without him, without the man he had hired to kill her, she would never have met David, would never have become the beautiful, vibrant woman of her dreams.

Somehow, Charlotte steeled her heart and dragged her gaze away from the earl to look upon the second person who stood a step behind his father—her stepbrother, Lord Henry. At first, she did not recognise him, for he had been but fifteen when Charles had been abducted. But as she stared, it was plain to see, merely from the way he strutted into the room, that he was made from exactly the same mould as his father.

Again, Charlotte shivered with revulsion as her mind flashed back to that terrible day when Henry had forced Charles into a trunk and had locked him in. Charles had nearly suffocated and had only survived the ordeal because one of the upstairs maids had heard his cries.

In a way, Charlotte had hoped Henry might have matured into a more affable person, but an instinct that was rarely wrong told her that this was a person that would be easy to anger. Oh, there was no doubt that he had grown into an undeniably handsome man, but Henry still had that same superior look in his eyes, the predatory expression of a bully designed to make those around him cower in his merest presence. How she hated such men.

Finally, Charlotte glanced at Lady Amelia, and this time her heart actually ceased to beat for a moment. For, even if she had not known who the young woman was, she would have instantly recognised her as the daughter of the Countess of Weybridge, Charlotte's very own mother.

Amelia was small, almost petite in stature and was extremely beautiful. Styled so that it draped loosely in delightful curls, her auburn hair shimmered in the candlelight and framed an elfin face that was dominated by the most gorgeous pair of golden-brown eyes. They were the eyes of her mother—the smiling, loving eyes that Charles remembered from his childhood; the eyes that had gazed lovingly at him; the eyes that had cried endless tears when his father had been killed. There was also an air of innocence about Amelia, an easy smile of a genial lady that suggested she had not only inherited her eyes from her mother but her temperament too.

Then and only then did Charlotte realise that the one person she had truly hoped to see, the Countess of Weybridge, her mother, was not in attendance.

****

James had been watching Charlotte intently as the Hamilton family entered the room, and his heart had gone out to his godchild as he saw the colour drain from her face. He, too, was nervous, although his expression would never betray the fact. After all, he was the only one who knew Lady Charlotte's true identity and the dangerous game she played, and it was he who had engineered the evening, despite the animosity he felt for the earl.

He now waited with bated breath, fully prepared for the earl's enraged outburst when he recognised Lady Charlotte for who she really was. His body tensed, but he forced himself to be civil as he moved across the room to greet the newly arrived guests.

"Beaufort," the earl said. Politely he dipped his head in a bow, yet a bow so slight it was almost insulting.

"Hamilton," James responded with an equally icy bow, choosing to ignore the man's discourtesy at not using his title. "What, no Countess Weybridge this evening?"

"Alas, no. My wife sends her regrets and her apologies. The woman is suffering from the most dreadful megrim and feels in no fit state to be of company this evening."

James stared at the earl, for he had not missed the lack of sympathy in the man's voice, nor his lack of respect towards his wife, certain that he held absolutely no concern for her condition. But he kept his displeasure in check, for it would certainly not do to make a scene and, as good manners dictated, James forced his expression to remain stoically neutral.

"What a shame, for it has been several years since I have had the chance to be in the company of Lady Olivia. I would have dearly loved to make her acquaintance once more, for as you may remember, her first husband and I were great childhood friends," James said.

"Indeed, and a great loss, too," the earl replied with little conviction. "But as my daughter is to debut this season alongside your own, I am certain there will be many more opportunities for you to reacquaint yourself with her. Now, the others here I know already, but who is that lovely young lady sat over there with Lady Anne?"

"Come, let me introduce you." Turning his back on the earl in a gesture of superiority, James stepped out across the room towards his godchild and swallowed hard to fight back his growing apprehension.

****

Once more, Charlotte felt herself close to apoplexy as she watched the duke and the earl approach, with Lord Henry and Lady Amelia following behind. As the group drew closer, both Lady Anne and Lady Jane stood in a flurry of skirts, so Charlotte stood as well, her knees almost betraying her as she came to her feet. The only one who did not stand was the dowager duchess, who sat resolutely, a scowl on her face.

"Your Grace." The earl bowed in greeting to the duchess first, with little warmth, then he turned to three ladies standing before him. "Lady Anne," he continued obsequiously, "many happy returns of the day, and might I say you look even more beautiful with each passing day."

"Thank you, my lord," Anne said, respectfully curtsying as she did so.

"Lady Jane you know," the duke interceded formally, "but may I present Lady Charlotte Winters, wife of the late Sir David Winters. Lady Winters, may I present the Earl of Weybridge, his son, Lord Henry Hamilton, and his daughter, Lady Amelia Hamilton."

"The honour is mine. It is wonderful to finally meet the enigmatic and mysterious Lady Winters," the earl replied as he took Charlotte's gloved hand and lightly kissed the back of it.

Inwardly, Charlotte shuddered with revulsion at this man's touch. But the larger part of her trilled with triumph as she looked back at the one man in the whole world that she truly hated. For, even though the man was studying her face, it was not an expression of recognition that suffused his eyes, but one of attraction and covetousness instead.

Charlotte curtsied, just a little more deeply than she had first intended. "Hardly enigmatic, my lord, only new to London society. Lord Hamilton, Lady Amelia, it is a pleasure to meet you."

As she spoke, Charlotte quite deliberately avoided making eye contact with her stepbrother, turning instead to her half sister.

"That is a pretty gown you are wearing Lady Amelia," she said.

"Thank you, Lady Winters." Amelia smiled demurely. "And might I say that I love that cameo you are wearing."

"Why, thank you. It was a present from my late husband who had it commissioned to be a likeness of me." For a moment she fingered the pendant that hung on a long golden chain around her neck, the cameo being one of her favourite pieces of jewellery. "Now, you must call me Charlotte if we are to be friends." Charlotte grinned as she took hold of the girl's gloved hand. "But what of your mother, of Lady

Hamilton? I was taken to believe that she was to attend this evening's gathering."

"Alas, my stepmother is unwell. Is she not, Amelia?"Henry interjected, his voice holding more than a hint of a threat.

For a fraction of a second, Amelia glanced at her father, almost as if she harboured some guilty secret, a secret that the earl had warned her not to divulge. It was a look that Charlotte could not mistake, instantly recognising there was more to this than did meet the eye.

"Yes" — the tint in Amelia's cheeks belied the truth of her words — "a terrible megrim, I am afraid. She sends her apologies to all," she added in a remorseful yet genuine tone.

Charlotte turned away for a moment to gain control of her ire. Bitter disappointment washed through her like the flood waters of the Nile, and her hand came to her mouth politely so she could cough away the frustration of having missed the opportunity of seeing her mother for the first time in nearly twenty tears. But her discontent was tempered by anger too, for Amelia, obviously coached by her father, had quite clearly not told the whole truth about her mother's condition.

For a moment, Charlotte felt her heart harden towards the young woman, her first instinct to believe that her sister had become more like her father than her mother. Yet as she looked back at Amelia once more, she found she could not remain angry with her, for the girl's face was like an open book, and she appeared more than a little embarrassed and completely ashamed at being forced into using an untruth.

"That is a shame, Lady Amelia," Charlotte offered politely as she recovered herself. "Please, do send your mother my regards and my wishes that she recovers quickly. Now, Gentlemen, if you would excuse us for a moment, I feel the need for us ladies to spend a little time in the mutual admiration of our gowns. Viscountess Holmes" — she turned to the lady who still stood next to her husband — "would you care to join us? I would beg to guess that a chair might be of some comfort to you at this very moment." She grinned as she turned her back on the earl to lead her troupe of ladies to a seating area to one side of the room, effectively giving him the cut.

Now sitting amongst the other ladies, Charlotte finally felt comfortable enough to look around her and felt the colour slowly returning to her cheeks. Bereft of his wife, Viscount Holmes had moved to join the duke and the earl, with Lord Henry standing awkwardly to one side. It was now to him that Charlotte paid attention.

Henry, she knew, was two years older than her, which would make him three and thirty years of age, and other than the fact that he was now in possession of Thorpe Hall and its estates, she knew little more. One thing was certain, however, and that was the fact that since he had walked into the room, he had hardly taken his eyes from Anne. So it was, that lost in thought, she nearly missed a comment directed at her by Anne.

" . . . And the material is the most gorgeous shade of golden silk, is it not, Lady Charlotte?" Anne gushed.

"What? Oh, yes, it is." Charlotte smiled as she dragged her mind back to the conversation that was flowing around her. "Now, Lady Amelia, Anne tells me that you are to make your debut with her. That must be terribly exciting for you."

"Why, yes, and I am so much looking forward to my season, too," the young girl prattled, obviously relieved that the conversation had moved on from the subject of her mother. "But I am still ever so jealous that Anne has managed to get Madame LeClerc to make her gown for her. In fact I might never forgive you for arranging it," she teased with a playful twinkle in her eyes. "I shall just have to make do with the drab brown sack that Mrs Quentin's emporium is making for me."

Charlotte laughed, genuinely amused. "Oh, I would dare to wager that a beautiful young woman like yourself would make even a burlap sack look wonderful, and I daresay that you will have gentlemen climbing over themselves to make an offer for your hand."

"Perhaps," Amelia agreed, her beautiful smile telling Charlotte that her sister was more than a little pleased with the compliment.

"Oh Amelia, you know full well that you have a tendre for Lord William, and he for you also," Anne teased."I for one would gladly wager a whole month's pin money that the two of you will be betrothed long before the season ends."

"Lord William?" Viscountess Holmes asked. "Do you mean Lord William Jameson, son of the Earl of Manchester?"

"Yes, that is he," Anne acknowledged on behalf of her friend, as Amelia grinned and placed her gloved hands over her reddening cheeks. "And quite a catch, too."

"Well, I for one am pleased for you, Amelia," Charlotte said, unable to resist joining in the gentle teasing. "For I am much in favour of marriage starting as a love match, and judging by the colour of your cheeks, I would say that you are very much in love with this young man."

"Yes, I am, but please don't say anything in front of my father," Amelia murmured with a touch of misery in her tone."He and the Earl of Manchester do not always see eye to eye, and I am not at all confident that he will approve the match."

"What about you, Lady Jane? Have you anyone special in mind as a husband?" Charlotte asked.

"I had my *come out* and my first season last year and had a wonderful time," she replied.

"And no less than four offers of marriage, too," Anne said.

"Yes, but I am in no hurry to marry, and like you say, Lady Charlotte, I too believe that a love match should be the basis for a happy marriage. For that, I am content to wait a while longer."

Charlotte smiled knowingly at her new friend and watched as the girl now blushed prettily, a sure sign that she was not telling the whole truth. Charlotte could not resist.

"Now why, Lady Jane, do I think that you may have already found your someone special?" she teased as she leant into the girl sitting next to her, her words so soft that none of the other might hear them.

It was at that very moment that Stevens, the butler, pushed open the large connecting doors that led into the dining room and announced that dinner was served.

Two things happened almost immediately on the words being spoken. Almost instantly, Lord Henry moved from where he had been conversing with his father, to stand directly in front of Anne, his intentions plain for everyone to see.

"May I have the honour of escorting you into dinner, Lady Anne?" he asked curtly. Charlotte felt herself glare at the man, but as he was practically blocking her path, Anne had little choice but to take his offered arm.

At the same time, Charlotte saw the earl turn towards her, his obvious intention to ask the same. But Charlotte was in no mood to allow this man anywhere near her, so before it could appear to be impolite, she turned to the dowager duchess instead.

"Your Grace," she said in a voice that was deliberately a little louder than polite. "As we are, er, a *little light on gentlemen* this evening, would you do me the honour of accompanying me into dinner?"

To Charlotte's surprise, the dowager's face softened, and she offered a knowing smile. With practised grace and the agility of a much younger woman, she stood and took Charlotte's proffered arm. Then, as they started towards the dining room, leaving the earl firmly in their wake, her free hand came 'round to pat Charlotte on the back of her hand.

"That is the second time tonight that I have seen you give the earl the cut, my gal," she confided with a twinkle in her eye. "But as I don't much like Hamilton either, I will forgive you." She smiled, then added at a whisper, "I will say, however, that despite my earlier grumpiness, I do approve of the way you have befriended Anne and her friends. In fact, I have a feeling that you and I are going to be such good friends, too."

It did not take long for the party to be seated, the place setting for the absent countess having already been removed. Of course, the duke sat at the head of the table with the guest of honour, Lady Anne, at the other. As for Charlotte, she found herself to the right of Lady Anne and to the left of her stepbrother, whilst opposite her, on the other side of the table, was Lady Amelia.

As was to be expected, the table was lavishly set, with crystal glasses twinkling in the myriad of candles that lit the room, and soon a whole army of footmen came trouping in to serve dinner.

It was as the desert was served, no less than a bowl of delicious creamed ice accompanied with pineapple, that Lady Amelia turned to Charlotte.

"Lady Charlotte, would you tell us a little more about your home. I would love to hear more about Jamaica."

"It would be my pleasure," Charlotte said, warming even more towards her sister. "Jamaica is a wonderful island, one full of unbelievable contrasts. My principal home is in the Blue Mountains, so called for the early morning and evening mists that give them a bluish tint. It is there that trees of such magnificence flourish, and also flowers of such beauty and colours that defy the imagination. It is also much cooler in the mountains, particularly in the summer months.

"Then there are the coastal regions, where my sugar plantations are mainly located. It is much flatter there, the land leading down to the sea, to endless beaches of golden sand edged by palm trees bearing the biggest coconuts imaginable. For me, there is nothing to compare to walking along such a beach as the sea swallows the golden sun. Oh, and the sea! It is so blue and clear and warm that one might close one's eyes and imagine oneself to be in a copper bath."

"You have been in the sea?" Jane gasped, totally captivated by Lady Charlotte's description.

"Yes, I have," Charlotte replied.

She blushed a little as she thought of that wonderful day when she and David, on finding themselves totally alone on a beach, had stripped down to their undergarments so as to swim in the sea together. The water had been so warm, so crystal clear, that even now Charlotte could picture the brilliant blues and yellows of the fish that had swum beneath her. Then she blushed a little more as she remembered how, mindless of the risk they took, her husband had made love to her in the shallows of the sea. "And it was wonderful," she sighed.

"And you met your husband there?" Lady Jane asked.

"Yes," she answered, now going into the story she had rehearsed over and over again. "My father is, or should I say was, as he has now passed, a gentleman merchant who did business with my late husband, Sir David Winters. It was how we met, and, although he was somewhat older than I, ours was most definitely a love match. It was he that introduced me to the delights of walking barefoot along a sandy beach," she mused.

"Of swimming in the sea as well, no doubt," Anne said. "Oh, you make it sound such a paradise, Lady Charlotte."

"It is, but one which has many problems too. For instance, were you aware that there are over three hundred thousand slaves on the island?"

"Yet it is those very slaves that work the plantations you

own and make you the blunt that you now spend. And to think that there are those idiots in Parliament who, not content with banning slavery in England, now plan to abolish slavery throughout the British Empire. What would you do without them, Lady Winters?" the earl sneered as he threw back yet another glass of wine.

"Perfectly well, thank you, my lord, for I own no slaves. Every man and woman on my estates is free to come and go as they please." There was no smugness in Charlotte's voice, only a passionate belief that what had been done was right, and her words held the attention of all around her.

With one exception!

"Pah, stuff and nonsense," the earl replied.

"Not so," Viscount Holmes interjected. "Slavery is a vile and immoral practice and I, for one, support its abolition."

"As do I, my lord," Charlotte said. "As did my late husband. After deciding to free our workers and to pay them a basic wage, the productivity of our plantations increased three-fold in ten years, which more than compensated for the cost of wages. Now, on my plantations, we have schools for the children, rudimentary housing, and a workforce that is happy and productive," she added with pride. "I only wish I could persuade other plantation owners as to the benefits of doing the same."

"Well said, my dear," the Viscount called out, holding up his wine glass in salute. "We should have you as our Prime Minister."

"And rightly so, my lord" Charlotte replied in deadly seriousness. "For a country run by a woman could only be a better place."

"I, for one, agree with my father," Lord Henry said, suddenly interjecting into the conversation. "There would be chaos and anarchy if all the slaves were freed, and the price of commodities such as sugar would soar. Anyway, they are all just a bunch of heathen ignorant savages, if you ask me."

"They are only ignorant because they lack the education that you have been so fortunate to receive, Lord Henry. Take my companion, Phoebe, for example. She is highly intelligent and can read and write as well as any educated man. I also question who are the real savages, when it is the white man who steals these men, women, and children from their own countries, from their own families, puts them in chains and transports them halfway across the world in conditions that not even a cockroach would endure. Then, when they arrive on the island, obviously hoping that things might improve, they are put to work in the fields of Jamaica with the threat of flogging, or worse, should they not co-operate. It is a life sentence, without appeal. And what is their crime? Having black skin, that is what."

Charlotte stopped and breathed deeply to calm herself, realising that the whole table had suddenly gone quiet at her outburst. She turned to the duke and nodded apologetically.

"I am sorry, your grace," she murmured, "for whilst this is a subject about which I am so obviously passionate, it is not a suitable topic for the birthday celebration of Lady Anne. Please accept my apologies."

"No apologies needed Lady Charlotte, for I happen to agree with you," the duke replied.

"And I still think that some people should not meddle in the order of things," Lord Henry hissed under his breath, but still loud enough for Charlotte to hear. "These people are nothing but heathens."

"I wouldn't say that to my man, Samson, Lord Henry," Charlotte warned.

"And why ever not," he sneered.

"For Samson, who was a slave himself, is nearly seven feet tall," the duke replied on her behalf, "and is built like the Colossus of Rhodes."

CHAPTER SEVEN

Charlotte slept late on the next morning and was finally awoken by Phoebe with a breakfast tray at about eleven. Having slept extremely soundly, she found herself stretching languishingly as Phoebe placed the tray on the bed before she went tutting all around the room, collecting this item of clothing and that shoe from where Charlotte had carelessly discarded them after undressing herself on returning home.

"So how was your evening?" Phoebe asked as she picked up Charlotte's gown to hang it up in the mahogany wardrobe.

"It could not have gone any better, Phoebe, but for one exception," Charlotte gushed. "Neither the earl nor his bastard son had the slightest inkling as to who I am, nor did they do anything to convince me that either of them may have changed their ways since the day I was abducted. The earl is just as arrogant as he has always been, and my stepbrother seems to have grown to be just like his father. Now my halfsister, on the other hand, is a darling girl and is, as we suspected, an innocent."

"And what of your mother?"

"That was the exception I mentioned, for sadly she did not attend. A megrim, seemingly."

"Which is probably why the earl thought he could get away with sending you flowers. He had a large bouquet delivered to you this morning."

"Did he, by God, the arrogant, egotistical, conceited . . ." Charlotte ranted, for she knew exactly what was going through the earl's mind when sending her the flowers. But then she laughed out loud, her heart doing a little dance of victory.

"Which means that the man saw you only as a beautiful, wealthy young widow, ripe for the picking. He probably believes that he can have you *picking up* your skirts for him in no time at all," Phoebe teased.

"Only to get the shock of his life when he discovers what is under there." Charlotte giggled. "Phoebe, would you pop downstairs and tell Samson that under no circumstances is the Earl of Weybridge to be allowed admittance, should he call? Could you then have a bath drawn for me, please?"

"That might have to wait, Lady Charlotte, for Mr Abernathy is waiting downstairs to see you."

That news had Charlotte throwing back her bedclothes and leaping out of bed in a flurry of satin nightdress.

"Why did you not say sooner? Come, help me dress."

Breakfast now forgotten, Charlotte quickly stripped out of her nightgown, not caring for one moment Phoebe would see her in a naked state, and mindless of the tiny penis that hung between her legs. After all, Phoebe had often seen her this way and was entirely responsible for the pert little breasts, the narrow waist, the lovely rounded bottom, and the long slim legs that Charlotte now possessed.

Being reminded as to exactly why she had these feminine characteristics, Charlotte grimaced as Phoebe force-fed her with her special medicine. Then she dressed in a clean chemise and the simple day gown Phoebe had selected for her. As there was no time to dress her hair, Phoebe also quickly brushed her hair so it hung loosely behind her back before stuffing a pretty lace mob cap onto Charlotte's head, something entirely appropriate for a widowed lady, but something that Charlotte normally hated to wear.

"There, you'll do." Phoebe grinned as she held out a pair of simple slippers for Charlotte to put on.

Moments later, Charlotte walked into the room she used as a study, to find Mr Abernathy perched inelegantly on a chair waiting patiently for her to arrive. As she entered, he stood and bowed politely, giving her a moment to observe the man. To say that he was nondescript was an understatement. Of indeterminate middle age, he was average height and build. His clothes were clean but plain, the sort of thing a clerk might wear in a counting-house, and his face was the type that no one would ever say would stand out in a crowd. Yet it was for that very reason, Charlotte suspected, that he was so very successful at his profession.

"Mr Abernathy, please do sit. I see someone has already brought you tea."

"Yes, thank you, my lady." The man's voice was somewhat high and nasally in tone and was the one thing that Charlotte disliked about the man.

"So, what do you have to report?"

The man reached for a black leather document folio that was on the floor beside his chair. Quite slowly and deliberately, he unfastened the brass buckles and flipped open the case to extract a thick sheave of carefully handwritten pages.

"Here are my notes, Lady Winters, you will find them most comprehensive," the man drawled.

"A précis, if you please, Mr Abernathy."

"Very well. Let me begin with the earl. His main source of income, as you know, is the tin mine on his Cornish estate. However, my sources tell me that the mine is virtually played out and that, for the last few months, the earl has employed geologists, without success, to prospect the area in the vain hope of finding more. The mine is simply leeching funds at the moment.

"As you requested, I have also viewed Haycock Abbey, his principal home, and whilst I saw no evidence of the countess, I did manage to make a number of observations on spending the evening in a local tavern with the earl's steward. As you know, the earl controls the estates of both Haycock and Thorpe Hall, which are mainly farmed by tenant farmers. By all accounts, these farmers are close to mutiny, as the earl has almost doubled the rents over the past three years, meaning that his tenants are barely subsisting. It would also suggest that the earl is desperate for money."

"So it would seem," Charlotte agreed.

"The steward was also quite forthcoming about Lord Henry Hamilton. It would seem that the earl keeps his son on a very tight financial lead. Whilst his lordship resides at Thorpe Hall, his father takes responsibility for the house finances. All Henry gets is a monthly stipend, which disappears almost as soon as he receives it. Lord Henry, it seems, like his father, is something of a gambler and is often seen in the gaming rooms at Whites, or some such establishment. It seems that the earl has had to bail out his son no less than three times in the past ten years, even once when Henry had actually been *called out* over an outstanding debt of over one thousand pounds.

"Now that is interesting," Charlotte mused.

"And it gets even more so. The steward told me, after a little financial incentive on my part, there had been rumour that in recent months the earl has been seen in the company of a notorious money lender, one Silas Green, and it is said that he has borrowed heavily against the value of the Thorpe Hall estate."

For a moment, Charlotte sat in silence, listening to the heavy thud of her excited heart, knowing that this news was even more than she had possibly hoped for. Whilst it did not surprise her to hear of the financial difficulties of both the earl and his son, the size of those difficulties was like music to her ears. But to find out that her stepfather had borrowed money against *her* estate was the icing on the cake.

"Now we come to the final part of my report. You asked me to investigate the demise of one Sir Oliver Royce. Well, I managed to track down the constable, a Mr Jarvis Jones, who investigated the accident, and despite his now advanced years, he seemed to remember the incident with remarkable clarity. Apparently, Sir Oliver's fall was witnessed by just one other rider."

"Let me guess. The Earl of Weybridge." She whispered the words in horror, hardly daring to believe what was being said.

"Quite. According to the constable, there was no reason to suspect any foul play, but, in truth, I suspect the man's honesty. For you see, shortly after the accident, Jones left the constabulary and then bought the Dog and Duck, a hostelry in Kings Langley, and for cash no less."

"Which suggests he might have been in receipt of some sort of bribe." Charlotte hissed through clenched teeth, the shock of what she was hearing, sending her mind into a spin.

"My conclusion exactly, my lady. For it would be very unlikely that a mere constable could ever amass sufficient funds to buy such a place outright."

"Which, in turn, suggests that the earl might somehow be responsible for Sir Oliver's demise."

"Quite."

Stunned, Charlotte sat there, and for a few moments, contemplated what this new information might entail. Everyone, Charles included, had assumed that her father's death had been a simple hunting accident, yet another rider falling and hitting their head on some rock or wall. But now it was as plain as the hairs on the end of a wart that the earl had somehow been involved, even if there was no direct evidence to support this conjecture. Slowly, Charlotte composed herself, once more fixing her expression into something akin to a hospitable lady of the *ton*.

"Well, Mr Abernathy. May I say that you have completely exceeded my expectations with your *fact-finding* mission. You have my gratitude."

"Thank you, my lady." Abernathy bowed his head in deference. "You will find all the details of my findings in my written report." He handed her the weighty document. "Along with, er, my, er, invoice."

Carefully, Charlotte opened the folded sheet of paper to see a very detailed account of agreed pay and incidental expenses occurred, amounting to exactly fifty-six pounds, fourteen shillings and sixpence. So, pulling open a drawer in her desk, she retrieved a hidden key and unlocked a small cash box that she kept there. Pulling out a money pouch, she handed it to Abernathy and watched as he opened it to pour the golden sovereigns it contained into his hand.

"Lady Winters, you have given me too much. There must be a hundred guineas here!"

"And I would have paid you double that amount for the information you have provided me with. You will keep the difference as a bonus, Mr Abernathy."

"Well then, thank you, my lady." Carefully, so as to not drop a coin, he poured the money back into the pouch and made to stand.

"Mr Abernathy," Charlotte began slowly and softly, "before you go, I do have one more task for you, should you care to undertake it. Might I add, that it is also a task that is worth another one hundred pounds on completion."

The man smiled as he sat back down on his chair. "You have but to name it, my lady."

"I would like you to arrange for me to meet this Silas Green."

Charlotte quietly sat alone after Mr Abernathy's departure and spent some time reading through the precise and accurate observations he had made. Then she sat back in her chair with her fingers intertwined as her mind began to move the chess pieces on her metaphorical board.

If Abernathy was to be believed, the earl was obviously experiencing some serious financial difficulties, especially if he had been forced to resort to borrowing from money lenders.

Mmm, I definitely need more information on that score.

Then there was Lord Henry, a notorious rake, whom, from all accounts, was, himself, continuously short of funds.

Which is why he was paying so much attention to Anne.

All evening, she had observed the man's posturing and had even heard Anne's gentle rebuff when he had asked if he could call on her or take her for a ride in his Phaeton. In fact, the man had been persistent throughout the entire evening, being far less than subtle in his advances towards the daughter of the duke.

I guess he needs to find himself a rich wife and quick, one with a dowry the size of a country as well. Who better than the beautiful Lady Anne? And the earl! He needs money as well, even more so than his son. Perhaps he sees the rich widow in town as a way of getting it. Flowers indeed, and from a married man, too.

Then a sudden thought crossed her mind. Perhaps this had been the earl's plan all along, the opportunity of the dinner party too good to miss. Perhaps it had been he that had demanded Henry court Anne, just so that the earl could get his hands on her dowry, a dowry which was surely big enough to alleviate some, if not all, of their financial difficulties. Then, should this fail, Charlotte could easily see Henry trying compromise Anne in some way, to force her to marry him or ruin her reputation amongst the *ton* so he could get his hands on her money. It would be so easy for him to do so, especially considering how endearingly naive Anne could be at times. All he would need to do would be to get her alone at some ball or other, to force his attentions on her, somehow arranging for them to be discovered so that her reputation would be ruined unless she married him. It certainly would not be the first time something like that had happened, nor probably the last.

And as for the earl himself, perhaps Charlotte was about to become his chosen victim in an effort to raise funds. Perhaps he saw her as the rich widow ripe for the picking, and he was certainly egotistical enough to think that he was so manly that *Lady Winters* would be unable to resist.

It was then a thought of such horror flitted through Charlotte's mind that she actually gasped aloud. Perhaps, if the circumstances warranted it, the earl would even be of a mind to actually dispose of the wife he already had, so that she could be replaced by someone with funds enough for several lifetimes. After all, it would not be the first time he had tried to commit murder for financial gain.

"Oh, Father," she whispered to herself as a single tear dripped down her face. "Did he murder you too?" She looked up at the ceiling, almost as if she was expecting a reply from on high.

Sudden anger scythed through her chest, and Charlotte stood so violently that her chair actually toppled to the ground behind her.

"This will not do! This will simply not do!" she yelled. "Phoebe!"

Almost instantly, Phoebe was in the room with her, a look of real concern on her face, and she was followed, almost immediately by Samson, who dashed in, his fists already curled as if spoiling for a fight.

"Phoebe, my bath, then you must help me dress for I must go and see the duke."

****

"Lady Winters, your grace," Stevens announced as he

showed the woman into the drawing room.

James watched as Charlotte breezed into the room, once more completely amazed at the poise and confidence that emanated from every pore of her body. Politely he dipped his head in greeting, pleased to see her curtsy in return, especially as Stevens was looking on.

"That will be all, Stevens,"

Yes, your grace. Shall I have a tea tray sent up?"

"Please . . . erm . . . please," he mumbled as he pointed towards a chair, still not quite comfortable with the whole situation.

In fact, for the last few nights, his sleep had been very much disturbed as he tried, in vain, to come to terms with what had become of his godson. Now here he was again, and once more James stared at him . . . her . . . in something akin to awe.

Charlotte sat on an armchair, her back straight, her shoulders square, looking every inch the lady. Her hair had been beautifully styled into a simple chignon, and she again wore a touch of face paint to embellish her feminine features. Her dress was in the empire style, a ribbon high on her chest under her bust, the neckline cut low enough to show the perfect swell of her breasts. Why, she even smelled beautiful, with the soft scent of lavender pervading his senses. And as he stared at her, like a teenage boy experiencing his first crush, he felt his body respond to the vision he saw.

He just could not help it!

Even knowing who and what she was, even knowing that this person was a child when compared to him, and was his godchild to boot, he could not stop the response he was experiencing, the sudden surge of attraction. Even with the iron self-control he prided himself on, it was the instinctive and inescapable primal attraction that a man had for a beautiful woman, and the thought scared him to the very core.

Had she been a woman . . .

He silenced his groan as he sat, pulling the tails of his coat over his lap to effectively hide the arousal he was experiencing. He coughed then, to cover his embarrassment, hoping beyond hope that Charlotte had not noticed anything amiss, then forced a smile upon his face.

"What can I do for you this morning, Lady Charlotte?" he asked.

"I . . . er . . . I have come into some information that I wish to share with you," she murmured.

She pulled some documents from her reticule and carefully handed them to him, and James could not help but note that she had deliberately avoided any physical contact between them, just by the way she snatched away her fingers.

James pulled out a pair of halfmoon, wire-framed spectacles, and for a few moments, he sat in silence to read through the document, his eyebrows rising as he took in the disclosure of the facts. Then, once more pulling the glasses very deliberately from his nose, he looked back at Charlotte.

"Where did you get this?" he demanded.

"I have had a man investigating the earl and Lord Henry," Charlotte replied.

"And do you believe this? I can scarce believe that the earl may have been responsible for your father's death."

"Whilst I have no proof, I have no reason to doubt his findings. But retribution for this will have to wait, for what we now need to do is to look to the future, to decide exactly how we are going to thwart whatever schemes they may now be concocting."

"Go on," he demanded.

Charlotte took a deep breath. "Did you notice how attentive Lord Henry was to Anne last night? Once the party resumed for cards, after dinner, he hardly left her side for a moment, even insisting that he partner her for whist."

"As a matter of fact, I did so note, and this morning a large bouquet of flowers was delivered for Anne, from him of course."

"As did I, from the earl," Charlotte grumbled. "A dozen coral coloured roses, no less. Hardly a subtle gesture."

"Did you, by God?" James cursed. "Whilst I am not well versed in the language of flowers, do not coral roses mean desire?"

"They do indeed."

"Well, I can cap that," said James. "The baron also had the audacity to call this morning to ask permission for him to take Anne on a carriage ride this afternoon."

"And?"

"I turned him down of course. It would not have been appropriate, even with a chaperon, until Anne has made her come out and has been presented at court."

"Thank goodness for that. For if you ask me, Lord Henry is in desperate need of funds and may have set his sights on Anne. Perhaps he thinks to seduce her, to make her fall in love with him before she has the opportunity of meeting any other eligible *gentlemen*. He is certainly handsome enough to do it, to turn the head of a pretty, yet naive, young woman. Nevertheless, I certainly would not put it past him to even try and compromise Lady Anne in order to force her to marry him, just so he can get his hands on her dowry."

With a sudden surge of anger, James stood quickly and paced across the room."I will kill him if he tries anything like that with Anne," he growled. "But what of you and that blackguard, the Earl of bloody Weybridge? He is a married man, for God's sake, married to your mother!"

"Well, one thing is for certain, and that is he has absolutely no clue as to my true identity. For had he known who I am, what I am, he would most probably have sent me deadly nightshade instead of roses."

"Quite. So what do you think the earl is trying to achieve?"

"I can think of three possible reasons for his behaviour. Firstly, he may see me as another notch on his bedpost, an available widow ripe for him to make his mistress. Secondly, he might be trying to use my friendship with Lady Anne to further Lord Henry's pursuit of her. Thirdly, and this notion I find the most disturbing, he may even try to court me, in order to make me *fall in love* with him. Imagine what he might do to the countess if he had a rich and willing widow ready to take her place."

"By God, yes, and if what you have told me of his past is to be believed, I certainly would not put it past him to do that. So, what to do? What to do? We have to stop them, Charlotte. We have to."

For a moment, James stood and stared at Charlotte as her brilliant blue eyes captured his once more. Again, he felt a surge of attraction, but this time it had nothing to do with his godchild's beauty. No, this time it had everything to do with the genuine concern that she had shown for his daughter.

And he no longer doubted her, either. He no longer doubted her ability to be the woman Charles had become, and moreover, he no longer doubted if he could trust her.

"Do you have faith in me, your grace?" she whispered.

"Yes, I do," he quickly replied. "It is the earl and the baron I do not trust."

"I, more than most, have cause to agree with you there. There is no need to worry about me, your grace, for you have my word that I can handle the earl. Consequently, my only concern is for us to protect Anne. So here is what I propose . . ."

****

Charlotte exited the duke's home, and Samson was waiting, as per usual, to escort her along the short walk back to her house. However, as they walked together, no words were spoken, for she was lost in thought, having been caught completely off guard by the unmistakable reaction of her godfather to her presence that morning.

Strangely, it had not been the content of their discussion that had surprised her. It had, instead, been the way James had physically reacted to her presence. The signs of it were undeniable—the dilated pupils, a soft bead of sweat on his brow, the beginnings of a bulge in his breeches that suggested a man might be experiencing some sort of physical attraction. But no! Her Uncle James? How could it be? It was simply inconceivable. He could not possibly be attracted to her... could he? After all, he knew her secret, he knew what lay beneath the gowns and crinolines.

Abruptly she coughed, to hide her thoughts, shaking her head to clear it of such imaginings and to force herself to focus on the real reason she had visited that morning. At least the duke had agreed with her assessment of the situation, even if it had taken every ounce of persuasive power she possessed to convince him of the course of action that was needed.

It was because her thoughts had been consumed with the duke that Charlotte hardly noticed, then dismissed, the wry smile that played on Samson's face for the entire journey back to her home.

That was until she walked into her bedchamber and called for Phoebe. For as she did so, a whirlwind of skirts and arms and legs and thick curly black hair swept her off her feet, swinging her around in girlish glee.

Phoebe shrieked in happiness. "He asked me, Charlotte! Samson asked me!"

CHAPTER EIGHT

When Charlotte had first returned to London, it had been her intention to use whatever means at her disposal to achieve her goals. Hatred for the earl had eaten deep into her very soul, and she knew that she would have no qualms at using every tool available to her, to achieve his downfall. Even the duke and his daughter would be used if she deemed it necessary.

But the more she had come to know Anne, the more she started to care for the girl, and it now it seemed like her return to London had been timed most fortuitously, if her suspicions about Lord Henry were correct.

So now, instead of exploiting the duke and his daughter, she determined to be Anne's guardian angel instead. She would be there to see her safely through the social maelstrom. She would be there to protect Anne from any unsavoury advances, especially from Lord Henry. She would attend balls and parties with her, would shadow her if a gentleman called to take her for a walk or to take her for a ride, as was the want in the *ton*.

Of course, in a more subtle way, this would also allow Charlotte to move forward with her quest. After all, Anne was close friends with her sister, Amelia, and through them, Charlotte was certain that she could once more find herself in the company of her mother.

And so it was, and with the dowager duchess's approval and blessing, Charlotte agreed to be chaperon to Lady Anne Beaufort for the whole of her first season.

At first, the duke had refused her offer, not wanting to risk the potential for scandal. But after extensive and persuasive discussion—although Charlotte had omitted several pertinent facts—even he had to admit that Lady Charlotte would be the perfect person to take on the role.

Anne had been overjoyed, and Charlotte had spent the next few days in her company. They had visited Madame LeClerc's establishment once more, for the final fittings of their gowns, and just that morning, Anne's coming out gown had been delivered and was now in her bedroom on a dress maker's mannequin.

"Oh, Lotte," Anne gushed, "I can't stop smiling. Isn't the dress simply breathtaking?"

"Yes, and it will only be more so with you wearing it next week," Charlotte teased.

There were just six more days to go before the start of the season, and preparations had the entire household in a frenzy. On the actual day, the season's debutantes would be formally presented at court. This was to be followed, on the next evening, by the Duchess of Harrow's ball, at which, it was rumoured, even the Prince Regent would be attending.

"Oh, I can't wait. I can see it now. There will be hundreds of eligible bachelors queuing up for the privilege of taking me for a ride in Hyde Park, hundreds of handsome men falling at my feet." Anne flopped back onto her bed in a very unlady-like way and giggled, wriggling her toes inside her satin slippers just for effect.

"And several of them, the rakes amongst them, evilly waiting for their opportunity to ruin your good name," Charlotte warned as she sat down on the bed next to her.

"And I cannot believe that anyone would be so cruel to do so," Anne said."Lotte, can I ask you a personal question?" She turned onto her side and propped her head up on one bent arm, a mischievous look in her eyes.

"If you must, but I retain the right to refuse an answer."

"Why do you always wear powders on your face when it is not really the fashion? Are you not afraid of being labelled a painted lady or even a demimonde?"

Charlotte laughed. "No, I am not, for I care not what the vacant minded ladies of the *ton* think of me. I wear makeup for a number of reasons. Whilst it may not be the fashion here, it was in Jamaican society, so I have become used to doing so. But mainly I wear makeup because I like the way it makes me look. The trick is to be subtle, to not use too much, just a little powder here, a little rouge there."

"Well, I happen to agree with you, for, in my opinion, your makeup serves only to enhance your beauty."

Inwardly Charlotte smiled, loving the compliment in a way that Anne would never understand. But she also held her breath, knowing the question that was about to come.

"So . . ." Anne paused innocently. "Do you think father would let me wear a little kohl around my eyes, like you do?"

"Oh, darling, I think there are two chances of that happening . . . no chance and absolutely no chance at all. Besides, it is only us *old maids* that need to use face paints. You, my darling, need nothing but what God gave you to look beautiful. So, have you decided what jewellery you will wear for the evening?" she asked, artfully changing the subject as she did so.

"Grandmama would like me to wear the family's emeralds, but they are far too garish for my tastes. So, my mother's diamond headpiece, and her pearls, I think. Oh, and your eardrops, too."

"That sounds perfect. Now I have a suggestion to make. As you are to make your debut at the same time as Lady Amelia, what say you to inviting her and her mother to tea at my house tomorrow? I thought it would be a good opportunity for us all to get to know each other a little better, especially now that I am to be your chaperon. And," she whispered,

tapping her nose in a most conspiratorial way, "if you promise not to tell your father, perhaps I can get Phoebe to give you
a lesson in the application of cosmetics," she added to
sweeten the pot.

Abruptly, Anne sat up on her bed and Charlotte could not
help but laugh as the girl grinned broadly.

"That, my dear Lady Winters, is a splendid idea. Let me get
pen and paper," she gushed with her natural exuberance.
"We must send an invitation immediately."

Wryly, Charlotte smiled and watched Anne dash to her
writing slope as part one of her little plan came to fruition.
She was beginning to hate the idea of using Anne this way,
but she could see no other way of gaining contact with her
mother. After all, she could hardly march up to the earl's residence and demand to see her without raising a great deal of
suspicion. This way was far more subtle, and much safer, too.

There was another good reason for wanting to make contact with the countess as well, for Charlotte saw this as one
avenue to discouraging the earl's *attentions,* which were becoming something of a dangerous nuisance. Just that morning, the earl had once more sent flowers, so perhaps appearing to befriend the countess might have the effect of keeping
the vile man at arm's length, without having to resort to a
more physical form of dissuasion.

The letter had been delivered, and to Charlotte's delight,
an acceptance received. Despite the fact Charlotte had been
prepared for disappointment, the note had said that Countess
Weybridge and Lady Amelia would be delighted to attend at
the agreed time of three in the afternoon.

So the plan was set, and that morning Charlotte was sitting
alone in her drawing room, nervously filling in the time by
dipping into one of Miss Jane Austin's more recent novels,
Pride and Prejudice. The only problem was that her mind was

so occupied with the impending visit of her mother and sister, that she often had to read a line three or four times before the words even registered.

It was a little after eleven in the morning when there was a knock on the door, and Samson let himself into the room with a grim expression on his face.

"Missy Charlotte. Earl Weybridge is here, *demanding* to see you. Do you want fo' me to send him away?" His slight smile suggested he would enjoy the opportunity of flexing his muscles.

Charlotte snapped her book shut and quite deliberately placed it on a tea table before she looked back at Samson, a theatrical sigh slipping from her lips as her heart ratcheted up by several beats.

"No, I think it is time for me to start dealing with this man, Samson, but no matter what happens, I do not want you to leave the room. Is that understood?"

"Yes, Missy Charlotte." Samson grinned.

"Then you had better show him in."

Samson retreated through the parlour door and Charlotte found herself closing her eyes and breathing deeply in order to quell her rapidly rising pulse.

When she opened her eyes once more, it was to see that Phoebe had let herself, uninvited, into the room, nodding respectfully as she placed herself strategically in a chair next to Charlotte, picking up a piece of embroidery to make it look as if she had been there all morning. Then she looked at Charlotte with an expression which said *I'm here for you* as she handed her mistress her book once more. Charlotte's heart soared at this tiny little show of moral support.

"The Earl of Weybridge, Lady Winters," Samson's deep voice called, and Charlotte lifted her head from the now open book.

George Hamilton, Earl of Weybridge, strutted into the

room as if he owned it, and Charlotte experienced an involuntary shudder of revulsion as she once more saw the smug, superior expression the man always seemed to sport. He was, she had to admit, quite the dashing figure. He was finely dressed — his jacket perfectly tailored, his boots gleaming in the sunshine that streamed through the door. Yet there was something about him, as always, that suggested he was anything but a gentleman. Reluctantly, Charlotte stood and gave a perfunctory curtsey, the merest dip of her knees, and he proffered the slightest bow of his head in return.

"Good morning, Lady Winters."

The earl smiled a sweet sickly smile, once more making Charlotte shudder, her whole body now tense for the confrontation that was surely about to come.

"Good morning, my lord. To what do we owe the pleasure of your visit?" she replied

Not wanting the man anywhere near her, she quite deliberately indicated a chair for him to sit on, a chair somewhat distant from her own. Then she smiled a tentative little smile when she saw the earl look with displeasure around the room, to observe Samson standing respectfully by a wall, to see Phoebe sitting by her mistress, her attention entirely focussed on her embroidery.

"I was hoping to have a word with you in private, Lady Charlotte. In fact, I insist I speak to you alone," he demanded.

Inwardly, Charlotte winced, for his voice was pitched in such a manner as to make anyone believe he must be obeyed. Then she stared at the man with as much indignation as she could muster, whilst she fought to disguise the rising anger she felt. This was the man she remembered so well from childhood, the man who had thought nothing of taking a belt to a small boy for even the smallest of infringements. This was the man who believed his station in life made him so superior that he could demand instant gratification from all those around him. This was the man who had delighted in allowing his own son to bully a young and vulnerable child all because, in his world, it would *build character*.

And this was the man who had ordered that very same boy killed for a mere parcel of land.

Charlotte composed her answer carefully and deliberately kept her voice low with a hint of menace and malice. "I think not, sir, and I suggest you think twice before *insisting* on anything in my own home. Besides, anything you have to say to me can and will be said in front of Samson and Phoebe, for they are no mere servants. They are my friends and I have no secrets from either of them."

"But . . . bu- . . . they are . . . they are niggers . . ." the earl blustered.

"I would advise that you be careful what you say, my lord, really careful," Charlotte snarled. "I for one detest the use of that word, and I will have you know that Samson will not take it at all kindly if you are anything but a gentleman towards myself or my companion. Now perhaps you would be kind enough to come to the point of your visit."

"But . . . but . . . What I have to discuss with you is of a very personal nature. Not something I would want to speak of in front of your . . . of your . . . er . . . servants, Lady Charlotte," he huffed.

Quite intentionally, Charlotte giggled to pre-empt the earl. "Oh, Lord Hamilton." She sighed dramatically. "Now I see your intentions for your visit this morning. It has not escaped my attention that you have formed something of a tendre for me, that perhaps you would like me for your mistress. After all, have you not twice sent me coral roses, which, if I'm not mistaken, means *desire* in the language of flowers, does it not?"

"But . . . but . . ." the earl muttered.

Charlotte watched as the man's face turned an interesting

shade of purple, knowing that her words, having been said in front of Phoebe and Samson, must be the cause of great embarrassment for him. Her mind smiled once more as she realised that now was the perfect time *to turn the screw.*

"But, my lord, I must inform you, with much regret, that I do not, cannot return those affections, no matter how much I might like to do so."

"And why not, by God!" he demanded, almost as if it was his God-given right to have her do so.

"Well, you may not have heard, but I am to be chaperon to Lady Anne for the entire season, and Anne, of course, is best friends with your daughter, Amelia. In fact, both Lady Amelia and Lady Olivia, *your wife,* are expected here for tea this afternoon. Therefore, I think that it might be somewhat inappropriate if you and I . . . well . . . you being married . . . well, perhaps you understand."

Charlotte deliberately kept her reply vague as she allowed her voice to tail off into nothingness and once more she smiled as she observed the play of emotion that danced across the earl's face. There was anger, much anger, and frustration, too. Nor had his arrogance disappeared, almost as if the man had truly thought that she would have, should have, fallen at his feet.

"Ah . . . er . . . yes . . . well . . ." he coughed, and obviously fought for self-control.

She could practically see the man's mind working and wondered if he had already prepared a secondary reason for his visit, *just in case.*

She was not wrong either!

"Perhaps, yes . . . that . . . erm . . . yes . . . perhaps it might be wiser . . . if . . . well. I, erm, had not heard that you had taken on this responsibility." He coughed. "However, in light of this, perhaps I could discuss an entirely different matter with you?" The earl adopted a more benevolent yet still supercilious expression.

"If I may be of service," Charlotte replied, lying through her teeth.

"Well, my son, Baron Weybridge, Henry, whom you met at Lady Anne's dinner party, has formed something of an attachment for the girl. As her chaperon, you have it within your power to facilitate the courtship he so desires, something I would deem as a great personal favour."

Charlotte, quite on purpose, sighed theatrically. "Oh, my lord, shame on you for asking such a thing. Of course, should Lady Anne find favour in your son's *gentlemanly* advances, then I will be glad to chaperone them when they are together. But the lady has a mind of her own, and I, for one, will do nothing to try and sway her towards one suitor or another. Besides, I am not certain that the duke would approve of the match. He is, after all, only a baron."

"And heir to an earldom," the man sneered.

"Yet I fancy the duke sees his daughter as a marchioness at the very least, or maybe even a duchess."

Once more Charlotte could see the anger bubbling beneath the surface, and a quick glance towards Samson had her man on the balls of his feet.

Charlotte stood politely.

Right then, Lotte . . . Time to end this, I think. For doing so is truly going to piss off the little fucker.

Inwardly, she giggled at that delicious thought, especially as the language she had used would have been much more appropriate for the brothels of Kingston.

"Now, my lord, I pray you will have to forgive me, but I shortly have another pressing engagement. Samson, if you would be so kind as to show the earl out."

For the briefest of moments, Charlotte truly believed the earl was not going to take the hint, and that he was going to remain to argue the toss with her. But then she saw him glance at Samson, who had gleefully taken a step towards him.

Judging by the change of expression on the earl's face, he had instantly decided better, even though he was obviously annoyed at being given the *cut*. He stood and bowed perfunctorily and then, without another word, he turned on his heel to march out of the room once more.

"Why don't you let me slip some hemlock into his tea next time he visits," Phoebe said, her words spoken in a voice that left Charlotte in no doubt that she would be happy to do that very thing and lose no sleep over the deed either.

"Oh, fear not, my darling, his time will come soon enough."

Shortly before three in the afternoon, Charlotte had changed her day dress, and Phoebe had styled her hair into something a little more sophisticated, and the two of them now sat together in the drawing room, waiting for their guests to arrive.

And Charlotte was more nervous than she could ever remember having been before.

"But what if she recognises me," Charlotte moaned to Phoebe who, once more, had her embroidery in her hands. "She is my mother. If anyone was to recognise me, it will be her."

"Would it be so bad if she did?" Phoebe asked. She put down her embroidery frame and took Charlotte's hand between her own in the most comforting of ways. "You are her child, and if what the duke has said is correct, she grieved your loss for many years."

"I know, but how could she possibly accept me the way I am now. God, if she recognises me, everything will be lost . . . all my plans . . . everything." Charlotte moaned again. "This is ridiculous! I must cancel this . . . this . . . farce."

Phoebe smiled and patted the back of her hand. "I don't think that will be possible, Lady Charlotte, for no matter what, you will have to face her sometime. Better you do so in private if you ask me. Besides, if I am not very much mistaken, I can hear your guests even now."

Moments later, a very excited Anne came bouncing into the room, curtsying to Charlotte as she did so. And, as Charlotte held her breath, her heart pounding so violently she felt almost as if she were about to give birth to it, Anne was followed by Lady Amelia on whose arm was another woman who, to Charlotte's genuine dismay, she hardly recognised.

Lady Olivia Hamilton, Countess of Weybridge, Charlotte's mother, appeared as a shadow of the woman she had once been. Her face had aged terribly, and despite the powder she wore, the worry lines and pensive look and dark circles under her eyes were more than evident. Her dark hair, whilst stylishly arranged, was shot through with grey, all of which made her appear much older than she was in reality. And, whilst she was smartly dressed, it was in a gown that appeared to be three or four years out of fashion. But of all the things Charlotte noticed, it was her mother's demeanour that shocked her the most. Clutching onto her daughter's arm, she walked stiffly, almost as if she were in great pain, and from the sad and vacant look in her eyes, it seemed almost as if she were suffering from some great melancholy.

"Lady Charlotte, may I introduce my mother, Lady Olivia Hamilton," said Amelia softly as she too curtsied.

"It is my honour to meet you, Lady Hamilton," Charlotte replied. "Please, do sit. Oh, and before we continue, might I beseech everyone to dispense with formal titles. We are all to be friends here, so I think, if everyone agrees, first names should be appropriate."

"Thank you, Lady Charlotte, and thank you for your kind invitation this afternoon so that I can now put a face to the name. I must declare that Amelia has hardly stopped talking about you since you met at Anne's dinner party."

Charlotte watched as her mother gingerly lowered herself down into a chair, the pain she was clearly experiencing etched onto her face. From behind her, she heard Phoebe hiss, the healer in her always ready to recognise someone in need. But before Phoebe could intervene, Charlotte turned and gave her a look that simply said *not yet.*

"In truth, I find both of these two young ladies quite charming company." Charlotte smiled as she turned to Anne and Amelia, who now sat together on a settee. "It warms the heart of an old widow like me to see such beauty and youthful enthusiasm. You should be quite proud of Amelia, for she is sure to be a hit with the *ton* when she makes her debut."

"Oh, I am, I am very proud. There will be a great sadness in my heart when she leaves me to marry, as marry she must," Olivia said with more strength and conviction in her voice than Charlotte had expected. "Or, perhaps, great rejoicing," she added in an enigmatic tone.

"So how are your preparations going, Amelia?" Anne asked. "Madame LeClerc delivered my dress two days ago, and I must say I am quite pleased with the result, quite pleased."

"*Pleased* is hardly the word, Anne," Charlotte teased. "If you must, Amelia, imagine a little girl being given her first pony, and that might tell you exactly how Anne reacted when her gown arrived. Now what of your gown, Amelia, are you as thrilled as Anne?"

Again, Charlotte sensed something amiss as Amelia and the countess exchanged a look, almost as if the two of them had pre-arranged an answer to this most obvious question.

"My ballgown is not quite complete, but Mrs Quentin, my modiste, has promised it will be ready on time," Amelia answered. "However, I am certain it will be nowhere near as beautiful as yours, Anne."

"It is not the gown that will be beautiful, Amelia, but the

woman wearing it," Charlotte said.

It was then Charlotte noticed something out of the ordinary. As she spoke, Amelia turned her head away, her cheeks reddening a little in embarrassment, her expression an exact mirror of when she had been forced into a lie at Anne's dinner party. Instantly Charlotte perceived that something was seriously amiss with her sister, for any young woman about to make her debut should be far more excited about the gown she was to wear for the occasion. Just then, a maid opened the door and entered with a large and ornate silver tea tray. "Ah good, tea! Phoebe, if you would please."

The four ladies chatted amiably as tea and cakes were consumed, with Phoebe acting as maid to serve them. The conversation was light and feminine and focussed on such topics as the current crop of eligible gentlemen and how the young debutantes would be expected to behave when in their company.

As time progressed, Charlotte felt the tension in her body begin to ebb away, for nothing seemed to suggest that the countess, her mother, suspected anything about her, even when she asked Charlotte about her own family.

"Alas, I have no children," she responded. "I loved my husband dearly, but unfortunately, due to a very severe dose of the mumps as a young man, he was unable to father a child."

Anne gasped. "But you are still young, Lotte. You could remarry and have children with your new husband."

For some reason, Anne had a glint in her eye, which almost suggested to Charlotte that she might have someone in mind to fill that very role.

"I think not, Anne. I have had my one true love and am content now with my lot. Besides, Phoebe and my man, Samson, are soon to marry, and I expect to have hundreds of little ones running around for me to play godmother to. Don't I,

Phoebe?"

"Yes'm." Phoebe grinned in a way that made Charlotte laugh silently for she knew full well that, since Samson had proposed, the two of them had been sharing a bed each night.

"Now Phoebe," Charlotte said as they finished their tea, "I believe that you have arranged a little demonstration for these two young ladies. Might I suggest that you take them upstairs, whilst Lady Olivia and I get better acquainted."

Charlotte watched as Amelia instantly looked back at her mother, her bottom lip caught nervously between her lips whilst she obviously sought her approval.

"Oh dear. Is this the face painting you were talking about, Amelia? I don't think my husband would approve, Lady Charlotte."

"Don't worry, my lady," Phoebe said. "'Tis only for fun, and I guarantee by the time both ladies come back downstairs, neither of them will have the slightest mark of makeup remaining on their faces."

"Oh," Anne said, completely unable to hide the disappointment from her face.

Charlotte laughed and playfully wagged her finger. "And don't even think of trying to persuade Phoebe otherwise, Anne. The duke would have my hide for a new riding saddle if you go home wearing kohl around your eyes."

"Yes'm." Anne grinned with a devilish glint in her eye.

Again, Charlotte found her heart pounding as, for the first time, she found herself alone with her mother. For a few moments, they sat in companionable silence. Then, in a completely irrational moment, Charlotte suddenly found herself fighting the urge to blurt out everything, to yell to the heavens that she was Charles, that she had come home. After all, it was her mother who sat before her—the woman who given birth to her, the woman who, until the death of her father, had showered her with love. Oh, how she longed, how she ached, to be held by her mama once again, to feel the comfort and warmth of her arms, to hear her whisper words of love and reassurance, just like she had done when Charles had been a child. How she longed for her mother.

But how could she? How could she reveal herself? After all, her mother was married to the man who had tried to have her killed. Her mother was married to the man who, earlier, had made a very clumsy attempt to persuade her to be his mistress. How could she, when to do so would risk everything, and maybe even put lives in jeopardy? No, she would stick to her plan and deal with the earl before making any decision as to what to tell her mother.

It was the countess who finally broke the silence as she moved a little on her chair, almost as if she were trying to find a more comfortable position with which she could sit.

"You have a lovely home here, Charlotte." Her words were spoken softly yet tinged with the discomfort she obviously felt, something that Charlotte did not miss for one second.

"Thank you, but alas I take no credit for any of the furnishings. I am merely renting the house for the season."

"Does this mean you will be returning to, where was it . . . ah yes, Jamaica, when the season is over?" she asked.

"No, I do not think so. I have an extremely capable man overseeing my business interests there, and whilst I have not ruled out the possibility of returning one day, as I love the island so, I think I am going to make my home in England. In fact, I even intend, perhaps, on buying an estate in the country somewhere."

"My husband's estate is only a few miles outside of Kings Langley in Hertfordshire. Haycock Abbey is a hulking great Tudor mansion with far more rooms than we could possibly need. In truth, I dislike the house intensely. I once lived in the home my stepson now occupies, Thorpe Hall, which is but a few miles from Haycock, a much more homely home, if you understand my meaning."

Charlotte knew her eyes must have glazed over for a second as she remembered Thorpe Hall with great fondness. Charles had had such a happy childhood, right up until the moment of his father's death, and Charlotte's memories of it were as clear as day.

"And that is exactly the sort of home I long for, Olivia." Charlotte sighed heavily, before deliberately changing the subject. "Now, would you like the grand tour of the house, whilst the girls *play* upstairs? Perhaps we could call in on them to see how ridiculous they have made themselves look."

Charlotte was happy to see a smile flicker over her mother's face, and just for a second, she saw the woman she remembered, a woman that had been full of life and love and happiness. But then, as Lady Olivia reach forward to place her teacup onto the table, Charlotte clearly saw her wince once more, the pain she was feeling more than obvious from the hiss that escaped her lips. Concern flooded her heart and now she had to ask.

"Are you in discomfort, Lady Olivia?"

"Er . . . ah . . . 'Tis only my back. I seem to have tweaked a muscle or something."

Charlotte stared at her, instantly knowing that the woman was lying to her. This was no mere pulled muscle, but instead, something much more painful. Reaching over to her side, Charlotte pulled on a bell chord and seconds later, Millie, the downstairs maid, poked her head in through the door.

"Millie, would you pop upstairs and ask Phoebe if she would join us for a moment."

The girl curtsied and disappeared as Charlotte turned back to her mother.

"Phoebe is something of a healer," she explained. "She might be able to help alleviate the pain for you."

Fear flickered through her mother's eyes, a look that was

almost akin to panic, and for a moment, Charlotte actually thought she was going to flee.

"It is not necessary," Olivia began only for Charlotte to interrupt her.

"I insist, Lady Olivia, I will not have a guest of mine in pain if there is something I can do about it."

The door to the sitting room opened a few moments later, and Phoebe entered holding small silver tray containing two fresh teacups, a small wooden box, a small pot of honey, and a silver jug of what appeared to be freshly boiled water. Carefully she placed her tray on the tea table and then sat beside the countess as empathy flickered through her deep brown eyes.

"I noticed your pain, my lady, so I had a tray prepared. May I?" she asked.

Putting her hands on Olivia's shoulders, Phoebe gave her no choice as she eased the countess away from the back of her chair, her hand gently reaching for her back.

Very gently, through the fabric of her dress, Phoebe examined the countess, her fingers lightly probing her spine and the muscles of her back, more than once causing the countess to wince in pain. Even though there was real fear in her eyes, Olivia sat there stoically until Phoebe had finished. Then Phoebe turned to her tray. Taking a small silver spoon, she opened the wooden box and carefully deposited two heaped spoonfuls of a herbal mix into the teacup. She then filled the cup with boiling water, adding a generous amount of honey, before stirring the cup vigorously. Finally, after giving the mixture a few moments to steep, Phoebe took a tea strainer from the other tea tray and filtered the mixture into yet another clean cup.

"Drink this, mistress," Phoebe ordered. "'Tis mainly a mixture of willow bark and chamomile, with a little honey to sweeten it. It is a much gentler remedy than laudanum and will ease your discomfort."She smiled encouragingly, as she handed Olivia the cup.

For a few moments, the countess sipped at the hot infusion, surely feeling its warmth and comfort as she swallowed. Charlotte knew that Phoebe was itching to examine the woman further, that given the chance, she would have had Lady Olivia stripped and naked so she could investigate her injuries properly. Instead, Charlotte secretly signalled that what they had already done would have to be enough for the moment. After all, the last thing Charlotte wanted to do was to embarrass her mother further.

She had been right too, for moments later, with relief showing on her face that neither Charlotte nor Phoebe had tried to investigate matters further, the countess placed her now empty cup down onto the tea table.

It was an hour later by the time Anne and Amelia had finished experimenting and had cleansed their faces of all traces of powders and paints. By this time, Phoebe's medicine had worked its magic and the countess was looking considerably more comfortable, the pain in her back no longer evident as she moved. Then, after Phoebe had presented the countess with a box of her herbal medicine and had given her a promise to supply her with more should she need it, Charlotte's guests had departed, leaving the two of them alone together.

"Well?" Charlotte demanded as she looked at Phoebe.

"Someone, the earl I would guess, had beaten the countess across the upper and lower back, possibly with a birch or with a riding crop," Phoebe replied, her face now deadly serious and extremely angry.

It was the following morning when, after a short coach ride, Charlotte and Phoebe, accompanied by Samson of course, entered Mrs Quentin's dress shop. It was nothing like

Madam LeClerc's establishment, but plain and simple, like the woman who came from the back of the shop to meet them. Yet she had a warm, open face and greeted them with a smile as she curtsied respectfully to Charlotte, who in turn, got right to the point of her visit.

"Mrs Quentin?" Charlotte enquired. "My name is Lady Winters. I believe that a friend of mine, Lady Amelia Hamilton, is a client of yours and that you are making her *coming out* gown for her.

"Why, yes, my lady. Is there some problem with this?" she asked.

"Not as such, but may I ask to see the gown?"

The woman looked somewhat mystified, but she nodded and disappeared behind a curtain, returning a few minutes later with a gown over her arm which she proceeded to lay out on the counter before her.

"It is not quite finished yet, my lady. My seamstress still has some of the hems to complete."

Charlotte stepped forward to examine the garment, already knowing what she would find. Of its kind it was well enough made, a simple white gown fabricated from fine muslin with uncomplicated embellishments in blue silk ribbon. This was gown perfect for a musicale or a visit to Almack's on a Wednesday evening but would simply not do for her presentation to the Prince Regent, nor for her come out ball.

"What is this? A pattern for her real gown?" Charlotte asked.

"No, my lady," Mrs Quentin spluttered somewhat indignantly. "It is what the young lady ordered specifically. In truth, I think it was all she could afford."

That simple statement was all Charlotte needed to verify her suspicions. Amelia had so obviously been embarrassed when talking about her gown that Charlotte had instantly assumed that her father was unwilling or unable to pay for anything better.

And that simply would not do.

"Well it will have to be done over, I'm afraid. Do you have silk in an ivory colour?" she asked.

"Yes, but it is very expensive, my lady."

For a moment, Charlotte rummaged in her reticule for her purse and then tipped several gold coins into her hand.

"There, fifty pounds. That should be sufficient, should it not?"

Mrs Quentin gasped when she saw the gold, her eyes practically out on stalks. "This is too much, Lady Winters. Even using the finest material I have, the gown would only amount to twenty guineas."

Charlotte grinned. "Then you may keep the rest but on two conditions. The first is that not one, but two gowns must be complete by Wednesday evening at the latest, one gown for her presentation at court and one for her come out ball on the following evening. I would like her presentation gown in white satin and her ball gown in the ivory silk that we discussed, both to be delivered and fitted to Lady Amelia personally. And second, you must *not* tell the lady who paid for this cotton gown to be transformed into two of the most beautiful gowns you have ever made. Do I make myself clear?"

"Yes, but . . . whatever am I going to tell her?" Mrs Quentin spluttered.

"How about this," Phoebe said, entering the conversation for the first time. "Tell her that you had both gowns made at cost, in exchange for her occasionally promoting your establishment to all her friends during the season. That way you will both profit from the deal."

"Yes," Mrs Quentin grinned. "I think that would do very nicely, miss."

CHAPTER NINE

When Charlotte and Phoebe entered the attic, Samson was already there, and for a moment, both women stood silently and watched him in awe. He was naked except for a pair of cotton pantaloons, his muscular body glistening with sweat as he went through a series of spins and kicks and punches, his imaginary foes lying in their death throws all around him. Despite his size, Samson was so light on his feet, every move he made, every punch, every step, like a well-rehearsed ballet.

Whilst a slave in Jamaica, Samson had been befriended by another man, a proud native of the Fulani tribe of West Africa, and it was he who had taught Samson the ancient ways of a tribal warrior. Already possessing an incredible physique, thanks to the endless toil in the fields of Jamaica, Samson had proved himself to be an outstanding pupil and soon became an adept in the martial arts of his people. It had been David who had first discovered this fact about Samson, shortly after Charlotte had purchased him in order to save his life. It was also David who had instructed Samson to teach Charlotte how to defend herself, should the occasion arise.

"Oh, Lor'," Phoebe whispered as she stared at Samson in sheer wonder, whilst gripping Charlotte's hand. "Is he not beautiful!"

Charlotte grinned in return as her gaze once more roamed over to Samson. He was indeed a faultless specimen of manhood, every muscle, every sinew, honed to perfection. Yet that perfection was sadly marred by the scars he carried, the scars of the whip used upon his back when he worked in the fields of Jamaica, scars which she knew Samson wore with a mixture of pride and anger.

As they continued to watch, Samson finally stopped and turned towards them, his muscles still rippling from the violence of his exercise.

"Good morning, Missy Charlotte, Phoebe," he said, as he bowed his head politely. "I hope the day finds you both well rested."

"Yes, thank you," Charlotte replied.

"Good, for we have much to do, and as it is sometime since we have trained, I think it best that we start with Dambe today."

Charlotte rolled her eyes and groaned, for Dambe was her least favourite style of fighting, a style that involved punching and kicking at an opponent. It was hard and physically demanding, and she did not really feel robust enough to comply. Yet she also knew the value of such skill, for, in the heat of the moment, a well-placed kick or punch could disable even the largest of men.

So without complaining any further, she simply nodded in compliance to Samson, for it was he who was now the undisputed master in the room.

Knowing what was in store for her that morning, Charlotte had dressed for the part. Instead of stays and a dress, Charlotte was wearing a simple pair of cotton trousers that had been matched with a tight padded tunic that constrained her breasts perfectly. Her hair had been woven into a single thick rope, and she wore a pair of light, soft leather shoes that had been designed specifically for her to wear during training.

"You too, Phoebe." Samson grinned, as he noted his woman laughing at her mistress's discomfort.

This time it was Phoebe's turn to groan. But she too did as she was told and started to take off her skirt to show that, like

Charlotte, she was wearing trousers beneath.

For a gruelling and tortuous hour, Samson put them through their paces, using himself as the antagonist for the ladies to practice on, his obvious skill making it difficult for either of them to press home an attack. It was only when he was satisfied with their Dambe routines that he called a halt to change the activity, handing each of his students a pair of short hickory fighting sticks.

Charlotte was in her element now, for whilst Phoebe had never really taken to the sticks, they were by far Charlotte's favourite weapon, and her expertise very nearly rivalled that of Samson. She stood for a moment, spinning her sticks expertly in each hand, before eagerly adopting a classic sideways stance in front Samson, the sticks held out before her like a pair of short swords.

"Engarde," she shouted.

With a wild grin on her face, Charlotte attacked, knowing that Samson was an advocate of the surprise attack, her sticks whirling and slashing at him as she took a step forward. She watched him grin with pleasure too as he took a step back to easily counter her strikes with blows of his own, the force of hickory on hickory sending vibrations deep into Charlotte's body.

"Good, Missy Charlotte, good!" Samson shouted thirty minutes later, when, for the second time, she had managed to penetrate his defences, lightly hitting him on the upper arm. "You improve each time we train."

"Thank you," Charlotte replied. She took a step back, her chest heaving as she gulped in huge lungs full of air, every muscle in her body now trembling with delicious fatigue. "But I think that will do for today. Come, Phoebe."

Later that day, Charlotte, her body still aching delightfully from her earlier exercise, sat in a window seat in her study, lost in the words she was reading. In her lap was a book of poems by Percy Shelly that had once belonged to her husband, and she had turned to the page on which was printed her favourite poem. It was a verse she knew by heart, for it was a verse that David would often read to her. And for a moment, she closed her eyes, her lips silently mouthing the words as she allowed herself to reminisce.

As clear as daylight, she remembered the very first day Charles had been taken to David's home, for it was the very first day he had met Phoebe. Whilst relieved to be free of the brothel, Charles had been under no illusions as to why he was there. After all, Sir David Winters had visited him several times in the brothel, each time with Charles dressed as a girl, as per his request. Now he had been sold to that very same man, one of the biggest slave owners on the island, and was once more, it seemed, destined to become some man's sexual plaything.

However, David's instructions had been clear and precise, and to Charles' everlasting surprise, he had not been treated harshly, but with kindness and respect instead. On that first day, Phoebe had gently undressed him and had bathed him in sweet-smelling oils before tenderly shaving his entire body with a straight razor. Then she had washed and dressed his shoulder-length hair into a feminine style and had subtly painted his face before dressing him in a simple gown of white muslin.

Only then had Phoebe taken him to David.

Not knowing what to expect, Charles had been more than a little nervous.

Throughout all their previous encounters, unlike many of her customers, Sir David had been kind and gentle. At all times he had treated her like the girl she had appeared to be, his love making tender and almost reverent. But two years of living in a brothel had hardened Charles like a hot knife in quenching oil. It had left him with little trust and even less self-esteem, and he had convinced himself that, now Sir David had purchased him, his life was once more about to take a turn for the worst.

How wrong he had been.

A small intimate dining room had been prepared with a table set for two. Even from the first, David had treated her as a lady, holding her chair for her so that she could sit. Then, as they shared a simple meal, served to them by Phoebe, David had set about the task of putting Charles at ease like he might a frightened stray animal. His voice was gentle and teasing, his sense of humour making Charles smile and then laugh as the anxiety he felt ebbed away into nothingness.

And when the meal had finished, David had taken Charles into his private garden, a space filled with the heady perfume of the tropical blooms, which grew in perfusion. They had walked, and much to the delight of Charles' beating heart, David had taken his hand within his own as they wandered through the oasis.

Then, as the sun had set behind the Blue Mountains, David had taken Charles into his arms and had kissed him, a soft, slow, gentle embrace that had every cell in his body screaming for more. Then, without speaking another word, David had taken him to his bed, and with a gentleness that belied his size, had shown him the true meaning of what it was to be a woman.

It was that very day that Charles had ceased to exist, and Charlotte had been born, just as it was, on that very day, that Charlotte had once more begun to believe in love.

Suddenly, the silence of the room was shattered by a loud knock on the door, and Charlotte's heart leapt in surprise. She sniffed, then wiped away the tear that had unwittingly rolled down her cheek before calling to whosoever was behind the door.

"Come," she croaked.

Her voice was thick with emotion as she closed her book, so she stood and turned her back on the door to take a moment to compose herself. When, but a few moments later, she turned around once more, three men had entered the room. Samson and Mr Abernathy she knew, of course, but the third was a complete stranger. The man was dressed as a gentleman, his clothes fine and well made, but there was something about him, an air of danger, that suggested he was anything but. Perhaps it was the once broken and flat nose, or perhaps the unshaven chin that instantly reminded her of some of the men who had once visited a young boy in a brothel in Kingston. Whatever it was, Charlotte knew, despite the fine clothes, this man was no gentleman and was someone not lightly to be trusted.

"Mr Abernathy and Mr Green, Missy Charlotte. You gave instruction to let them in when they got here," Samson rumbled, his wary gaze not leaving Green for a second.

Charlotte smiled. "Yes, thank you, Samson. If you could wait outside for me, please. Mr Abernathy will be leaving in a few moments, and I would like you to show him out." Charlotte had been expecting the men after receiving a note from Mr Abernathy, so she already had his payment ready. "Thank you, Mr Abernathy," she said as she handed him the purse. "Your services have been entirely satisfactory and worth every penny."

The man bowed respectfully as he took the money from her hand.

"The pleasure has been all mine, Lady Winters. Should you ever need my services again . . ."

"I will not hesitate to call on you," Charlotte said, finishing the sentence for him as he backed towards the door.

Charlotte then turned to the other man who, without waiting to be asked, had taken a chair placed by the desk Charlotte used. He was a big man, in middle age, with a thick shock of unruly grey hair, and was undoubtedly the sort of man that a lady would normally cross the street to avoid. For Charlotte, however, he was exactly the man she needed to see.

"Abernathy tells me you have business you wish to discuss. Well then. 'Ow much do ya need?"

Charlotte stared at him and smiled softly as she weighed the man up. His voice was deep and gravelly, suggesting the heavy use of tobacco, and his crooked nose told the story of a violent past. One thing was for certain, just from the way he perched on his chair. This was a man who held women such as her in contempt, simply because she appeared to be a member of the ton. But he was also a man who valued money above all else, if the heavy gold chain across his chest was anything to go by, and this was something she put to her advantage. She smiled confidently.

"Whilst it is only supposition, Mr Green," she began, "I have heard a rumour that one George Hamilton, Earl of Weybridge, has borrowed a considerable sum of money from you."

As Charlotte had expected, her words instantly caught the man's attention, and he sat upright, his body automatically adopting an aggressive posture. Instinctively, she almost called for Samson.

"What is that to you?" the man growled.

"And it is also rumoured that he has used Thorpe Hall, and its estate, as collateral to secure that loan, a loan that I am told is about to come due."

"You are remarkably well informed. Again, what is it to you?" Green grumbled.

"As my late husband used to say, information is the key to success in any venture, Mr Green. Whilst, as you surmise, I am quite well informed, there is still much more I would like to know, and I now find myself in the position of needing information which only you can provide. Information for which, by the way, I am willing to pay quite handsomely."

As she watched the man's face, Charlotte nearly laughed out loud, for she knew the way his emotions showed within his eyes would have made him the worst card player the world had ever seen. At first, there was a flash of anger, of irritation, his temper nearly getting the better of him. But then Green, a man who was obviously no one's fool, must have thought better of allowing his displeasure to rule over business, for he sat back in his chair and forced himself to adopt a more relaxed posture.

"Very well, Lady Winters. Tell me what you have in mind."

"First of all, Mr Green, I would like you to tell me exactly how much the earl owes you."

Charlotte allowed a little steel to enter her voice, to make it clear she would not take *no* for an answer to this question. Yet she also tempered that steel in a way that suggested that, if he gave her the information she wanted, she would make it worth his while.

For a moment or two, Green looked at her suspiciously. Then, his mind seemingly made up, he glanced furtively around the room, almost as if he were expecting to see a constable behind a curtain somewhere before fishing into his jacket pocket for a small black leather-bound notebook. Slowly and quite deliberately, after licking one finger, he leafed through the book until he found the page he wanted.

"He originally borrowed eight thousand pounds, but the loan is now nine thousand, six hundred and forty-two pounds, sixteen shillings and sixpence." Very deliberately, he then flipped the book closed and slipped it back into his inner jacket pocket. "Including interest," he added, as he looked straight into Charlotte's eyes.

Even Charlotte paled a little at that figure.

"That is not an insubstantial sum of money, Mr Green. And would you say that he owes money to anyone else?"

"Of that, I have little doubt, for, at the interest rates I charge, I am not the sort of person who's first choice when it comes to borrowing money."

Charlotte opened the drawer to her desk once more and extracted another large pouch of coins, sliding it onto the desk, its presence an obvious and deliberate temptation to the man who sat before her.

"Very well, Mr Green. In there, as a testament of my good faith, is two hundred pounds in gold coin, which you may keep as, let's say, a down payment, no matter what the outcome of our negotiations."

Charlotte watched the man carefully as he eyed the bag greedily, his hand twitching to reach out and take it. It was at that moment Charlotte knew she had won the man over and that his greed and her money would bend him to her will.

"And in return?" he asked without moving.

"The earl is in possession of something I hold very dear, and it is my intention to use the debt he owes you to force him to sell it to me. You see, I happen to know that he is in no financial position to repay the money he has borrowed from you. So, when you call in the debt, and the earl becomes desperate for funds, I will offer to purchase this . . . erm . . . object from him, thus forcing him to sell. This will then give him the money, which will enable you to recover the full value of what is owed, including the accrued interest. 'Tis a win-win situation for both of us, don't you think?"

"And you have the coin to do this?" the man demanded.

"Yes," Charlotte replied. "And as an incentive, I will pay you an additional five percent of the value of the debt as a way of, shall we say, expressing my gratitude for your help in this matter."

"Ten percent!" Green growled.

"No," Charlotte said firmly. "I will pay you seven percent and not a penny more. But for that, I have two non-negotiable demands. The first, and most important, is that you do not call in this debt until a time of *my* choosing, for timing in this matter will be paramount. However, when the moment is right, I would expect you to do so with as much menace as you can possibly muster. Secondly, it is imperative that neither the earl nor his son, the baron, must hear any word of my involvement in this matter."

Green sat and rubbed his chin with the palm of his hand as he considered the offer.

Charlotte, knowing she had already won the argument, sat in silence and waited for Mr Green's brain to catch up with her. It did not take long for a crooked smile to appear on his face, and her heart danced a little jig of victory as it did so.

"Agreed," he said. "But I am not a patient man, my lady. I will not wait on this matter forever, and if we shake on this, then you take on final responsibility for the entire debt."

"Agreed. But might I also add that I will not take it kindly if you try and cross me on this matter, Mr Green. For you see, I was not always the *lady* that you see before you, and I am quite capable of arranging for serious and violent repercussions to occur, just as you are. Perhaps you remember my man from when you arrived."

"Yes, and a big bugger he is too. I could use a man like that."

"He is not only big, Mr Green, but very, very dangerous, too, and entirely loyal to me. Once, upon my command, I saw him crush a man's skull between his two bare hands. It simply went *pop,* like a ripe melon would when dropped from a great height."

Despite his obvious bravado and the undoubted ability to call upon any number of unsavoury characters from the slums of London, Green swallowed hard. Her words had been a thinly disguised threat, and, judging by Green's reaction, it was apparent that he was beginning to realise the woman before him was made of sterner stuff than he had first thought.

Then, much to Charlotte's relief, Green grinned, a scar on his cheek showing white as he did so.

"Oh, I think we have an understanding, my lady, and with that, I think our business is concluded."

He made to stand, and as if by magic, the pouch of gold coins disappeared into a voluminous jacket pocket. At the same time, Charlotte leant forward and picked up a silver bell from her desk, and as she sounded it, the hulking figure of Samson appeared instantly through the door.

"Could you please show Mr Green out, Samson," she said.

Green lurched to his feet, his stocky body at least twelve inches shorter than Samson. Then, after they left the room and Samson had closed the door behind them, Charlotte sat back in her chair and closed her eyes for a moment.

The awful memory of what Samson was capable of came flooding back. The incident had occurred some six months after David had passed away. She had been shopping in Kingston when she had seen a man alighting from a recently arrived slaver that was docked in the harbour. It was a man that Charlotte recognised immediately, for the hatred of him was permanently engraved upon her mind.

Later that night, as Captain Thaddeus Jones staggered blind drunk back towards his ship, she and Samson had caught up to him in a dark alley, and her retribution, served by a very willing Samson, had been awful to watch. But watch it she had, unable to tear her eyes away from the scene. At her command, Samson had taken the man's head between his hands, and as the captain screamed in his death throes, he had literally crushed the man's skull.

And to her eternal shame, even to that day, Charlotte felt not one ounce of regret.

CHAPTER TEN

James was pacing back and forth in the receiving room of his townhouse, an empty sherry glass in one hand, an embossed invitation in the other, as the moment of the debutante's ball approached. In celebration of the event, his valet had taken great care dressing him that evening. He wore a new suit of clothes specially tailored for the evening, and his boots shone like black polished glass. His cravat was perfectly tied and fixed with a large diamond tie pin, and he had even allowed his man to trim his hair a little.

The presentation at court had proceeded exactly as he had expected. As the daughter of a duke, Anne had been one of the first to be presented, and his heart had swelled with pride as he watched his daughter perform a serenely elegant curtsey in front of the Prince Regent.

But now, just a day later, he waited, alongside the dowager duchess, upon his daughter as she prepared for her first ball, for which occasion she had been secreted upstairs with her maid for the last three hours. He also awaited the arrival of Lady Charlotte, who, of course, would be Anne's chaperon for the evening, so they might all travel to the Duchess of Harrow's ball together.

In truth, he was not certain which of them he was most nervous to see first.

"Damn it," he cursed to himself as that thought flickered through his mind.

"What was that you said?"

The duchess was perched on a chair, looking resplendent

in a beautiful purple velvet gown, which she had matched with an outrageously lavish feather headdress. Like she had when he had been a child, she gave him a piercing glare for having cursed out loud, and James could not help but curse once more, silently this time.

"Nothing, Mother, nothing," James muttered as he turned towards the empty fireplace.

But it was indeed anything but *nothing* that was bothering him. Over the past few days, James had deliberately distanced himself from Lady Charlotte Winters. Now he was even beginning to truly regret his decision to allow her to be Anne's chaperon, for the simple reason that it would bring him into close contact with the blasted *woman*.

The predicament he faced was a straightforward one.

The simple fact of the matter was that Lady Charlotte was his *godson*. The simple fact of the matter was that his *godson* was now an undeniably beautiful woman. The simple fact of the matter was that each time he found himself in Lady bloody Charlotte's presence, his accursed body seemed to betray him, reacting with an uncontrollable lust that disturbed him greatly.

And he hated the fact that he just couldn't seem to help himself!

"God, what a bloody mess."

He groaned silently to himself, and in his confusion, tried to down a sherry that had already been consumed, somehow snapping the stem of the glass as he did so.

"Bugger," he said softly to himself, as he threw the remains of the glass into the fire.

"Ahem," a soft voice called.

James started a little in surprise, and he turned to see Lady Charlotte entering the room, her gloved hand on the handle of the door as she closed it behind her.

Once more, James felt his breath catch in his throat as he

saw her for the first time that evening. His godchild was dressed in a stunning gown in the palest of pinks, the material lavishly decorated with swirls of raised embroidery that must have been individually and expensively hand sewn to the dress. The neckline was modest, but there was no denying the soft swell of breasts beneath, and around her elegant neck, she wore a superb necklace of matched natural pearls that must have cost a king's ransom. Even her hair had been perfectly dressed, and she sported a simple headdress of feathers in a style most befitting a *widow* of her age.

Yet, despite all the opulence and finery, there was but one thing about her that captured his eyes. Once more she had defied convention and was wearing makeup upon her face. But instead of it being garish, like some women he had seen, hers was delicately applied, a touch of kohl to highlight the vivid blue of her eyes, a little rouge on her cheeks, a little ruby stain on her lips that had the duke wondering what she might taste like should he kiss her. Once more James groaned inwardly as he bowed respectfully.

"Please forgive me for entering unannounced. All the servants are so busy that I took the liberty of showing myself in."

"Lady Charlotte, you look . . . you look . . ."

For some reason, James found himself mumbling, his mind strangely and embarrassingly devoid of words. The awkwardness of it brought colour to his cheeks as he suddenly felt but thirteen years of age once more.

"What my idiot of a son is trying to say, Lady Charlotte, is that you look lovely, my dear." The duchess nodded towards James with a hint of a knowing smile, having obviously not missed one second of the little byplay.

Once more James groaned inwardly, as he noted a hint of mischievousness in his mother's eye that suggested he might need to be wary of her scheming to have him marry once more . . .and with Lady Charlotte her intended victim.

Charlotte turned and gave the duchess a polite little curt-sey.

"Thank you, your grace, and might I say you look incredibly beautiful tonight as well. I love that headdress you are wearing. It is, erm . . ."

"Outrageous, I know. The Duchess of Harrow is one of my closest friends, my dear, and each year we have a little competition as to who can find the most ridiculous headdress. Last year she wore the entire plumage of a peacock."

"I was going to say eye-catching, but yes, perhaps outrageous might be a good word." She turned to him once more with a shy smile that was, to James, anything but innocent. "And you, your grace. Might I be permitted to say how handsome you look this evening?"

"Thank you. One has to make the effort occasionally. Besides, Anne would never have forgiven me had I been dressed in sack-cloth."

"Talking of Lady Anne, is she ready?" Charlotte asked.

"I hope so, for it is almost time for us to depart."

As Charlotte walked elegantly into the centre of the room, he rang a bell to fetch a maid who might find out what the delay could be. But instead of a maid, it was Stevens who entered the room, and for once, his normally sombre expression had been replaced by the sort of wide smile generally reserved for a doting grandfather.

"Lady Anne is waiting for you in the hallway, your graces, Lady Winters," he announced. "And might I be so bold as to say that I believe she is feeling somewhat apprehensive."

Instantly, James made to stride across the room to the door, only to be stopped by Charlotte, who placed a gentle hand on his arm.

"No, let me," she whispered.

****

Charlotte actually gasped out loud when she saw Lady Anne sitting on a stool in the hallway, for her beauty was beyond anything she could ever remember having seen before. This was the first time she had seen Anne dressed in her gown, and Charlotte could not think of anything more perfect — the golden highlights of the lace and jewels that she wore a wonderful match to the flecks of gold in her eyes. Her lady's maid had expertly dressed her hair so that elegant golden tendrils framed her face to perfection, all topped off with the most delicious gold, diamond, and sapphire headpiece. She was even wearing the diamond eardrops that Charlotte had given her as a birthday gift.

But it was Lady Anne's face that truly captivated Charlotte's heart, that beautiful, gorgeous face, which, despite Anne's normal exuberant self-confidence, suddenly looked so young, so pensive. Quietly, Charlotte walked over to her and with a little nudge of her hips, pushed Anne to one side of the stool so she could sit next to her, taking her gloved hand in her own as she did so.

"Oh Lotte, what if I make a fool of myself? What if no one asks me to dance? What if I forget the steps and worse still trip over this stupid gown? What if . . ."

Genuine pain lanced through Charlotte's heart as she heard these words, and she knew Anne was on the verge of tears. It was only natural for a young woman to be nervous before her first ball, but, from the way that Anne's hands were shaking, Charlotte knew Anne would require all the support and confidence that she could give her if she was to get through this moment."

"No, Anne. No." Charlotte insisted. "Now you listen to me, young lady. Tonight is to be your greatest triumph. You are the most beautiful and accomplished young woman I have ever known, and every eligible bachelor in the *ton* will be lining up to beg you for the privilege of a dance. Yes, you have every right to be a little nervous. I, for one, should know that, for I was so nervous when I made my debut in Kingston that I was sick three times beforehand. But trust me when I say that you are going to have the most incredible time tonight, especially when you have your father and grandmother and me to watch out for you. Isn't that right, your grace?"

She turned to the duke and dowager, who were now in the hallway, only to see the duke fighting back tears that were brimming in his own eyes.

Supportively, Charlotte smiled as the duke walked over to Anne to take each of her hands in his own, holding them as he gently helped her to her feet. Only then did he appear to find enough voice to speak.

"You look so much like your mother, my darling," he croaked. "She would have been so proud of the woman you have grown to be. Lady Charlotte is right as well. No matter what, this is to be your night." He leant forward and kissed his daughter on the cheek.

"Thank you, Papa." Suddenly, she pushed herself into his arms and hugged him tightly. "I'm sorry." she sniffed. "I was only having a moment. Now come, everyone. If you keep me waiting any longer, I will be late for the first dance!"

Charlotte watched as Anne slipped her arm into her grandmother's, then paused respectfully to allow Lady Anne and the dowager to walk first towards the front door. She was about to join them when she felt a hand placed gently on her arm. She stopped and turned to see the duke staring at her, a fiercely protective look of love in his eyes.

"Promise me that you will keep my baby safe, Charlotte. Promise me," he whispered.

The ride to Hanover Square took longer than anyone had expected, as the roads were filled with lines of carriages all trying heading to do the same. Eventually, the carriage drew up outside a brightly lit town mansion, whereupon an army of footmen descended to help the ladies alight. Within moments they were inside and passing a short reception line, the duchess going first, followed by the duke, Lady Anne, and finally herself. James had presented Charlotte to the Duchess of Harrow, and as she had curtsied, trying to hide her own nervous apprehension, she suddenly found herself fighting to suppress a nervous giggle. For, just as the dowager had predicted, the Duchess of Harrow's headdress was something of an architectural masterpiece, consisting of what looked like the tail feathers from several ornamental pheasants.

Soon they entered the crush, and what a crush it was too, with what seemed like every possible member of the *ton* in attendance. Names and faces passed in a blur for Charlotte as she was introduced to this viscount and that lord and this duchess and that lady. By the time she actually saw a couple of friendly faces, her head was positively spinning. But there, standing to one side of the room, talking amiably to each other, were the Countess of Weybridge and Lady Amelia, along with Lady Jane and her parents, Lord and Lady Chalmers. There was also another young gentleman with them, a young man who, with the confidence born of nobility, looked every inch the gentleman. Of the earl and Lord Henry, however, there was no sign.

To nobody's surprise, Anne grabbed Charlotte's hand and dragged her over to her friends.

"Gosh, what a crush it is," Anne announced as she kissed both Amelia and Jane on the cheeks in greeting. "And don't you both look wonderful," she gushed as she took her friends by the hand. "My goodness, Amelia, that gown you are wearing is stunning."

Amelia's gown was, without doubt, a masterpiece, made from the most gorgeous shimmering ivory silk. In the empire style, the dress was gathered just beneath her ample bosom with a matching ribbon before draping itself elegantly over her slim body. In short, she looked every inch as beautiful as Anne, her dark hair a perfect contrast to Anne's golden ringlets.

Charlotte smiled proudly, knowing that her fifty pounds had been extremely well spent.

Amelia grinned with inane happiness. "Yes, I do love it so, although it was not quite what I had expected. My original dress was to be somewhat simpler, but it seems that my modiste, Mrs Quentin, has recently taken on a new seamstress. This gown and the gown I wore to court yesterday were her first for Mrs Quentin and were to showcase her talents."

"Well I for one, feel completely overshadowed by both of you, just as it should be for your first ball," Jane said without a hint of resentment.

"Well, that is stuff and nonsense, Lady Jane," Charlotte declared as she looked at the lovely gown that Jane was wearing. "Your gown is every inch as beautiful, and I dare say that there isn't a single woman here, Anne and Amelia included, that could overshadow you, my sweet girl."

"Perhaps with the exception of yourself, Lady Winters," a rich baritone voice added.

Charlotte turned and cocked an eyebrow at the handsome young man who stood patiently next to Lady Olivia. He was tall and impeccably dressed, with a breadth of shoulders that almost rivalled that of Samson, yet an easy and confident mouth readily identified him as a man of superior breeding. As for Lady Olivia, she too looked resplendent, although in a dress that had obviously been worn before, and she appeared to be in decidedly better health than on the previous occasion on which they had met. It was she who made the introductions.

"Lady Charlotte, may I present Lord William Jameson,

Lord William, may I present Lady Charlotte Winters."

Charlotte looked on approvingly as her mother smiled at Amelia and William, her whole demeanour suggesting that she wholeheartedly approved of the young man.

"Lady Winters, 'tis a pleasure." Lord William bowed politely in return, his voice surprisingly deep. "Lady Amelia has already told me so much about you."

"And I of you," Charlotte retorted, as she curtsied in return.

At that moment, the duke appeared at their side. With him was another man of similar age to himself who was accompanied by a very handsome young man in full military uniform, the golden buttons of which gleamed in the myriad of candles that lit the ballroom.

"Ladies, may I present my old friend, the Marquess of Blandford, George Harvey, and his son Major Lord Peter Harvey of the Fifth Hussars. My lords, may I present Countess of Weybridge and Lady Amelia Weybridge, Lord and Lady Chalmers and their daughter, Lady Jane Chalmers, my daughter, Lady Anne, and last but not least, Lady Charlotte Winters."

As Charlotte observed the little scene play out, she had to hide a smirk behind the fan she carried, lest anyone see her amusement. For the moment Anne set eyes on Lord Peter, her pupils widened, and her mouth dropped open briefly, as she viewed the young man in front of her with something akin to awe. Nor did Charlotte blame Anne for reacting so. For he was indeed a truly beautiful young man with an athletic build that was a testament to genuine labour, a strong jaw, and intelligent deep brown eyes, all set off by the dazzling elegance of his uniform.

In return, Lord Peter also appeared flustered as he returned Anne's gaze. With cheeks that looked like he had spent too much time in the sun, he presented a deep bow, almost as if he too needed a moment to compose himself.

"Lady Anne, . . . er . . . , I was wondering if you might do me the honour of favouring me with a dance tonight?" he asked, somewhat bluntly.

Anne hesitated for a moment, glancing first at her father and then at her chaperon, and Charlotte had to battle with herself to maintain a serious expression on her face. However, everything was right and proper, for the family was known to the duke, and Lord Peter had been properly introduced, so Charlotte simply nodded her approval.

"I would be delighted," Anne squeaked as she handed him her dance card.

"And you, Olivia, how wonderful it is you see you again. It has been too long," the duke said.

"Indeed it has, James, indeed it has. I believe the last time was at your dear Margaret's funeral. But now we have renewed our acquaintance, I hope you will no longer be a stranger to us."

"I will endeavour to make it so," the duke replied with a polite nod.

And that set the pattern for the evening. Charlotte sat with the countess and Lady Helena, whilst all three girls were practically mobbed by gentlemen, all wanting to claim a dance. In fact, within minutes, each one of them had their dance cards complete, with only the waltzes left out, as they were deemed to be too risqué for the debutantes. But even Charlotte had to give a knowing little smile when she realised that Amelia had daringly promised no less than three dances to William, the first dance, the dinner dance, then the most romantic of all, the last dance of the evening.

"May I say, Lady Olivia, that your back appears to be much improved," Charlotte ventured.

She had dutifully watched Amelia, Jane, and Anne safely

escorted to the dance floor, each one of them grinning with happiness as they started on yet another promenade. Secure in the knowledge that, at least for a few minutes, all three girls were engaged in their dance, she felt able to focus her attention on her mother for the first time that evening.

"Oh, it is, thanks to that girl of yours. Her medicine has worked wonders," Olivia gushed.

"Medicine?" Lady Helena asked.

"Lady Charlotte's companion is a black girl she brought with her from Jamaica." Olivia paused. "Oh! I hope that is not an impolite term for her."

"Well, her skin is black, but I think she prefers the term *African*, as that is where she originates."

"Anyway, Phoebe, for that is her name, prepared me some medicine for my back pain, which has worked miracles. Better than any London quack, I can tell you," Olivia expounded.

"Talking of backs. Where are the earl and your stepson this evening?"

"Henry is somewhere about, but my husband has already retired to the gaming rooms. He does not like these events very much. It is a good thing, too, for he doesn't seem to care very much for Lord William."

"But why? Lord William seems like a fine and upstanding young gentleman. Heir to an earldom, too. He would be such a good match for Amelia," Lady Helena said.

"Yes, he would. But it is so much more than that," Olivia said. "Did you not see the way he looks at Amelia and the way she looks at him? I know that Amelia is only nineteen and that Lord William has just turned three and twenty, but I very much believe and hope that theirs is nothing short of a meeting of hearts."

In the background, the reel that had been playing ended, and after a flurry of bows and curtsies, three gentlemen delivered three tired and very flushed young ladies back to their chaperons.

It was then that the first waltz of the evening was announced, and Charlotte found herself once more sighing loudly.

When Charlotte had agreed to be chaperon to Anne, she had made the decision not to dance at all, on the pretext that that she might keep a close eye upon proceedings. As a consequence, she had been required to turn down more than one request from a hopeful partner. Now, despite the fact she loved the waltz more than any other dance, it appeared that she would have to do the same once more, as, from the corner of her eye, she glimpsed the duke's friend, the Marquess of Blandford as he approached.

"Lady Winters, I was wondering if you would do me the honour of this dance?" he asked.

****

On arrival, James had deliberately distanced himself from the rest of his family, thinking that Anne and her friends would have much more fun without an old man such as he watching over them. Ostensibly, he was there to protect the reputation of his daughter. But whilst she was in the company of her friends, she was more than safe enough from compromise, and he reasoned he could keep an eye on her from afar. Nevertheless, as he stood with a group of acquaintances, he could not help but constantly keep a weather eye on proceedings, knowing, in his heart, that there was yet another reason — an important, beguiling, frustrating reason — behind his vigilance.

Lady bloody Charlotte!

Her presence had caused quite a stir amongst the *ton*, and more than once, an acquaintance had approached him to enquire as to their involvement. Several times, he had also seen this or that gentleman try to engage Lady Charlotte in a dance, only to have her, much to his relief, politely decline, giving the excuse that she needed to watch out for Anne.

Then a waltz had been announced, and he groaned to himself as he saw George bloody Harvey approach Lady Charlotte, a gleam in his eye and a smile on his face. As the waltz was the one dance forbidden to the debutantes, the marquess, who was a widower himself, had obviously decided this would be the one dance open to Lady Charlotte and he seemed intent on prevailing with her to join him.

"God's teeth! Surely she can see the dangers of this!" he groaned to himself

Without even realising he was doing so, he stepped out across the room, an irrational surge of protective jealousy hitting him hard. Within seconds, he was standing in front of his godchild, a smile more akin to a grimace again fixed to his face as he replied to the marquess' request on her behalf.

"I'm sorry, George, but I'm afraid Lady Charlotte has promised *me* this dance."

"I have?" Charlotte asked with mock innocence. Her head tilted up to look at him with something akin to amusement. "Oh yes, *of course* I have. Perhaps, my lord, you might ask me to dance the next waltz with you instead," she added as she took James's proffered hand.

Without speaking, James led Charlotte onto the dance floor, his heart pounding from the audacity of what he was about to do. He bowed to her whilst she elegantly curtsied back to him, just as the music began to play.

Not since his very first dance with his late wife had something felt so perfect to James. Taking the lead, he gently took her dainty hand into his, a hand he could not help but notice was trembling. Then, as he slipped his free hand around her tiny waist, he stepped off in time to the music. To his amazement, Charlotte simply followed, every step taken and every movement of her body so perfectly attuned to his own that it was as if they had practised together for hours. And as they danced, he dared to look down at her, only to find she was gazing back at him, her eyes soft, her pupils large, a gentle smile playing across her lips.

Once more he groaned inwardly, deliberately distancing his body from hers and keeping his steps to the simplest of forms. But he soon realised Charlotte would have none of that, and even though it was he who was leading, she used every device — a tip of her head, a push of her hand — to urge him on. What choice did he have? Little by little, he began to pick up the pace as he recognised the expertise of his partner, and soon they were spinning effortlessly around the dance floor, every step he made fluently matched.

Suddenly, every sense he possessed seemed to come alive. His nostrils were filled with the soft scent of sweet perfume, and it was almost as if he could hear the pounding pulse of her heart as his gaze feasted on her beautiful face. With each turn and spin, the gap between them closed, and, much to his growing torment, he felt the soft caress of her breasts against his chest as they moved in perfect harmony to the music.

And James could not have stopped the blood from suffusing to his groin, even if he had wanted to.

When the music finally came to an end, his mind was so befuddled that he did not know whether to feel relieved or disappointed. Instead, he took a respectful step back as he once more bowed to her and she curtsied in return. Surprisingly, it was not her normal graceful dip, but one that suggested that her knees might threaten to give out beneath her, as if she, too, had almost been overtaken by the pure and barely disguised covetousness of the moment they had just shared.

Ever mindful of proper etiquette, James forced himself to escort Lady Charlotte through the crowd and back to her seat.

No words were spoken between them, for even if he had wanted to speak, he was certain it would be impossible for him to string together anything resembling a cohesive sentence through the befuddlement of his brain. So once he had returned Charlotte to her friends, instead of staying for a few moments, as any decent gentleman might do, he turned and stalked off through the crowd.

Without knowing how he got there, James found himself in the gentleman's retiring room, where a motionless footman, holding a silver tray, provided him with exactly what he needed—a large brandy. In a single gulp, he tossed it back, relishing the burn of the spirits before reaching for a second. Only then did he look for a quiet corner, a place where he could hide as he collected his thoughts.

Cradling his drink, James sat in a high-backed chair and tried to make sense of his feelings, wondering what on earth had possessed him to dance with Charlotte. Part of him was so angry for allowing that minx to manipulate him, incensed that he had allowed himself to be seduced into dancing with his godchild. But then, as his hand rubbed his face, he groaned with the memory of it, knowing that it had been he who had asked her, knowing that she had done nothing to bring about the situation. Of course, the dance just had to be perfect, as had the partner he had danced with, and even he could not deny that his body had reacted to his godchild as if she were the woman she appeared to be.

He sipped at his brandy and groaned once more.

****

As expected, once the dinner dance had concluded, there was a general crush towards the dining room, where a veritable feast had been laid out. Plates were laden and lemonade procured and soon their party, which once more included Lord

William—who Charlotte was beginning to like more and more with every passing second—had retaken their seats in the ballroom.

It was then that the atmosphere around them took a sudden chill.

"Lady Anne," a voice called with slurred words suggesting the consumption of more than a little ardent spirit. "I was hoping you might favour me with a dance after dinner."

Charlotte looked up to see Lord Henry standing in front of them. He was swaying a little, his eyes glazed and bloodshot, and even from a distance, she could smell the spirits the man had found from somewhere. Charlotte was quick to react. Indignantly, she stared at the man, then waved her fan before her face to attract his attention. Only then did she speak.

"I'm sorry, my lord, but you have missed your chance for this evening. I'm afraid to say that Lady Anne's dance card is already completely full, as is Lady Jane's," she added, in case he turned his attentions to her next.

"I'll bet it is. My father said you were going to be difficult, *my lady*," Henry scoffed.

His words were little more than a sneer, his tone of voice showing anything but deference, and Charlotte had to suppress a shiver of loathing for the man. At Anne's birthday party, he had been nothing but polite and ingratiating. But now, in his cups, his true colours were definitely beginning to show, and Charlotte felt a sliver of steel float down her back in response.

"Henry," Lady Olivia hissed. "Please show some respect."

"Respect! Ha! You talk about respect. My father knows how to instil respect, doesn't he, *stepmother*," he snarled.

"That is enough," Lord William said as he moved to stand next to Charlotte. "If you can't behave like a gentleman, then I suggest you leave, Lord Hamilton."

His words were spoken in a voice that made Charlotte stare

at the man in admiration. This young man might have been several years younger than Henry, but he was a head taller and very broad in the shoulder, and the calm reassurance in his voice suggested that he was more than capable of looking out for himself.

"Jameson, what the hell are you doing here? Sniffing around my sister again, I see," Henry growled.

Standing by her as he was, Charlotte sensed the whole of William's body tense, his fingers automatically curling into solid looking fists. This was something Charlotte could not allow and, instinctively, she reacted to defuse the situation, just as she had been taught to do when ensconced in the brothel.

Divide and conquer, Lotte, divide and conquer.

When but a child, Charles had been petrified of Henry. As the older of the two, Henry had bullied Charles mercilessly and had made the years after his father died almost unbearable. But Charlotte was not afraid of this man now, or any man, for that matter. After all, if she could survive the brothels of Kingston and deal with the men who used them, she could certainly deal with the Henrys of this world. She simply placed her hand on William's arm to steady him, then stood to face Henry, fixing her eyes firmly on his as she did so.

"Lord Henry, might I have a private word with you?"

Not waiting for a reply, Charlotte took his arm, turning him and leading him away from the group. Before he even realised what she was doing, she had taken him from the ballroom, through the open French windows, and onto a secluded veranda. It was only then that he shrugged his arm away angrily.

"What!" he demanded.

"Am I to believe that you intend to court Lady Anne?" Charlotte kept her voice low but edged with the irritation she felt as she fastened her gaze firmly upon his eyes.

"What is it to you if I am," he snarled.

"Because if you are, my lord, I would like to suggest that you are going the wrong way about making an impression on her. Being rude and aggressive is hardly going to endear her to you, now is it? Besides, as you know, I am to be her chaperon for the entire season. I would like you to understand that I take that duty very seriously, and I have promised the duke that I will protect Anne's honour and reputation over everything else." She deliberately kept her voice light and gentle in an attempt to placate the man. It did not work

"As if you could," Henry sneered. "If I want the girl, I shall have her. Better still, now that you have turned down my father, I could take you instead. After all, your money is a good as hers."

Charlotte stood perfectly still as Henry took a threatening step towards her, her hand already inside her reticule. She had anticipated Henry's reaction from the very first moment he had approached them in the dining hall. He was a bully and had always used his station in life and his physical size to pick on those less fortunate than himself. However, for two long years, first Charles and then Charlotte had survived in the brothels of Kinston, where there had been an endless stream of drunks and thugs. Whilst the lessons had been hard, she had learned them well, and with the help of Samson, she now knew how to protect herself from harm. Inwardly she smiled, for she knew she was to enjoy the moment that would surely come.

Just as she had expected, Henry took another step towards her, his body now practically touching hers, every muscle in his face contorted into a mixture of lust and dominance, leaving no doubt in Charlotte's mind that he meant to do her harm. Despite his obvious intoxication, the move had been quite deliberate and one that was designed to frighten and intimidate.

"What say you to that, *Lady Winters*," he growled as he

made to grab her. "I bet you could do with a real man between your legs."

Like lightning, Charlotte's hand flashed out from her reticule, the silver of the razor-sharp stiletto blade she held glinting in the moonlight. It was a move that took Henry completely by surprise, and he screeched as he looked down, all the colour draining from his face as he felt the wicked point of the knife press against his cock. Instinctively, he took a step back, but Charlotte moved with him, denying him the space to swing a fist, pressing home her advance until his back was against a wall, her knife perfectly poised.

"Think you not that I am one of those simpering ladies of the *ton*, Henry Hamilton," she growled as she pushed her blade even harder against his manhood so the sharp point of the stiletto actually penetrated the fabric of his trousers. "As you can see, I am more than prepared to defend myself and my friends against the likes of you."

Like a bag of wind pricked by a needle, Henry deflated.

"Fuck . . . Y-yes . . . yes," he stammered as he held up his hands in a gesture of submission.

"I would also suggest that you do not misjudge my resolve in this matter, either."

Henry winced as Charlotte pressed even harder, yet there was still anger and defiance in his eyes that made Charlotte resolve to end this matter once and for all. Now she moved the blade, its razor edge resting right beneath his testicles.

"Christ . . . watch what you are doing with that thing,"

Charlotte growled. "Oh, you need not worry about me, Henry. My little blade is only to ensure you behave yourself. No, the person you should worry about is my man, Samson. You have not met Samson yet, have you? But trust me when I say that he is the biggest and most dangerous man I have ever met and is a man who would gladly kill at my command, without missing a heartbeat."

"You would not dare."

"Oh, but I would, Henry. Now, I am not one who normally resorts to violence or threats, Lord Henry, but I think you seriously underestimate me and what I am capable of. You *will* behave as a gentleman, or one night, as you return from your club or from whatever mistress you keep, Samson will, at my instruction, take great delight in teaching you some manners. Tell me, my lord, have you ever seen what a mahogany cudgel will do to a man when wielded by someone with Samson's strength and proclivity to violence?"

"No" he grimaced through clenched teeth, suppressed anger threatening to burst a blood vessel in his neck.

"It is not a pretty sight, I can tell you. The last person, *baron*, who suffered my displeasure, *baron*, lost all his front teeth with a single blow. I would imagine that a member of the *ton* with no teeth would find himself quite the figure of ridicule, don't you think, *baron*?"

Now Charlotte was beginning to enjoy herself, for each time she mentioned his title, her hand pushed on the blade a little harder, and she inwardly smiled each time she saw him wince in fear.

Time to really let him know who he is really dealing with, Lotte.

Instantly, Charlotte's whole character changed from that of a confident lady of the *ton* to one of a whore in the brothels of Kingston, one used to dealing with men such as Henry. She narrowed her eyes menacingly as her demeanour hardened into something akin to cast iron, any trace of a polite smile vanishing as she again pressed her knife into his groin, just for emphasis.

"What say you to that, you pathetic excuse for a piece of dog shit? Do I need arrange for Samson to pay you a visit?"

"No ... no ..." he stammered. "I ... I do not ... do not think that will be necessary," he squeaked.

"Well then, I would strongly suggest that you go over to Lady Anne and make a heartfelt apology before I deem it necessary to make it so. Do . . . I . . . make . . . myself . . . clear, Henry?"

For a moment, Henry simply stood and stared back, and from the look in his eyes, Charlotte knew the man was still teetering on the edge of the cliff, part of him still wanting to argue, to reply with the violence that bubbled beneath the skin. But she held his glare in her own, daring him to try.

"Make a choice, baron, before this gets out of hand," she warned.

Charlotte saw a change in the man as his gaze darted towards the open doors that led to the ballroom, and instinctively she knew he had made his decision. Accordingly, Charlotte relaxed her hand by a fraction and took a half step back to give Henry the chance to escape.

"Yes . . . yes, Lady Winters, yes, of course," he blustered as he moved away from her.

Charlotte stood still and watched her stepbrother walk unsteadily back into the ballroom and towards her party of guests, which, by then, had been joined by Lord Peter Harvey. She followed Henry inside and saw him stand before the group, his voice lost amongst the hubbub of the crowd whilst he made an obvious yet forced apology. Only then did he turn to stalk from the room, his parting look of pure loathing enough to make even Charlotte shudder.

"By God, Lady Winters, what on earth did you say him?" Peter asked as Charlotte re-joined the group. "The man was as white as a sheet!"

"Oh, I merely *pointed* out the perils of not behaving like a gentleman, my lord." Charlotte smiled sweetly.

****

Having returned to the ballroom with the intention of politely joining the party for dinner, James witnessed the moment Lord Henry approached his daughter. Whilst he could not hear the words that were being spoken, it was obvious, just from the way that young Jameson had reacted, that Henry was being anything but polite.

However, what happened next was not at all what he expected. Lady Charlotte had stood and had taken the man by the arm to lead him away from the party. To James, it was a brilliant move, for in an instant Charlotte had removed the threat, and he found himself grinning as he supposed the situation to be dealt with.

But then he cursed out loud as he watched Charlotte take Henry out on the veranda.

Knowing the danger she had placed herself in, James practically ran from the ballroom, his fists curled as if ready for a fight. But as he ran out into the darkness, unseen by either of them, something made him stop short — a flash of silver metal in the moonlight. Instinctively, he ducked behind a huge stone column, and from the shadows, he watched with approbation.

It was obvious that Charlotte held no fear for the man, for it was she that had the man cowering against a wall, it was she that threatened him with a stiletto blade that she held pressed firmly against that man's groin. In fact, if anyone was in danger of harm, it was Lord Henry, and the thought of it nearly made James laugh out loud. In the end, the man had simply deflated, his arrogant and conceited manner evaporating before his very eyes.

Unseen, James followed them back into the ballroom. Standing well behind Charlotte, he watched her as she watched the baron make his apology. But the look of hatred that the baron had subsequently given Charlotte could not go unanswered, and as the man made to leave the ballroom, James, without really giving the matter much consideration, intercepted him, watching the man's eyes widen as he confronted him.

"Baron," he called, deliberately keeping his voice low and menacing. "What I have just witnessed, out on the veranda, leaves me in no doubt as to your despicable character and it has gladdened my heart to see you humiliated by a mere slip of a woman. Now you listen, and listen good. If you ever come near my daughter again, or for that matter, Lady Charlotte, I will make it my solemn duty to destroy you and everything you stand for. Do I make myself clear?"

CHAPTER ELEVEN

As they drove home from the ball, Charlotte sensed that the mood in the carriage had become a mix of contradicting emotions. Anne was simply jubilant, a huge broad smile fixed permanently onto her face. The night had been nothing short of a triumph for her, and she had danced all night, discreetly flirting with those gentlemen who had caught her fancy, one Lord Peter Harvey in particular.

As for the duchess? She had promenaded a little, had laughed and reminisced with her friends of when they had been debutantes, had drunk more than her fair share of wine and had won several guineas playing Faro in the gaming room. She was now snoring gently, her head resting against Anne's shoulder as she dozed.

Her godfather, however, was staring stoically out of the window, his face placid and emotionless, and Charlotte was finding it difficult to read the man. Yes, they had shared a moment on the dance floor, a moment she knew she would cherish for a very long time. But that had been all. For the rest of the evening, much to her displeasure, the duke had ignored her, had kept his distance, even when she had been forced to deal with Lord Henry.

Charlotte sighed loudly and watched as the duke's gaze flittered over to her. She, in return, glanced at him, their eyes making contact for the briefest of moments as, once more, she tried to discern his thoughts. Then his lips formed the merest hint of a smile, forcing her to look away as a surge of irrational desire made her heart beat even faster than it had when she had shared the dance with him. Surreptitiously, she glanced at him once more, this time to see the look of disdain and the practised expression of indifference, and once more she sighed as she recognised it for what it was.

Perhaps it is for the best, Lotte, for there could never be anything between us. He is Anne's father and my godfather. He knows my secret . . . he knows who and what I am! He is five and twenty years older than me! He is a man! So no, it could never be, could it?

But would you, Lotte? Would you, if he gave you the chance?

Charlotte smiled to herself as she thought of the answer to her rhetorical question. Charles's time at sea and his tenure in the brothel had been awful, even if it had been the time where she had found herself.

But then David had come into his life.

David had moulded Charles into Charlotte and had then shown her how wonderful making love as a woman could be. Yes, the ship and the brothel, at times, had been brutal. But David had changed all that, and Charlotte could not help but smile to herself as she remembered how much she had come to enjoy the physical act of making love. In fact, for Charlotte, their coupling had soon become the ultimate expression of her femininity, and she had adored nothing more than to have David take her into his arms so as to make love to her as if she were the most precious woman in the world. For that, Charlotte knew she would always love David, no matter who came into her life in the future. But now that he was gone, she missed the intimacy of making love to a man, and even more, she missed the validation of her femininity that making love to a man could bring.

Again, she furtively glanced at the duke, just a fleeting look from the corner of her eye. Yes, he might be many years her senior, but there was no denying that she found him immensely attractive, and more than once she had imagined what it might be like to make love with him. However, there was more to him than just his rugged handsomeness. He was also kind, strong-willed, and loyal to a fault, especially to his family, traits of character Charlotte valued above all else.

So yes, you would, wouldn't you, Lotte.

Still lost in thought, Charlotte started a little as the carriage jerked to a halt outside the duke's house, the dowager lifting her head as she came groggily awake. The four of them sat in silence for a moment, until a footman opened the carriage door before reaching in towards the duchess as he offered a helping hand. It was then, and only then, that the duke spoke, his words catching Charlotte completely by surprise.

"Mother, would you please ensure that Anne gets inside safely? For I think I should escort Lady Winters home." His voice was somewhat gruff as he turned to her. "That is, by your leave, Lady Charlotte."

For a moment, Charlotte stared at the duke intently, trying to read, in his dark, brooding eyes, what his intentions might be. He was a difficult man to fathom, but she shivered a little with excitement when she saw the undeniable traces of lust — lust that was, at the same time, matched by undeniable traces of confusion and doubt.

Charlotte's heart began to pound with growing excitement."I would deem it an honour, James," she replied.

Moments later, Charlotte found herself being escorted by the duke up to the front door of her townhouse. The portal was opened almost as if by magic by a very alert Samson, who had obviously been waiting up for her. He said nothing as the two of them entered.

"Thank you, Samson," Charlotte said as Samson opened the door to the sitting room to reveal that the room was still well illuminated by several candles that had been left alight. "You may retire now. Oh, and when you go to bed, pray, tell Phoebe that I would like my breakfast at eleven in the morning, please."

"Thank you, Missy Charlotte," he replied. For an instant, a

sheepish grin appeared on Samson's face, a grin that almost made him look boyish. But as he backed out of the room, Charlotte saw him scowl at James, forcing her to hide a smile behind her hand.

"Oh, that man," Charlotte said. "As subtle as a stone thrown through a hothouse window. The two of them thought I had no idea that they have been sharing a bed, ever since he proposed to her."

"You are lucky to have them both. Samson is so obviously devoted to you."

"And I to him. Like I said, he is my protector, and I would not know what to do without him."

The duke laughed as she said those words. "I am not sure about that. From what I witnessed this evening, with Baron Henry Hamilton, you are quite capable of looking after yourself."

"Ah, you saw that, did you?" Charlotte winced a little, then shrugged her shoulders in a very matter-of-fact way. "It was a situation that needed dealing with, so I dealt with it!"

"And you have my thanks for doing so, Charlotte. Did Samson teach you how to do that?"

"Mmm. Shortly after David and I were *married*, I had occasion to save Samson's life. One of the estate overseers on another plantation was beating a young female slave with a whip, quite violently in fact, and I watched Samson charge from his field to put a fist in the man's face. The overseer, who was well within his rights, wanted Samson hung, but I managed to intervene on his behalf. I bribed the overseer and then persuaded Samson's owner to sell him to me. It turned out that Samson was an adept in the fighting styles of his tribe, and he has taught me much about how to protect myself. I would trust him with my life, and he and was but the third person in the world to whom I trusted my secret."

"Ah yes, your secret," James mumbled. "I am, in truth,

having a very hard time with that."

"What? What do you mean? I thought that you had accepted—"

"What I mean," James interrupted, "is that I am now not certain. I have doubt, Charlotte, real doubt, especially after what I have been witness to this evening."

Charlotte's heart literally stopped when she heard him utter these words, for not only had he said so much, he had left an equal amount unspoken, too, and she felt her mouth go dry at what he might be trying to intimate. And to make matters worse, he then took a half step closer, forcing her to tilt her head upwards so she could retain eye contact with him.

James groaned and ran his hand nervously through his greying hair.

"Do you not think my rational mind knows that you are neither one thing nor the other? No longer are you the boy I once knew, but neither are you the real woman you purport to be."

He groaned once more, sounding something akin to a wounded animal pain, and then closed his eyes, almost as if he no longer dared to look at her.

"Please, James, what is it you are trying to say?" Charlotte beseeched.

"How the hell am I supposed to know? You look like a bloody woman. You move like a bloody woman. You dance like a bloody woman. You even smell like a bloody woman," he groaned. "But you are not. You are a man, and a man quite capable of looking after himself at that."

"No, I am not," she insisted. "I am a woman and have been for several years now. That, you must believe."

"But . . . but . . ." he spluttered.

"Yes, there are some things about me that will always be part of the boy I once was. For that, there is no potion, no remedy. But in my heart and in my mind, I am every inch a *real* woman."

"I know . . . but . . . God . . . this is so confusing for me. Neither does it help one jot that I find everything about you intoxicating. You are so beautiful, Charlotte . . . but . . . but . . ."

"Are you attracted to me, James? Is that what you are trying to say? For I am most certainly attracted to you," she murmured.

"No . . . Yes . . ." he whispered. "I don't . . . I don't know! My rational mind tells me I shouldn't be, if you are who you claim to be. It would be wrong, so very wrong. But my body tells me different, and I bloody well don't seem to be able to stop myself!"He groaned again in clear frustration.

And there it was. His message was clear. James wanted her, wanted the woman she had become. But what he didn't want was the boy she had once been.

Charlotte stood absolutely still, as though she was stalking a wild bird she wished to capture, knowing that any sudden move was sure to spook him. Tentatively, she lifted a hand to his cheek.

"Well, there is no confusion in my mind as to what I want, James," she whispered as she lightly stroked his skin. "Tell me, do my fingers feel like the fingers of a man?"

"N . . . no," he replied, his voice shaky and uncertain.

Boldly, Charlotte went up onto her tiptoes and lightly brushed her lips against his, hearing him moan a little as her flesh made contact with his.

"And do I taste like a man?" she asked.

"No," James admitted.

Then, feeling more audacious than she had ever before, Charlotte took hold of both of his large hands and lifted them to her breasts, covering his hands with her own as she felt him cup her flesh.

"And does my chest feel like the chest of a man?"

"No!" he growled.

Leaving his hands where they were, Charlotte lifted her own arms and placed them around his neck, pulling him down to her. Slowly she kissed him, properly this time. It was a long, lingering embrace, and her lips traced the firmness of his own as she teased and licked and captured his bottom lip playfully between her teeth.

"And, my lord, does my kiss feel like the kiss of a man?" she whispered.

"No, by God," James roared, and this time his lips came crashing down on hers.

He pulled her closer, his kiss harsh and heady. Charlotte simply responded in kind, her own arms grasping him tighter so she could return his embrace in equal measure. It was a kiss that she never wanted to end, a kiss to end all kisses, and every cell she possessed, from the tips of her toes to the end of her nose, seemed to be sparkling like fine champagne. She tilted her head a little as he deepened the kiss, relishing the feel of his firm lips and the touch of his tongue against hers. Her heart was hammering in her chest and she felt her body respond as she felt her own little piece of flesh begin to swell and grow, every fibre, every sinew, every muscle, screaming out more. Again and again, their lips met, their embrace exhilarating and urgent, and as they kissed, James pulled her body firmly against his, two bodies melding into one. She felt her small breasts pressing delightfully against his chest and felt the enormity of his erection pressing against her thigh, the joy of it so great that she nearly lost herself in the moment.

And it was for that very reason, even with her befuddled mind, she knew she had to stop, that there were words that needed to be spoken. Slowly she pulled away from him, their lips momentarily connected by a silver thread of saliva.

"Be very clear, your grace, that I want nothing more than to have you make love to me tonight," she murmured. "But, should you feel the same way, please also be very clear, whilst

I am all woman, here, here, and here" — she pointed to her head, her heart, and her breasts — "there is still one tiny part that remains of the person I once was."

Charlotte paused to allow him to respond to her statement. But James stood before her, his eyes gazing down at her with an intensity that made her shiver with expectation.

"However," she continued, "in the event that you find yourself able to overlook that little defect, I want to reassure you of one thing. I learned the craft of lovemaking as a *woman* at the hands of a master, and you need to know that the pleasure I offer you will be like nothing you will have ever experienced before."

Seductively, as she spoke, her hand moved down, her fingers slowly tracing the outline of his massive erection beneath the soft yet tight material of his breeches. James hissed as his body shuddered.

Then, without waiting for his reply, Charlotte moved away from him, circling the room to snuff out each candle in turn with fingers that she dampened seductively between her lips. Soon there remained but a single candle in a silver candlestick, its flame casting soft and sensuous shadows onto every surface in the room.

"What are you doing?" James asked.

He looked somewhat confused as Charlotte carefully picked up the last remaining candle, so she smiled reassuringly.

"I am preparing to go to bed, your grace, and the only thing I now need to know is whether you intend to accompany me."

Reaching down with her free hand, Charlotte interlaced her fingers with his, and without the need for another word, she led him from the room. Meekly he followed, almost as if he was in a trance, any trace of self-restraint seemingly flown out the window the moment she had taken his hand.

Charlotte led them out into the hallway, and the duke

continued to follow. They walked up the stairs, onto the landing and through another door into a large well-appointed bedroom, where Charlotte carefully placed the candle onto a side table, its light now combining with several others that had been left to illuminate the room. Again, she turned to James and gazed into his beautiful, soulful, yet troubled eyes.

"Last chance, your grace," she said as she boldly placed her arms around his neck once more. "Whilst I would be extremely disappointed, I will not hold it against you if you now decide to leave."

"As if I had any choice," he sighed.

His mouth met with hers again, and for an eternity, they stood together as their lips made gentle love to each other, as their tongues danced their own type of waltz. As they kissed, Charlotte pressed her body ever closer to his, delighting in the way he responded to her, his excitement evident in the shortness of his breath, and in the massive erection he once more sported beneath his breeches.

And it was that very fact that gave Charlotte a clear idea of what to do next.

She broke their kiss and sank gracefully to her knees before him, the skirt of her dress pooling all around her as she did so. Looking up, she locked her gaze upon his as she lifted her hand, hearing him groan as her slender fingers drew lower to trace the impressive outline of his cock.

Then, one by one, she unfastened the buttons that secured his breeches.

"May I?" she whispered.

Without waiting for his reply, she slipped her hand inside his trousers, feeling the heat within. For a moment, her fingers searched for him, and she felt herself smile a lazy smile when she found her prize.

Delicately, as if his cock were a newborn babe, she took him into her hands, relishing the feel of its size. Again she looked up and smiled, her hands pulling his trousers down over his hips to free him completely. His magnificent cock jutted towards her, her fingers stroking his silky skin, and she felt James shiver in anticipation.

And who was she to disappoint?

As she pulled back the skin that covered its angry head, she moved her face forward, pursing her lips just a fraction to kiss the very end of his cock. James groaned at her touch, a sound which did nothing but encouraged her. She held him in one hand as the other cupped his balls, her tongue darting out to lick him and caress him and tease him. And when she thought he could stand it no longer, instead of pulling away from him, she simply opened her mouth and took him deep into her throat.

"Oh, my dear God!" he moaned.

With infinite care and patience, Charlotte began to fuck him with her mouth, mindful of her pace lest the pleasure become too great for him. Slowly she slipped her mouth up his length to the very tip, her tongue swirling around his crown as she did so. Then she began to rock her head backwards and forwards, her lips forming a perfect circle around his flesh. She brought her hand into play too, her fingers teasing at his length, moving in time with her lips, knowing the sensations she was creating would be almost too much to endure. She allowed her mouth to trace the contours of his bulbous head, and even though her lips remained around his cock, she smiled as she looked up to see the lust in his eyes — eyes that stared back at her with an intensity she found unbelievably intoxicating.

Like most men, it had been so easy to seduce him, and she knew if she were so inclined, she could have him reach his peak within moments. But that was not what she wanted. Instead, she slowed her pace, her lips now more of a caress as she took hold of his hands, bringing them to her hair, showing him what she wanted him to do as she directed him to a bejewelled pin.

Charlotte returned her attention to his cock as she felt James begin to search for the pins that secured her hair. The headdress went first, carelessly thrown onto the floor. Then he removed pin after pin, and with each, she felt yet another tress of hair fall around her face, until her long curls hung gloriously around her shoulders and face.

It was only when he had finished removing the very last pin that Charlotte finally released him from her mouth. She stood and turned her back to him, lifting her hair so he could reach the back of her dress. James needed no further encouragement. With fingers that trembled slightly, Charlotte felt him fumble at the bows and buttons of her gown until, with a shrug of her shoulders, she allowed her dress to slip from her body.

Demurely, Charlotte stood before the duke and posed for him, now dressed in nothing but her stays and petticoats, knowing how important it was for James to see her as the beautiful woman she was. The tight laces of her stays did little to hide the soft swell of her breasts, and for a moment, she allowed her hands to touch herself there, feeling her flesh with her fingers, shivering a little with expectation as she felt her nipples swell. Then she let her hands fall, her fingers tracing the outline of her slim body through the material of her petticoats, her tongue darting out nervously to moisten her lips. Again, she took a step towards him.

"Tonight, your grace, if this is to be, then there is to be nothing hidden between us," she whispered.

Garment by garment, Charlotte undressed him, almost as if she were his personal valet. His tailcoat went first, followed by his cravat, and then she unbuttoned his shirt, pleased to see that, whilst he no longer had the body of a young man, his muscles were lean and toned. Playfully she allowed her hands to roam through the soft down of hair that covered his chest, then heard him gasp as she took first one and then the other tiny nipple between her teeth, nipping at them and feeling them swell as she did so.

Then she knelt before him once more, to find herself sorely tempted to take his cock into her mouth. Instead, she removed his boots so that she could ease down his breeches over his shapely thighs and calves, carelessly discarding them onto a chair as she did so.

This time she did not resist temptation. As he stood there, as naked as the day he was born, his rampant cock standing proud before him, she reached for him, taking him lightly in her hand. Again she kissed him and tasted the first few drops of clear fluid oozing from its single eye, a sure indication of the state of his arousal. Again she slipped his glorious manhood into the warmth of her mouth, relishing its size, feeling herself gag a little as she took him deep into her throat. She caressed his cock, she licked and lapped, swirling her tongue around its head and listened to his groans and grunts of pleasure.

"Stop, Charlotte, stop."

His voice was gruff as he finally pulled himself away, and Charlotte smiled as she looked up at him from her subservient position. For a moment, she saw a flicker of indecision on his face, and her heart suddenly feared that he was about to put a halt to their liaison. Instead, his hand reached down to cup her face, gently smoothing her hair behind her ears as he motioned for her to stand.

"You have me at a disadvantage, madam," he whispered as he made her turn.

Charlotte sensed his hands as they reached delicately for the bow that fastened the top of her stays. She felt the pull of the ribbons as he loosened them, eyelet by eyelet, before he tugged at the soft silk of her bodice to uncover her shoulder blades beneath. She shivered, not with cold but with excitement, as he leant forward to kiss each small square of flesh he bared, finally burying his lips into her neck as the stays fell away to the floor.

Charlotte was now dressed in nothing but her floor-length chemise, the fine cotton of which was practically transparent in the candlelight that illuminated the room. Unexpectedly, James remained behind her and took a step back as Charlotte glanced coyly over her shoulder at him, wondering what he was doing. Realising that James simply wanted to look, she posed for him, knowing that through the material of her shift he could clearly see her outline. As she stood before him, Charlotte rejoiced in the woman she had become and the sensuous curves she now possessed. From hours of posing in front of the looking glass, she knew her back was slender and her waist was trim, which would do nothing but emphasise the swell of her buttocks, so round and enticing. She knew that she also possessed a pair of slim, shapely legs with calves that could drive a man to distraction.

And now it was time to let him see . . . to really let him see.

Charlotte giggled, and her shift pooled to the ground so that she too was completely undressed, her back still towards him.

Bashfully, Charlotte turned and heard James gasp when he saw her naked body for the first time.

In her mind, her body was simply perfect. Long tresses of auburn hair hung loosely over her small yet perfectly formed breasts, breasts that sported dark areolas and expectant nipples that stood proud from her flesh. Her arms were toned, her stomach flat, her hips slim yet rounded, and everything about her screamed, *I am woman.*

With one exception.

Between her legs, almost hidden beneath a triangle of soft, curly, auburn hair, was a tiny penis, a small, flaccid, and insubstantial piece of flesh. Initially, it was here that James's eyes were drawn, and it became Charlotte's turn to feel a little embarrassed whilst the man who stood before her stared at her nakedness. But then his eyes fixed upon her breasts, and she gasped inwardly as his hands reached forward to cup her flesh. Motionless, she stood, and as he felt the weight of them with his fingers, his eyes widened, almost as if he could not believe their existence.

"Remarkable, quite remarkable," he croaked as he fingered her nipples.

"I . . . er . . . I . . . as . . . as you can see, my lord, I am hardly a man after all," she whispered. "Ever since I started taking Phoebe's medicine, my breasts have grown, and I have . . . well . . . my . . . erm . . . has become smaller and smaller and will now no longer . . . well, you know . . . I no longer function normally as a man might . . . as you might . . . as you have, so magnificently." She pointed at his massive erection, her hand shaking with anticipation.

Boyishly, James grinned. Charlotte closed her eyes but felt him draw closer, his arms reaching around her waist to pull her into his body, his erection becoming trapped between them.

"Be quiet, *woman*," he demanded, and his lips crashed against hers once more.

One simple word, and Charlotte's world came together in pure unadulterated happiness. She, too, had suffered from doubt, her mind almost consumed with the worry that once he saw her naked body, he would reject her. But instead, he had called her *woman*. And her heart rejoiced.

"Come," she said as she took his hand.

Meekly James followed as Charlotte led him over to her bed, and together they clambered onto the mattress. Once more Charlotte took charge, encouraging James to stretch his legs out as she scrambled on her knees between them.

Tenderly, she took his cock in one hand, slowly running her fingers up and down its length, as she reached forward with her lips, searching for his to give him a long slow sensuous kiss, her heart rejoicing at how responsive he had become.

Suddenly, James twisted his body and flipped Charlotte onto her back, her long auburn hair pooling on the pillow beneath her. For what seemed like an eternity, they stared at each other like two star crossed lovers, until, slowly James lowered his head, bringing his lips to hers once more in a soft and gentle kiss.

Charlotte felt herself ascend to heaven. As James kissed her, she felt his hand begin to roam, cupping her breasts, teasing at her nipples before moving to the soft, smooth skin of her legs. He touched her everywhere—with one exception of course. But, in truth, she could not have cared less he avoided that unwanted part of her body, especially when his lips moved to suckle at her engorged nipples.

She, in turn, allowed her hands to roam. As her fingers traced the muscles of his back, her other hand grasped his length, her fingers gently playing with his flesh as her fist moved up and down. It was a beautiful, warm and tender moment, and with each touch, each kiss, Charlotte felt her need begin to climb.

She pushed him away. Then from the mahogany bedside table, she picked up a small crystal glass bottle with a silver lid and poured a little of the golden liquid it contained onto the palm of her hands.

"A little sweet oil, James," she whispered in explanation. "Olive oil, from the shores of the Mediterranean Sea."

She pushed him onto his back and then began to massage the oil onto his cock, a huge shiver of pleasure coursing through him as she touched him there.

"Holy Mother of God," he groaned. "That feels incredible," he whispered as she began to massage the slippery oil into his flesh, her hand stroking up and down.

"And it will make you taste even more wonderful than you already do, my lord." Charlotte grinned.

She leant forward to once more take him into her mouth, her hair pooling around her face as she did so. At first, she was tentative, just kissing the bulbous end of his cock, yet each time she moved, she took a little more of his length. Deeper and deeper she went, her tongue swirling around his flesh, the angle perfect to take the whole of his cock into the back of her throat, the oil just adding to the sensation in her mouth.

"My God. Stop, Charlotte, stop, for I do not think I can take much more of this, please, Charlotte," he beseeched.

"Very well," she pouted as she lifted her head. "Perhaps it is, after all, time for me to show you the real pleasures I have to offer you."

Reaching for the bottle once more, she rubbed a little more oil onto his cock and then reached behind herself to do the same at her own entrance. Then before James could utter a word, she straddled his legs, her arms snaking around his neck to steady herself.

"I hope you realise," she whispered, "that you are partly to blame for the person I am today." She sighed softly and then averted her eyes coyishly.

"What?"

"Even when I was but a boy, I think I knew that God had made a mistake with the body I had been given. Often, I would lay awake at night imagining what it might be like to be a girl, to have breasts, to have a cunny, to marry and beget a child, my belly growing fat as I increased. And it was you, my lord, who was the subject of my girlish imagination."

As she spoke, keeping her voice purposefully low and hypnotic, she lifted her body and positioned herself over his cock. Then without a moment's hesitation, she pushed her hips down firmly and took his cock deep inside her body.

"And now, I get to live some of my dreams," she panted.

Charlotte closed her eyes and winced a little with the pain she felt. But as his beautiful cock invaded her depths, despite the discomfort she felt, a broad smile flashed across her lips.

"Oh, my dear Lord," James whispered. "That feels . . . feels . . ."

"Mm, wonderful," Charlotte said, finishing his sentence for him. "God, James, you are so big."

Gently, as she sat on his lap waiting for the pain to subside, Charlotte pulled his head to her breast and sighed in pleasure as he suckled there, feeling her small nipple swell once more between his lips. She could not help but hiss in pleasure as his teeth nipped at her flesh — pleasure that simply melted away the discomfort she had felt only moments before.

As the hurting faded away into nothingness, Charlotte pulled him away from her breasts to find herself looking into those beautiful eyes once more, eyes that were now staring intently back at her. Very tenderly, her hands still on his face, she kissed him again, her lips in full contact with his as their tongues danced together. And as they embraced, she raised her hips up slightly and then pushed back down, wanting his approbation, listening for the growl of pleasure in the back of his throat.

He did not disappoint, and only then did she begin to show her lover the pleasure of making love to someone such as she.

Charlotte began to move her body in earnest. She lifted her hips, almost pulling his cock out from her body before once more pushing down, the oil she had used making his cock slide effortlessly into her depths. Up and down, up and down she went, and as she did so, she felt her own surge of pleasure shoot through her very core.

"God, that feels incredible," James moaned as Charlotte added yet another movement, a little thrust forward with her hips as she pushed herself down onto him. "Bloody hell!" he groaned.

But she was not yet finished with his *education,* so she pushed him down onto his back before lifting herself from him completely. Then turning so that her back was facing him — so that he could no longer see her little cock — she once more took him into her body. This time, however, there was no pain for her. Turning this way, she also achieved the perfect position for her as well, and she gave out a little whimper of ecstasy as his cock reached her most intimate and sensitive place.

She began to truly fuck him, and she felt the man beneath her grab her hips, to guide her, to help her, as his hips pushed up to meet her every time she thrust down. Faster and faster she went, her small breasts bouncing on her chest as the whole room filled with the sound of flesh on flesh to accompany the groans of a man and the moans of a woman in the throes of passion.

The end came much faster than even Charlotte had imagined it would, and with one last huge thrust, she felt his cock pulse. His whole body jerked and throbbed, a huge groan emanating from him as she felt jet after jet after jet of his essence spurt deep into her bowels. This just spurred her on. Within seconds of him, her own body convulsed in unison, a thin scream mewling from her throat as every muscle spasmed in pleasure around his girth.

Chapter Twelve

It was a little before two in the afternoon on the next day when an anxious yet serene Charlotte arrived at James's home. As was tradition, callers were to be received from three in the afternoon, and Charlotte, taking her duties as chaperon seriously was there to see that everyone behaved as they were expected too. Especially, Henry Hamilton, should he have the nerve to call!

The butler opened the door, and judging by the warm look on his face, he had been warned to expect her.

"Good afternoon, Lady Winters," he said as he took her cape from her.

"Good afternoon, Stevens. Is Lady Anne in the drawing room?"

"Yes, but his grace has instructed, or should I say requested, that I show you into his study first. I believe he desires a word with you," the butler replied with a slight bow.

Swallowing hard, she nodded her agreement, then followed as the man turned to walk down a corridor.

In truth, she had not expected to see James that afternoon. By the time they had finished making love, it had been nearly three in the morning, and she had fallen asleep in his arms, feeling loved and more than a little cherished. But when she had awoken, every sign that he had ever been in her room had simply vanished. He had not even had the courtesy to leave a note, giving her the distinct impression that he believed that what had happened between them had been nothing but a huge mistake.

Gracefully, her head held high despite the nerves she felt, Charlotte walked behind Stevens as he led her towards yet another large oak door. Charlotte recognised it as the door to the duke's study, behind which, undoubtedly, Charlotte was about to find out the truth of the matter, once and for all.

"Her Ladyship, your grace," Stevens announced.

Charlotte stayed behind the butler for a second to peer at James, noting that he looked tired and more than a little vexed. His face was long and serious, yet he still managed a tentative smile as he watched her enter the room.

"Thank you, Stevens, and could you shut the door behind you."

Charlotte remained standing, her hands before her as she nervously throttled her reticule, instantly sensing that something was amiss, just as she had expected it to be. When the door closed behind her with a solid thud, her heart fluttered as she once more found herself alone with James.

"Please, Charlotte, please take a seat," James stammered. His face showed more than a little embarrassment as he pointed to two chairs that had obviously been carefully positioned especially for this moment, and Charlotte could see that he was equally as nervous as she was.

"Is everything all right, James?" Charlotte asked as she sat demurely, her reticule now on her lap.

"Yes, well, no," he mumbled. "God, I don't know how to say this, especially after last night, which by the way was totally wonderful."

"Perhaps, then, you should simply say the words, James. If it is what I expect it to be, you can rest assured that I am no simpering woman who is going to fall at your feet crying over the matter."

James smiled sheepishly, then shrugged his shoulders as an expression akin to relief flickered through his eyes. It was an expression that spoke volumes, and even though she had prepared her mind for such an eventuality, Charlotte still felt a surge of disappointment.

"Yes, well. I'll just come out with it then, It's just that I have had time to, well, reflect on what happened last night, and I . . . erm . . . and whilst I truly enjoyed our time together, I don't think it is something we should repeat. In truth, I don't think it is something that I . . . we . . . can risk repeating," he murmured, his voice so low it was practically inaudible.

"I see."

"Please, understand that it is nothing that you have done. Throughout all of this, you have been totally honest with me, and I knew exactly what I was getting myself into last night. It is just that I do not wish to mislead you, Charlotte, and I cannot see myself having a . . . well . . . an affair with someone . . . with a person . . . well . . . like you."

"A boy, you mean."

"Mm yes, amongst other things. Being *associated* with you is one thing. But if it became known that I have taken you as my mistress and then your true identity came to be public knowledge, I would undoubtedly be ruined, as would Anne."

Her first reaction was one of anger, for his choice of words did little to please her — *Taken? Mistress?* — words unlikely to endear him to any lady. But then she laughed inwardly and cursed herself for being more than a little churlish.

Her second response was one of frustration and disappointment, as, just for a few short hours, she had allowed herself to dream that she might have found someone with whom she could share at least a part of her life. But, on the other hand, neither was she surprised at his decision. She had always known that James was as straight as one of Robin Hood's arrows, and she was someone who simply did not fit the mould. Spending the night with her must have been quite a conundrum for him for, as he had professed, he had never before slept with another *man*. He was right to fear discovery

155

and ridicule too, and despite her plans for the earl and his son, if she had to be truthful with herself, the last thing she desired was to bring dishonour and disgrace to James's family.

So it was that she smiled agreeably, in the hope she conveyed not the slightest hint of animosity.

"And now I appreciate your honesty, sir," she said. "Whilst I cannot pretend to not be disappointed in your decision, I will gladly abide by it." Charlotte paused, almost as if she were placing a full stop at the end of their potential relationship. Yet there were still other matters to be resolved. "But I have to ask," she continued "Will this affect my relationship with Anne, for whom I have developed a great fondness? Do you wish for me to stop spending time with her? After all, you have done as I have requested of you and have affected a meeting with both my mother and my halfsister, a service for which I shall remain eternally in your debt."

"No, I do not wish that, nor, I am sure, would Anne. In fact, I would deem it an honour if you would continue as her chaperon, just as I would deem it an honour if you would consider us as we were before, not as lovers, but as friends, as godfather and godchild."

Charlotte stood and walked over to the still seated duke, knowing how much it had cost him, how much he risked, to speak those words. She bent down and kissed him lightly on the cheek as if to affirm her agreement to this.

"I would like that very much, Uncle James," she whispered, once more noting the look of relief on his face. "Now, as it is close to the time for Anne to receive visitors, I think it would be for the best if I joined her."

Charlotte stood with a little more alacrity than was polite, knowing that if she were to hide the tears she felt, she needed to leave the duke's presence. She dipped a curtsey.

"Your grace," she said, as she turned and fled.

To Charlotte's surprise, not only was Lady Anne waiting for her when she was announced, but Amelia also, an Amelia who seemed to be having the greatest difficulty in keeping the biggest smile from her face. However, it was Anne who could not contain her excitement, and she practically shrieked as soon as Charlotte entered the drawing room.

"Oh, Lotte," she said as she jumped up to her feet. "We have wonderful news. I mean Amelia has wonderful news, don't you, Amelia?"

"Then perhaps we should let Amelia tell it," Charlotte said in return. She sat on a vacant chair and looked at her sister quizzically. Amelia was attired in a pretty green dress with matching spencer and bonnet, which suggested she had only just arrived herself, and she was sat next to Anne, the two of them practically bouncing up and down with excitement. "Well?" Charlotte asked, wondering which one of them was going to blurt out the news.

Amelia blushed delightfully. "William paid me a call this morning. He has asked me to marry him and I have said yes, Oh, Lotte," she gushed. "I am so happy, so unbelievably happy."

"Well, well, well, this is wonderful news, Amelia. But isn't this so very sudden, and you having only last night made your debut, too."

"I know, but William and I have been acquaintances for over a year, and when he saw me dancing with Lord Kirksteven last night, it appears that he had a fit of jealousy which prompted him to propose today, before, as he said, *I get snatched up by some other gentleman*. Oh, Lotte, I do love him so, and he loves me, too."

"Of course, he does." Charlotte grinned. "For you are eminently loveable."

"In truth, isn't that the most romantic thing you have ever heard, even though people are bound to speculate when the news comes out, as it is so early in the season?" Anne sighed.

"Which is why mother has said that we must keep this to ourselves for the moment, even from father," Amelia said. "Oh, Anne, you must promise!"

"So William has not spoken to your father yet, to ask for your hand?" Charlotte asked.

"No, not as yet. But that will be a mere formality, I hope. William is heir to an earldom and has ten-thousand a year, too, from his own estates in Lincolnshire. He has even said that he will permit me to put my dowry into a trust for myself and our children. To think, one day I will be a countess in my own right."

"And what of you, Anne? Has your morning been an interesting one?" By the expression on Anne's face, Charlotte was certain she could predict the answer to her question, for the girl was brimming over with the joy of the moment.

It was Amelia who responded before Anne could. "Oh, yes. She has had no less than eight bouquets delivered this morning. The day room looks like a veritable flower shop. Annnnnnd" — she drew out the word dramatically, her grin, if possible, becoming even wider — "then there is the gossip column in this morning's newspaper too. Have you seen it yet, Lady Charlotte?"

"No, but judging by the conspiratorial looks on your faces, you are about to show me, I should think."

From behind her back, Anne slowly drew forth the newspaper, its pages already turned to the gossip columns. She handed it to Charlotte, her finger pointing to the passage she wanted her to see.

"Please, Lotte, pray do read it aloud, for I will never cease wanting to hear it," Anne begged.

Charlotte duly obliged.

"At last night's debutantes' ball, held at the home of the Duchess of Harrow, there were two that stood out from all the rest as

diamonds of the first water. *The first, Lady H, it seems, much to the disappointment of many a rake, may already have lost her heart. For she danced no less than three dances with the handsome Lord W. The second, Lady B, who was dressed in a sumptuous cream and golden gown, was the undeniable incomparable of the evening and is a lady who is sure to attract the most eligible of bachelors. She, in turn, was chaperoned by the mysterious and beautiful Lady W who enjoyed but one dance all evening with none other than Lady B's father."*

"Oh, isn't it wonderful, Lotte." Anne giggled as she flopped back onto the settee in a most dramatic way. "Amelia is engaged, I am *incomparable*, and you are *mysterious and beautiful*."

"I just hope my father doesn't read the paper," Amelia groaned.

That very moment, Stevens knocked on the door, a silver tray in his hand with no less than three calling cards on it."

"There are some gentlemen in the vestibule, my lady," he said stoically as he handed Anne the tray. "All of whom are requesting an audience. Shall I permit them to enter?"

"And that" — Amelia giggled as she stood and kissed Anne on the cheek — "is my cue to take my leave. Mother is expecting me at home to receive callers, too, even if I have no interest in receiving them. Stevens, would you please fetch my maid and have my carriage brought round?"

CHAPTER THIRTEEN

The following three weeks were full of excitement for Anne and Amelia alike. There had been no end of gentleman callers and invitations to this house party and that dance. There had been carriage rides along the Ladies Mile in Hyde Park and promenades around the Serpentine.

For Amelia, the ready presence of her beloved Lord William was a continuous source of pleasure, even though they were both very careful to not cause any suspicion of scandal. Their meetings were always properly chaperoned by the countess herself, even though she seemed to always do what she could to encourage the match.

Both Amelia, and their friend, Jane, would often be found at the duke's townhouse, and with each passing day, Charlotte came to care for her sister more and more and more.

It also gave her endless opportunities to be with Lady Olivia, too, and they would often sit together as the girls danced at some function or other.

As Charlotte, once more, became closely acquainted with her mother, it soon became clear to her that everything was not as it should have been. It was almost as if her mother's state of mind seemed to change almost as often as her dress. When the earl was about, she was quiet, introverted and withdrawn, hardly ever interacting with others or entering into a conversation. On the other hand, when the earl was not in attendance, Olivia was far more like the woman Charlotte remembered from her childhood, the warm, gentle woman she had loved for all her life.

And the contrast between the two made Charlotte even more resolute in her quest.

As for Anne, there seemed to be one young gentleman for whom she was developing a special fondness, and that gentleman was none other than Lord Peter Harvey. As it turned out, even though he had appeared in dress uniform at the debutants ball, he had recently resigned his commission in the army so that he could spend more time helping his father with the management the families' estates.

Although he had not formally declared himself as Anne's suitor, Lord Peter became a regular visitor to James's home in Belgrave Square. He would often be seen driving his curricle madly along Rotten Row too, just as Anne and Charlotte would be *conveniently* taking a walk along the Serpentine at the same time. In fact, it happened so often that Charlotte began to suspect that he might have bribed one of the maids in James's household to tell him when they would be taking their walks. Much to her amusement, however, Charlotte soon discovered that it was actually Anne who was passing the information through her own lady's maid just so they could *accidentally* meet next to the river.

To Anne's evident excitement, her father approached the Patronesses of Almack's on her behalf, to secure vouchers for the Wednesday night ball, and to Charlotte's surprise, he had even secured her one as well. After all, to be found worthy of the privilege of buying a voucher, you had to be personally known to one of the seven powerful society hostesses who organised it, and she was hardly a leading light in the *ton*. Even though James had been conspicuously absent from the event — much to Charlotte's disappointment — their first evening at Almack's had been a complete triumph for the girls, who had gaily danced the night away, especially with both Lord William and Lord Peter, who were both in attendance.

The morning after Anne and Amelia's second jaunt to Almack's, Charlotte sat in Anne's drawing room with Anne in attendance. For once, her companion was quiet, almost subdued, the hint of black circles beneath her eyes an indication of the lack of sleep they all seemed to be getting

"Oh, Lotte." Anne sighed, confirming Charlotte's suspicions. "I am exhausted. It was so late when we returned from Almack's that I simply don't think I can face another function for at least a month."

Anne sat down heavily onto the settee in the library and groaned theatrically, her hand rubbing her temple almost as if to say *I am so tired that I am getting a megrim.*

Charlotte grinned inwardly as she heard these words, although she somehow managed to keep a straight face. Just that morning, she had been staring at a short but very significant list on a piece of paper before her, wondering what would be the next move in her great game. Thanks to the demands of being Anne's chaperon, her real quest had, for the time being, been put on hold. But earlier, she had received a message from Mr Green, *enquiring* as to the state of their business, and she had decided the time was right for her to make the next move. So it was that she had come to visit Anne that afternoon with one thought in mind, and now she wouldn't even have to try to engineer it herself, as Anne had presented her with the perfect opportunity.

"I totally agree, Anne, for I am exhausted, too. Perhaps we ought to take a few days in the countryside to recharge ourselves. A little break might do us all good, do you not think?" she said, working hard to keep the excitement from her voice.

Like a trout taking a fly, Anne took the bait and sat up with sudden enthusiasm.

"Oh, what a lovely idea. Where shall we go? I would love to offer my home, Wilton House, but I fear that will not be possible, as it is over a day's journey and Papa will not be pried from London whilst Parliament is in session — not for love nor money."

"I had thought of asking Lady Olivia and Lady Amelia to accompany us. Perhaps the countess would play hostess at her home for a few days," Charlotte suggested.

"That, my dear Lotte, is a splendid idea." Anne grinned. "Haycock Abbey, that is the earl's house, is but a three-hour carriage ride from London, and I am certain that Lady Olivia and Amelia would enjoy a break as much as we. Do you think they might take us up on the suggestion? In truth, I think that they may both relish the idea of time away from both the earl and Lord Henry, as neither of them is likely to be dragged away from the gaming tables."

"There is but one way of finding out," said Charlotte.

Two days later, arrangements had been made. As both she and Anne had suspected, their friends had jumped at the chance of a few days away, even though Amelia was loath to leave William in London. Lady Olivia had sent a message to the housekeeper at Haycock Abbey, and then the days had been filled with packing and preparations, the mood light and excited.

An early start was arranged, and by eight in the morning, the whole procession was on the road, the ladies sharing the first coach. Phoebe and the other maids were close behind in the second, driven by Samson, of course.

At first their progress was slow, but as they left the streets of London behind, the traffic cleared, and they began to move on at quite a clip. As they drove out into the countryside, the early morning mist, which had lingered longer than it should, cleared, and the day turned into one of those wonderful early English summer days that Charlotte loved.

Time passed quickly, and Charlotte soon began to feel her apprehension and excitement grow, even though she tried desperately not to show it. For as they drew nearer and nearer to Haycock Abbey, and to Thorpe Hall, she began to recognise the roads and landmarks along the way, causing memories — some good, some bad — to come flooding back to her.

The village of Kings Langley was just as she remembered it to be. A broad market street wound its way through the centre of the town, lined with half-timbered Elizabethan cottages and merchant shops of all shapes and sizes. They passed All Saints Church and the Dog and Duck coaching inn and were soon once more out in the countryside and making their way towards Haycock Abbey. It was as they turned a bend in the road that Lady Olivia exclaimed out loud.

"Look!" Her face lit with excitement as she pointed out of the carriage window when they passed a pretty viewpoint. "That is my old home, Thorpe Hall."

Just for a second, Charlotte turned away as a host of emotions threatened to overwhelm her, and she took a deep breath before she discovered the courage to look.

But look she did.

The house was exactly as she remembered it to be — a stunning limewashed Georgian mansion nestled perfectly into its surroundings. In the foreground, a lake glistened and sparkled in the sunshine, whilst mature oaks and elms and willows that were dotted haphazardly all over the landscape rustled in the summer's breeze.

Suddenly, tears threatened to fall as Charlotte recalled a particular memory with great fondness. It had been but a few weeks before Charles's father had died. The father had placed the son on his horse in front of him, and the two of them had travelled out onto the very road they were now proceeding along. Together they had ridden up into the hills overlooking Thorpe Hall and had stood side by side to admire the view, whilst his father had pointed out the boundaries to their property.

"That house belonged to my late husband. It was left in trust to my son but . . ." Olivia's voice trailed off into the wind, pain and loss in her words obvious to all.

"I was not aware that you had a son, Lady Amelia." Charlotte chose her words carefully, her heart now pounding violently, for this was a conversation she had, until now, deliberately avoided. After all, there was always the risk that when her mother spoke of her son, it might trigger some memory, some level of recognition. However, now that the countess had brought up the subject, there was no avoiding it, and she found herself holding her breath as she hoped, beyond hope, that the mother would not identify the son.

But surprisingly, instead of the countess, who seemed for a moment to choke with emotion, it was Amelia who continued the story.

"My halfbrother, it is believed, was *taken* by the press when he was but thirteen years of age and was never heard of again. It is presumed that the war at sea took his life, as it did so many. Is that not so, Mother?"

"Yes, my darling." Lady Olivia sighed. "When, after seven years, my son was declared legally dead, the property became entailed to my husband and is now my stepson's residence."

"Not that he is ever there to look after it properly," Amelia grumbled.

The carriage rumbled on, and as Thorpe Hall slipped out of view, Charlotte found herself able to breathe once more, realising that the moment was ripe for her to play her next card.

"Do you know, Lady Olivia, I think that whilst we are here, it might be nice to take a ride to Thorpe Hall," she said, thus planting the seed she wanted to sow. "It looks absolutely charming."

The driveway leading to Haycock Abbey was interminably

long, winding through park and woodland that appeared to be long overdue for maintenance. It was as if every occupant in the carriage sensed it as well, for the mood in the carriage was subdued, and for the first time in many a day, even the boundless enthusiasm Anne had for life seemed to be in decline.

As Haycock Abbey came into view, everything inside Charlotte tensed at the sight. It was large and ostentatious, its Tudor brickwork crumbling in disrepair, its towers and chimneys lording over their surroundings. What made the building so unusual was that each of the three main storeys had a higher ceiling than the one below, the ceiling height being indicative of the importance of the rooms' occupants — least noble at the bottom and the most important at the top. And, of course, the earl occupied not one room, but the entire west wing.

Even as a small boy, *she* had hated the house.

After his mother had married the earl, Charles had been required to move to Haycock Abbey, leaving behind everyone and everything he loved. Not even his beloved Hermes had been allowed to come, the earl deeming the pony too small for him.

His life had changed in an instant.

On arrival, he had been given into the care of a governess, a woman so dour it was rumoured she could curdle milk at a glance, and gone was the freedom he had enjoyed at Thorpe Hall. In its place, he found a structure so rigid that even the merest slip would result in a beating, the governess with her strap, the earl, if he deemed it necessary, with a cane. Charles had been allowed little independence — every waking hour seemingly occupied by meaningless task after meaningless task, and even his mother had seemed powerless to intervene.

To add to Charles's misery, there had been his stepbrother Henry who seemed to go out his way to deliberately make

Charles's life miserable, respite only coming when Henry had finally been sent off to boarding school.

No! Thorpe Hall held few happy memories for Charlotte, and she felt herself shudder as the carriage pulled up outside the main door, despite her resolve to keep the past in the past. Even though she had suggested this visit, every fibre of her being now resisted walking through that entrance once more.

But what choice did she have? She could hardly turn around and head back to London, not after travelling all that way. Besides, the visit to Haycock was an integral part of her master plan, an excuse for her to visit the one place she did want to see.

Thorpe Hall.

Having slept poorly, Charlotte arose early on the next morn. She had been given one of the grandest bedrooms at the top of the house, a room, thankfully, much removed from the ones she used to occupy as a child. Phoebe, of course, was in the small room next to hers.

Not wanting to awaken her friend, and also wishing to escape her companion's supervision, Charlotte crept silently around the room as she dressed in the riding habit she'd had specially designed for her. Then, as the sun was starting to rise, she tiptoed out of the room and made her way silently down to the stables.

The stables at Haycock had always been something of a refuge for Charles, the only place he seemed able to get away from the horrors of his daily life. He had loved the horses, and as often as he could, he would escape there to work alongside the grooms and the stable hands. Much to the disgust of his governess, he would help with grooming the horses and mucking out the stables, relishing the few minutes of camaraderie he would find with the men, even if it meant a flogging when he returned.

As Charlotte walked into the familiar stables, she could not help but smile as that unique scent hit her nostrils once more. She walked along the rows of stalls, stopping to admire the occasional snout as it peered over the door, adoring the feel of a horse's breath as it snorted at her. One horse, a beautiful grey mare, had demanded her attention and she was so lost in her thoughts as she scratched the horse behind the jaw, that when a voice spoke from behind her, she actually jumped in fright. With hand on heart and a rueful smile, she turned to see a boy, perhaps fifteen years of age, standing there staring at her.

"Can I help you, miss?" he asked politely.

"And you are?" Charlotte asked, as her pulse started to go back to normal.

"Billy, miss."

"Well, good morning, Billy. I am Lady Winters, and I was wondering if you might be so kind as to point out Lady Amelia's horse, Star. She has kindly agreed to allow me to borrow her for a ride this morning."

Somewhat red-faced, the boy led Charlotte to the very end stable where she found the most gorgeous thoroughbred bay mare, approximately fifteen hands tall.

"There she is, my lady," Billy said, an endearing grin now returning to his face "She is the sweetest 'orse in the stables. I can help get her tacked up if you want."

"That would be most kind of you, Billy."

Charlotte watched with a smile as the boy dashed over to the tack room, soon to return with bridle and side-saddle, a choice that made her frown.

"No, I'm afraid that will not do, Billy. I will require a gentleman's saddle if you please."

The boy stood looking dumbfounded as he stared at her attire. She was properly dressed in formal riding habit, her full skirt easily reaching the floor and entirely unsuitable for anything but side-saddle. But then Charlotte laughed at his expression and pulled her skirt apart to show that, in reality, it was two parts of a voluminous pair of trousers.

"Don't worry, Billy" — she conspiratorially tapped the side of her nose with a long elegant finger — "I won't tell anyone if you don't. But the truth is, I much prefer to ride astride."

"Yes, my lady," the boy said.

Billy disappeared back towards the tack room, leaving Charlotte alone in the stable. She could not resist. She reached out to stroke the soft muzzle of Star, her attention focussed entirely on the beautiful horse. So it was that she jumped once more when a deep masculine voice called out.

"And where do you think you are going without Samson, Missy Charlotte."

She whirled around to see Samson standing in the entrance to the stable, his massive form blocking most of the early morning light. It was also a very annoyed and harassed looking Samson who, judging by the state of his clothes, had obviously rushed to get dressed.

"Oh drat." Charlotte pouted with mock innocence. "I had hoped to ride out alone this morning. I suppose I woke Phoebe after all."

Then there was a crash, which had both of them whirling around, only to see Billy staring open-mouthed at Samson. In apparent shock, the boy had dropped the saddle he had been carrying onto the ground.

"Bloody hell," he whispered, his eyes wide with awe.

Charlotte tried very hard to control her amusement, but failed miserably, and ended up holding her hand over her mouth to try and spare the lad's blushes.

"That's all right, Billy, I pretty much reacted the same way when first I saw him. Samson, this is my new friend Billy. Billy, this is my man, Samson."

"I . . . I . . . I'm sorry sir . . . it's just that you are a big bugger, aren't you? Oh . . . God. I'm sorry." Billy moaned and turned as if he were about to run away.

This time Charlotte truly did laugh, a laugh which started as a giggle and turned into a chuckle and then ended in a rib aching guffaw that threatened to cause tears to pour down her face. Samson merely stood for a second before he, too, grinned, his perfect white teeth showing starkly in the dim light of the stables.

"I will forgive you, this time, boy." Samson scowled, now pretending to be angry. "That is provided you can find me a mount so that I may accompany my mistress on her ride."

For a moment, the boy remained perplexed as he once more looked Samson up and down with a dubious sort of expression on his face.

"I'm sorry sir, but the only mount we have that might be big enough for you is Satan, and he is, well, he is a bit of a handful, sir. Perhaps it might be better if you waited for Mr Hobbs to come in. He's the head groom, my lady."

"Show me," Samson demanded. "Show me this horse."

The stall to which Billy took them had both upper and lower doors closed. Behind them, Charlotte could hear a horse in the early stages of agitation—a hoof kicking out, a loud whinny, all suggesting that Satan was, indeed, already in a foul temper. Samson, however, only smiled with pleasure and opened the upper door to reveal the largest chestnut stallion Charlotte had ever seen.

If possible, Samson's grin just got wider and wider as he, too, spied the horse.

The beast was magnificent, at least nineteen hands high, with almost as many muscles as Samson, and he was pacing around in his stall as if he were a champion prize-fighter spoiling for a fight. Samson, however, without even the slightest hint of fear or hesitation, slowly unlocked the lower gate and stepped inside.

"Lord, Satan will kill him." Billy gasped, as he tried to step forward, perhaps thinking he could pull Samson back.

"Oh, worry not," Charlotte whispered as she caught the boy's arm. "Watch for a moment."

Charlotte had seen Samson do this before, on several occasions, but what he was about to attempt never failed to amaze her. For a few moments man and beast circled each other, neither one making eye contact with the other. However, it was clear that the horse seemed to fear Samson, for a light sweat appeared on his chest, and the beast's eyes almost appeared as if they were out on stalks.

Samson remained calm and completely in control. Even when the horse reared and kicked out, he did not flinch or react with anger. Instead, he simply began to talk to the animal. He kept his voice low and deep and hypnotic, the words soothing and calm. As Satan began to steady, Samson reached out a hand to allow the horse to smell him. Almost immediately Satan seemed to calm a little more, merely standing still as he tossed his magnificent head up and down. Samson took this as a sign to step closer, now rubbing the stallion's snout as he leant forward to breathe several times into the horse's nostrils. The effect was simply amazing. Almost as if he had been mesmerised, Satan suddenly became as placid as a cart horse, and the moment Samson turned his back to walk away, instead of rearing or kicking out, the horse walked tamely up to Samson and rested his head on the man's shoulder.

"Gawd," Billy whispered in awe, as he stood there opened mouthed once more. "Have you ever seen the like? Last time I went in there, the beast fair tried to kill me. Scares the living daylights out of me, he does. But look at him now, as meek as a lamb."

"It is a kind of magic, isn't it?" Charlotte smiled. "Samson is the finest horseman I know, and I am certain that Satan will be of no more trouble to him. Now then, young man, were you not about to saddle Star for me?"

But Billy was unable to comply, for at that very moment a very angry Samson confronted him.

"Tell me, boy, who has mistreated this horse?" Samson growled as he came out of Satan's stall.

"I, er . . ." Billy mumbled. Instantly, his face turned beetroot red, and from the fear that he displayed in his eyes, Charlotte knew that he was not sure how much he should say.

"It is all right, Billy," Charlotte said, her words almost as gentle as had been Samson's whilst he was taming Satan. "You can tell him. I won't let you get into trouble for doing so."

Billy gulped and looked nervously around him. "It was the baron, sir, Lord Henry. Satan threw him, so he whipped him, sir, something real bad," he whispered.

It had been nearly twenty years since Charlotte had last ridden the paths between Haycock Abbey and Thorpe Hall, yet the fields and tracks seemed to be as familiar as the lines on her own hand. The morning was bright and fresh, and she soon found herself leaning into her stirrups to urge Star on, a trot at first to loosen her mount's muscles, a canter, and then a full gallop. It had been months since she had ridden this way, and the sheer joy of having a horse between her legs once more had her whooping with excitement.

Samson, too, seemed to be enjoying himself immensely, and Satan's prodigious strength meant that he was easily able to keep up with his mistress, even when she cleared a drystone wall with ease. Slowly, though, after galloping for what was probably a full mile, Charlotte eased her mount back, not wanting to overdo things, and soon the two horses were walking companionably alongside each other as they cooled down in the early morning sun.

"Missy Charlotte, may I speak?" Samson asked.

Charlotte sighed dramatically and then looked at him with as much indignation she could muster.

"How many times do I have to tell both you and Phoebe . . . Of course, you may speak, and I will take it personally if you ever deem it necessary to ask again."

"It is of Phoebe that I wish to talk to you about. She did not want to ask you herself, but now that I have spoken for her, she would like to know when it might be possible for us to marry."

Charlotte looked up and beamed at him with genuine pleasure before nodding towards the large white house that was rapidly getting closer with every step of their horses.

"That is Thorpe Hall over there, Samson, the house that my father left for me in trust when he died. That is the house, along with its estates, which gave the earl cause to order my death so he could take ownership through marriage to my mother. That is the house which I intend to take back, whatever the cost. If you choose it to be so, Samson, that house will also be your home, a home where you and Phoebe can raise as many little Samsons as you like. However, the problem remains that before I can give all of that to you, and before you and Phoebe can marry, I have to *persuade* the earl to sell it to me."

"Perhaps, then, you might let me do the *persuading*, for I have a great need to take Phoebe as my wife, Missy Charlotte."

"I know, Samson, but please be patient. These things take time, even though my plans are moving along nicely."

He chuckled. "Oh, I can be patient, Missy Charlotte, but it is my Phoebe that you will have to worry about, for she is desperate for a child."

Side by side, they continued their progress towards Thorpe Hall, and as they came closer, they began to see signs of the day to day business of the house. In front of the Manor was a large lake where a gamekeeper was walking, presumably checking for signs of poachers. Dry-stone walls, most in a state of disrepair, lined the path they were on, and in the distance, she could see a team of horses shackled to a plough as a tenant farmer trudged behind. It was then that Charlotte saw the paddock that surrounded what she recognised as the Manor's stable block. Unlike the walls of the estate, the fences around the paddock were well maintained, and for some unknown reason, Charlotte found her eyes drawn to the horses that were peacefully grazing there.

Then she gasped, her eyes transfixed in shock, as she focussed upon one horse in particular.

"No! It can't be, it can't be!" she whispered.

Instantly, forgetting her status as a lady, she kicked her right foot from the stirrup and jumped down from Star as nimbly as any man might, before dashing over to the paddock.

Standing close to the railings, his head down so that he could crop the grass with worn and stained teeth, was an ancient Shetland pony. His back was bowed, his barrel fat and round, and the hair around his nose, which was more grey in colour than black, paid testament to his age.

"Oh, my days, Samson, look!"

"What is it, Missy Charlotte?" Samson hopped down from his mount and walked over to stand next to her.

"It can't be," she repeated. "I thought him long dead. But . . . I . . . I think . . . I think it's . . . it's . . . Hermes. My pony . . . from when I was but a boy."

Gently, Charlotte called to the old pony, holding out the flat of her hand as she saw the old horse's head lift. Then suddenly, it was as if boy and pony had never been apart. Hermes, with the apparent energy of a much younger horse, came running over, lifting his head over Charlotte's arm, just like he used to do when he wanted a young Charles to scratch him behind his ears, his lips greedily snuffling for the treat that Charles would always have for him before taking him for a ride.

"Oh my, Samson, he remembers me, he knows who I am," Charlotte whispered.

"Of course, he does, Missy Charlotte. That horse plainly loves you and will know you by your scent."

Then the tears began to well in the corner of her eyes whilst Hermes adopted a pose of adoration, and Charlotte scratched him in the place he loved the best, just below his jawbone.

"Hullo, and who might you two be?" called a croaky yet friendly voice from behind them.

Both Charlotte and Samson swivelled round to see an ancient looking man walking briskly towards them, a man whom Charlotte immediately recognised, despite his age. A wrinkled, leathery face sat beneath an old felt cap, and patched corduroy trousers, held up by string, covered bowed legs. Yet the man still had the same smile and twinkle in his eye that she remembered so well.

Once more Charlotte found herself holding her breath, waiting for the moment of recognition that might yet come, for this man had once been like a second father to Charles. In his youth, a young George Harris had worked for her grandfather and had been employed at the estate for most of his life. It had been he who had taught Charles to ride when but a child, and it had been he who had consoled a young boy who had lost his father — giving him jobs to do around the stable, keeping him busy, keeping his mind from the despair that threatened to overwhelm him.

"My name is Samson, and this is my mistress, Lady Winters," Samson replied, instinctively realising that his mistress was too emotional to reply for herself. "And you are?"

"The name's Harris, sir, George Harris. I look after the 'orses and the stables here." He gave a small smile as he respectfully doffed his cap to Charlotte. "Begging your pardon, milady. That's Hermes. He's a cantankerous old bugger, but he is partial to a bit of apple."

The man grinned fondly as he fished an ancient clasp knife and an old wrinkled apple out of one massive pocket in the patched coat he was wearing. Carefully he cut away a slice and then handed it to Charlotte.

Without uttering a word, Charlotte held out her hand and felt the soft muzzle of Hermes as he snuffled up the apple slice, as he had done so many times when Charles had been but a boy. Then, as she buried her head into the shaggy mane of the little horse that had captured her heart all those years ago, the tears truly began to fall, big, silent tears that Charlotte could not have stopped even if she had wanted to.

In the weeks and months following her father's death, Charles had poured out his heart to this pony, the bond that they had shared being far stronger than any simple friendship. But when her mother had married the earl and Charles had been forced to leave him behind, his heart had once more been broken all over again.

"Gaw, I have never seen old Hermes take to someone so quick. But don't take on so, lass." George's words were gentle, obviously taking her tears as sympathy for an old arthritic pony. "He's nigh on thirty-year'-old and has had a good life, and no matter what the young master here says, Hermes will live out his days here, too, if I have my way."

"Thank you . . . er . . . Mr Harris." Charlotte sniffed through her tears, barely stopping herself from blurting out the man's first name, as she had done as a child. "Thank you, Mr Harris," Charlotte repeated with more conviction. "You will never know how much it means for me to hear you say so."

Reluctant to leave Hermes behind, yet knowing she must to not reveal who she was, Charlotte turned and walked away. Still, she could not resist a backwards glance at her old friend, George, who was standing by the railings, feeding Hermes the rest of his apple. It was a simple act of kindness on his part, but one so poignant for Charlotte that a sudden surge of emotion once more threatened to overwhelm her. She could not help herself as another tear slipped from her eye, one that simply encompassed the lost innocence of her youth, and all she could do was to walk away as fast as her legs would carry her.

For the next hour, Charlotte and Samson wandered unchallenged through the grounds of Thorpe Hall. It was just as she remembered, albeit somewhat neglected. The vegetable garden was overgrown and unkempt, the beehives that her father had loved disused and empty. Only the stables and courtyard seemed to be well cared for, along with a cottage that Charlotte remembered as the one used by the estate manager. That building seemed to stand out from the rest as having some money spent on its upkeep. The outside of Thorpe Hall itself was in something of a sorry state. The brickwork was in sore need of a new coat of lime-wash, and many of the windows seemed in need of repair.

Despite this, as they wandered, Charlotte suddenly felt an acute sense of belonging. Everywhere she looked there were memories—Hermes in his field, the stone wall that she had failed to jump, the lake where her father, and James, had taught a young Charles to fish. Even the view over the English countryside was stunning, and for the first time in many a year, Charlotte realised that she truly felt at peace.

It was a peace that served only to stiffen her resolve.

CHAPTER FOURTEEN

From the shadows of a dark alley, Silas Green, flanked by two of his thugs, grinned to himself as he watched George Hamilton, Earl of Weybridge, stagger out of his club, only to find the carriage he had expected was nowhere to be seen. The man cursed loudly, his eyes scanning for a hack or a carriage, anything he could hire with the last few shillings he must have in his pocket. But there was none to be had, as the roads were empty.

Silas chuckled to himself, for this had been so easy to arrange. A so-called *message* from the earl to his coachman had sent his coach on a fool's errand across to the other side of the city, and a gruff word to the drivers of any hacks in the area had been enough to clear the street. And now the earl was walking straight towards him, exactly as he had planned, and the moment that he had been looking forward to for weeks drew near.

"Ah, my lord, a word, if you please."

Silas stepped out of the shadows, directly into the earl's path, noting with pleasure the immediate look of shock and fear that crossed the man's face, an expression that was quickly replaced by one of loathing as the earl recognised who stood before him.

The earl cursed. "Not now, Green, I'm not in the bloody mood."

Silas grinned and nodded to one of the men standing next to him.

Before the earl had time to react, a huge fist lashed out,

striking him firmly in the stomach, every last ounce of air in his lungs shooting out of his mouth as he doubled over in agony onto the muddy street.

As he desperately fought for breath, the two men flanked the earl, each taking an arm to hoist the gasping man back onto his feet. Now grinning with pleasure, Silas turned and walked towards the alley, followed by his men and a desperately struggling earl, whose eyes were frantically looking around for any hope of salvation. Only when they were deep into the shadows once more did Silas turn to face the earl once again.

"Now then, *my lord*," he said with as much sarcasm as he could muster. "You owe me nine thousand, six hundred, and forty-two pounds, sixteen shillings and sixpence, and I am here, on this lovely evening, to arrange payment."

"Well, you can't have it!" the earl yelled, words he should definitely not have said.

This time it was Silas's fist that lashed out, a short punishing punch to the solar plexus that left the earl gasping for breath once more.

"I will ask you but once more, my lord. I . . . want . . . my . . . fucking . . . money!" he growled.

This time, as the men hauled him back to his feet, Silas grinned as he saw the expression on the earl's face. It was no longer one of self-satisfied smugness, but instead, something more akin to fear and panic.

"I . . . I can't. I don't have it," the earl mumbled. "I can't pay it. I don't have the money."

Again, Silas lashed out with a fist, and again the earl fell to the ground, this time with blood streaming from his nose.

The earl now appeared to be dazed, so Silas knelt, his face scant inches from the earl so as to gain his attention. "Now you listen, and listen good," he growled, spittle spraying from his mouth as he spoke. "You have seven days to get me my money. I don't care where you get it from, but you will pay me in full, seven days from now, or I will cut off your balls and feed them to you. Better still, I will cut the balls off that bastard son of yours instead and fuck your pretty little daughter with them! Do I make myself clear, *my lord*?"

Panting, clearly unable to speak through his fear, the earl nodded in reply.

Silas stood and turned to his men. "Gentlemen, be so kind as to give Lord Hamilton a taste of what will happen if he tries to welch."

Once more, a fist lashed out.

****

Charlotte waited for exactly five days after she had arranged for Mr Green to *pay the earl a call,* and her plan seemed to be working perfectly. For, according to Mr Abernathy, whom she had watching the earl, the man had been seen all over town, trying desperately, yet failing, to raise the funds that he needed. So, when she deemed the time to be right, waiting until she knew that both the countess and Lady Amelia would be out, she arranged for Samson to drive both herself and Phoebe to the earl's rented townhouse. She and Phoebe were now sitting in the hallway of the earl's home, Phoebe looking as if she had not a care in the world, whilst Charlotte steeled herself for what was yet to come.

"Do you want me to come in with you?" Phoebe asked.

"No. I think it better for you to wait outside, for we both know what he thinks of people with your colour. Besides, I can handle the earl if things get *difficult.*"

"I know you can." Phoebe giggled. "After all, you have your parasol." She pointed to the furled sun umbrella that Charlotte would take with her, whenever she deemed it necessary.

Specially designed by Samson, the innocuous-looking parasol was, in fact, a fearsome weapon. The finial was made from solid silver whilst the shaft was made from a single piece of ivory. The result was a fighting stick formidable enough to take down any foe, and with it in her possession, Charlotte feared no man

It was at that moment the butler reappeared.

"If you would come this way, my lady. The earl will see you now," he said with a respectful nod of his head.

Charlotte followed the butler, and as she entered the room, she politely dipped a little curtsy, only to be ignored by the insufferable man who sat placidly behind his desk, pretending to shuffle through some papers. Only after a moment or two did he make believe to suddenly see her, before standing himself, still choosing not to bow in return as a gentleman should.

"Lady Winters. To what do I owe the pleasure?" he asked in a voice that conveyed anything but. "Have you finally come to your senses and decided to accept me as your lover?"

For a second, Charlotte glared indignantly at the insufferable man, amazed that he would have the gall to suggest such a thing. But as she looked she was pleased to see that, judging by bruises on his face and the stiffness he displayed in his body, the effects of the beating she had ordered had not worn off and, because of it, she allowed herself an indulgent smile.

"This is not a social call, my lord. I am here on business."

"Oh, yes, and what might that be?" the earl enquired.

"I have something you need, my lord."

"Oh, yes, and what might that be?" he repeated, trying to maintain an air of disinterest but failing badly.

"Money," she replied.

Charlotte sat herself on a chair, even though she had not been invited to do so, her hands resting lightly on the silver finial of her parasol as she observed the earl. The effect of her simple statement had been *interesting*, to say the least. With great satisfaction, she watched the play of emotions as they washed across his face. As incredulity turned to anger, the colour in the man's face turned from a pallid grey to an interesting shade of red, reminding her a little of an overripe tomato, and again Charlotte had to fight to stop herself from laughing out loud. Instead, she turned the screw.

"The word is that you owe a very unpleasant character a great deal of money, Lord Hamilton, and the word is that the man has made some quite serious threats too."

This time, Charlotte saw real anger flare in his eyes, and she suddenly found herself gripping her parasol around its shaft, preparing herself to strike, should she need to do so.

"What! How?" the earl spluttered as he dragged himself to his feet, his face now going from a red to something akin to a ripe plum.

Charlotte remained sitting serenely, even though her heart was pounding. "How is of no consequence, my lord. It is what to do that matters, for in truth, I would not see my dear friends, Lady Olivia and Lady Amelia, bereft of husband or father, or even put in danger themselves should you fail to act upon this matter. Surely you must realise how dangerous it can be to borrow money from such characters," she admonished as if she were talking to a child.

"What? How dare you —"

"This is what I propose." She deliberately cut him off in mid-sentence, enjoying every moment of doing so. "I have decided that I now wish to remain in England instead of returning to Jamaica at the end of the season. As I am more of a country girl at heart, I have resolved to purchase an estate, and in truth, after our visit to the countryside, I have taken a very strong fancy to Thorpe Hall. The house is charming and is the perfect size for me, although it might have been nice to have a little more land. The estate only has three-thousand acres, I believe."

"You want the entire estate? All three-thousand acres?" he spluttered.

"Yes, and I will give you a fair price too, let's say ten-thousand pounds for the house and a guinea an acre for the estate. That, I believe, comes to exactly thirteen thousand, one hundred and fifty pounds."

"But . . . but . . ." the earl blustered, "the estate is managed by my son, Henry. It is his home."

"Yet it is owned by you, is it not?"

"Yes . . . but . . ."

"Which means you are at liberty to sell, should you choose, does it not?" Charlotte said smugly.

"But . . . but . . ." he spluttered once more.

Charlotte stood with a calmness even she felt surprising. Then she smiled at the man she hated with every fibre of her being, trying very hard to assume the supercilious look that the earl himself would normally adopt.

"In truth, my lord, it matters little to me if you choose not to sell, for I will just go and find another estate somewhere else if you do not. However, I do harbour concern for my friends Amelia and Lady Olivia. After all, I have observed first-hand what a money lender will do to get back his loan, and what I saw did not paint a very pretty picture. Hence, the offer I make you now. What say you? Will you sell, or shall I leave you to think on it for a day or two?"

Charlotte deliberately paused, choosing to remain calmly silent in order to give the earl a moment to think. She knew full well that the earl did not have the luxury of time. After all, it had been she who had dictated the earl's deadline in the first place. Now, all she needed to do was to turn the screw once more.

"I take your silence to be your answer, my lord," she said.

"So be it. But please don't expect me to console Lady Olivia and Lady Amelia at your funeral."

Slowly she turned and made to walk from the room, knowing full well panic would suddenly grip the earl. She stood tall with her back to the earl and rested her hand on the handle of the door, pausing for dramatic effect. Then she sighed to herself with pleasure as she heard him call out.

"No . . . wait . . . Very well, Lady Winters," he spat, almost shouting the words at her back. "But it will cost you eighteen thousand for house and estate."

"Fifteen, for house, contents, and estate. My final offer," she retorted.

It took but a fraction of a second for the earl to decide, his words curt and angry as he sat down heavily onto his chair.

"Done! That is provided the transaction is completed by the end of the week. I shall have my lawyers contact you."

"Agreed." Charlotte nodded slightly and walked out.

****

His father, the earl, was sitting behind his desk when Lord Henry entered the room steaming, the anger he felt firmly affixed to his face.

"Father, you cannot do this," he shouted. "Thorpe Hall is my home, *my* estate."

"No, it is not!" his father shouted in return. "The estate is mine to do with as I please, and you are naught but a tenant, living there upon my whim. And not a very good tenant at that, might I add. I see hardly any income from the estate."

"That is because of those lazy godforsaken farmers who work the land. No good, the lot of 'em." Henry moaned. "But you can't sell the Hall, you simply can't."

"Oh, but I can. I have to, for, as you know, I need the blunt. But what rankles more than anything is that I have to sell to

Lady bloody Winters. Bitch!"

"I tell you, that woman is no *lady*! She is nothing but a pretentious widow of some pompous man of bloody trade in Jamaica. Yet she still seems to have the whole *ton* at her feet."

"Including that bitch of a stepmother of yours. 'Tis her fault that Lady Winters set her sights on Thorpe Hall in the first place."

"If you ask me, she needs to be taught a lesson." Henry sneered as he walked over to the liquor cabinet to pour himself a very large whiskey. "That woman needs to be taught her place."

"Who? Lady Winters, or your stepmother?"

For a moment, Henry remembered how Lady Winters had humiliated him at the debutantes' ball; remembered how he had been refused the chance to court Lady Anne; remembered how he was now about to be evicted from his own home.

"Lady Winters, of course," he snarled.

"Well, how about you deal with *that* little situation yourself, and leave the countess to me," his father suggested.

CHAPTER FIFTEEN

Exactly two days later, in the law offices of Drew, Drew, and Chalmers, a legal document was signed by both Lady Charlotte Winters and George Hamilton, Earl of Weybridge.

For Charlotte, it had been something of a strange meeting. The earl had not spoken a single word during the entirety of the conference, and had, instead, simply glared at Charlotte throughout the whole process, a whole host of emotions playing across his face.

At first, there had been a scowl of anger as he had presented the deeds of the property to Charlotte's lawyers. Next had come a look of relief as she, in turn, had presented him with a banker's draft for the full amount of fifteen thousand pounds. Then, as the earl had left, Charlotte could have sworn she saw a look of triumph and victory — a look that sent chills down her spine as she realised that, in the earl's mind, the *game* was not yet over.

Not a day later, Charlotte was once more at her desk in her study, having had yet another visit from Mr Green so he could collect his *seven percent*. The man had been in a jovial mood, for Charlotte had tipped him off that the earl would be leaving the solicitor's office with a bank draft large enough to pay off his debts. Charlotte had actually laughed out loud when Mr Green took great delight in describing the look on the earl's face when confronted by himself and his two henchmen.

For a few moments, Charlotte smiled as she allowed herself to bask in her victory.

Everything she had initially set out to do, she had achieved. She had befriended Lady Olivia and Lady Amelia. She had regained Thorpe Hall, hitting the earl where it hurt the most — his pride and in his pocket. Now, the only thing that was left on her list was to secure the future of her mother and her sister. Amelia, it seemed, would be taken care of by her marriage to William, and that thought pleased Charlotte immeasurably. As for her mother, all she had to do was to persuade her to leave the Earl, for she could and would provide her mother with enough funds to last a lifetime, should she choose to do so.

But then another thought crossed her mind, a thought that, in truth, had been plaguing her dreams. From a desk drawer, she pulled out her list and then dipped her pen into the inkwell before her. Slowly she began to write, adding just one more item to her list.

What to do about the duke?

****

It was a little after nine that evening by the time James had finally managed to extricate himself from the House of Lords. The sitting had been interminable, the business of the day banal and boring, and it had taken every ounce of fortitude to prevent him from leaving mid-session.

The problem was that, in his boredom, his mind had taken to thinking of other things, other issues, the first and foremost being what the hell he was going to do about Lady Charlotte Winters.

The truth of the matter was that the night they had spent together had disturbed him greatly, and on so many levels, as well.

On the one hand, he felt disgusted with himself. Lady Charlotte was no lady, of that he was now sure, and his proclivity had never before leant towards members of his own sex. She was his godchild, too, and the mere thought of the scandal all this might cause, should it become public knowledge, had caused several sleepless nights.

On the other hand, however, he had to admit to himself that the night they had spent together had been, without doubt, the most exciting, erotic and fulfilling sexual encounter of his life, and thoughts of the passion they had shared that night seemed to have him in a permanent state of arousal.

Of course, to complicate matters, he actually liked the *woman* that Charles had become. Charlotte was a wonderful influence on Anne, who had, for so long, been without a mother figure. And there was no doubt in his mind that Charlotte took her role as chaperon more seriously than he would have done. She was brave and intelligent, not to mention rich, and on more than one occasion, James had to admit to himself that he had simply enjoyed her company.

"Damn it," he muttered to himself as he entered the house, throwing his top hat and gloves at Stevens as he did so.

"Beg your pardon, your grace?" the butler asked as he closed the door behind James.

"Oh, nothing," James grumbled. "Can you please have someone put a plate together for me and bring it to my study? I have not eaten since luncheon."

"Ahem." Stevens coughed to attract his attention as he started towards his study. "Sir, Lady Winters is awaiting you in your study."

"Is she, by God?"

"Yes, she is. She said she had something of great importance to discuss with you and has been waiting for over an hour, your grace."

With sudden anger, James strode down the hallway, only to stop short as he threw open the door to his study. Charlotte was curled up on a chaise that had been conveniently placed next to the fireplace and was fast asleep. Despite the anger he felt at this person's intrusion into his private sanctuary, James could not help but smile ruefully as he looked down upon her. In her sleep, she looked so peaceful, so beautiful, so vulnerable, too, and in that very instant, James felt his heart reach out in a way he never thought would be possible again.

He could not help but stare, just as he had done on the night they had spent together. Whilst she had slept, he had studied her, part of him hoping to find something, some small insignificant feature that would identify her as the boy he had once known. But even in sleep, her face had been undeniably feminine, her long eyelashes flickering a little as her hidden eyes moved in time with some dream or other. Her nose was small, her cheekbones high and aristocratic, and even her lips were full and plump, swollen from the kisses they had shared.

"Oh God!" he groaned quietly. "You must stop this." His hand reached for his cock to adjust his growing erection within his breeches. "You have to stop this!" he admonished himself again.

Quietly, he walked over and knelt so he was at her level, breathing hard for a second to steady himself, to reassert the self-control that he felt slipping away. Then he reached out and shook her gently on the shoulder as he called her name.

He watched as Charlotte slowly came awake, her eyes opening sleepily, a soft smile playing on her face as she saw him kneeling before her in front of the fire.

Yet again his heart missed a beat.

She was dressed in a beautiful green gown, cut low enough that he could see the soft swell of her small pert breasts, and for a second, his whole body ached to reach out for her, just as he had done that night when they had made love.

For the longest time, he watched as Charlotte lay there, her head on a padded cushion as she returned his gaze, the focus of eyes travelling over his face almost as if she were trying to memorise each feature. Then her hand reached to his cheek and he shivered lightly as she caressed his skin.

"Hello," she murmured. "I was waiting for you, and it was so warm by the fire that I must have fallen asleep."

Reluctantly, he pulled her hand away and sighed inwardly at the loss of her touch.

"You wanted to see me?" he asked as he helped her to sit up before dropping her hand as quickly as he had taken it.

"Yes, I have some news."

For a second, James's irrational heart stopped as his mind leapt to the obvious conclusions. Someone had found out about Charlotte. That must be it! Someone knew the truth of it. Involuntarily, he groaned aloud. That had to be it. Someone knew about his godson, and the scandal that this would bring was about to ruin him. He groaned yet again.

"No, not that," Charlotte laughed as she seemed to read his mind. "My secret is still that . . . my secret. However, there is something I need to tell you, James, and you might not like it, I am sorry to say."

"And what might that be?" he asked as he sighed a little in relief.

"I am afraid that I have not been entirely truthful with the reasons for my return to England. Yes, my principal goal was to reconnect with my mother and my sister, and I truly thank you for facilitating this. But when I returned, I also had another goal in mind, and that was to recover what was mine all along. Thorpe Hall and its entire estate."

"Did you, by God! And you thought not to tell me this!"

"Yes, and for that, I am truly sorry," Charlotte said, her regret more than a little apparent. "However, my reasons for hiding this from you were clear. I thought you might try and dissuade me from this course of action."

"Which I would! Getting to know your mother and sister was dangerous enough, with you being who you are. But meddling in the earl's business affairs . . . that is a completely different matter. It is far too dangerous for you to be playing this game, Charlotte, and I insist that you stop this madness at once."

"Ah! Yes! I thought you might say that," Charlotte replied. "But you see, Uncle James, I have already managed to, how shall we put it, *engineer* the estate's purchase from the earl. I now legally own Thorpe Hall and all the land that should have been mine all along."

She smiled smugly.

"By God, Charlotte," James growled as he walked over to his drinks tray. "The earl must have been furious!" Carefully, he poured two small glasses of brandy, one of which he handed to Charlotte.

"He was, but he had no choice but to sell, for he needed the money. I do believe that Lord Henry was not best pleased either, for he has had to quit Thorpe Hall because of it."

"No loss there," said James.

"So, to my news."

"And that was not it!" he snorted

"No," Charlotte replied. "It is this. I will be shortly leaving London for a while, to take up residence in Thorpe Hall. And no, before you ask, I do not wish to relinquish my duties as Anne's chaperon. I will, however, miss the midsummer ball at Lady Felicia's."

Charlotte paused, then fished into her reticule to pull out a small stack of white embossed envelopes, which she then handed to him.

"But in return for missing the ball, I have these for you, instead. Invitations to Thorpe Hall for yourself, Lady Anne, and the dowager duchess, for the purpose of attending Phoebe and Samson's wedding. I would deem it a great honour if you would come and help them celebrate the occasion."

CHAPTER SIXTEEN

Two days later, Charlotte, Phoebe, and Samson took up residence at Thorpe Manor, and for Charlotte, it was as if she had never left. It was almost as if she had once more found the lost glove that had always fit perfectly, or the shoe in which you could walk miles without a blister. Whilst there were the signs of neglect and lack of upkeep everywhere, every room, every piece of furniture, seemed to be as she remembered, and Charlotte, for the first time in many a year, simply felt at home.

The first thing Charlotte did when she arrived was to visit Hermes, and it was then she had her first shock. Many of the horses she had expected to find there were gone, presumably removed by the earl or his son, something that was quickly corroborated by old George Harris. The only horses left to her were those of age, but in truth, Charlotte did not mind, for putting a stable of horses together would give Samson something productive to do.

Only then did she assemble the staff, to unsurprisingly find that the number she had to call on was woefully inadequate. There was no butler, nor housekeeper, with Mrs White, the cook, doing her best to keep things ticking over with only two maids and two footmen to help. So naturally, the first thing Charlotte did was to make Phoebe her housekeeper and Samson her temporary butler. This, at first, had caused a little consternation with Mrs White, mainly because of the colour of their skin. But both Samson and Phoebe soon won her over, just by their sheer energy and devotion to the new mistress of the house. Neither did it harm that Charlotte also doubled the cook's wages, in recognition of her lengthy service, and also hired on an extra maid to work in the kitchen.

To the other senior member of her staff, Mr Frederick Whitfield, the estate's steward, Charlotte took an instant dislike. He was a big brute of a man, and by all accounts, was quick to use his whip when things did not go as he wanted them to. Nor did it take her long to discover that his dealings with the tenant farmers were far from honest.

One such farmer, a Mr Edward Sykes, on hearing that the estate had a new owner, had begged to see Charlotte in person. She, of course, had been only too pleased to receive the man. But when he had told her how Whitfield had been demanding *payments* to *insure* the farm and its livestock, payments that were obviously going straight into the man's pockets, her pleasure quickly turned to anger. Charlotte had dismissed the steward on the spot, and then Samson had taken great delight in escorting the man violently from the premises, especially after hearing some of the choice language that Whitfield had used towards his mistress.

To Charlotte's delight, each day began to develop its own rhythm as the estate once more came to life. With Samson's expert eye to guide her, horses were purchased to replace those which Lord Henry had taken with him, even though they had not officially belonged to him, and Charlotte had spent a pleasant few days riding around the estate, once more familiarising herself with the property. She, of course, renewed her acquaintance with Hermes daily, for whom she always had an apple, and intriguingly, the more time she spent with the old horse, the more she came to believe that he was the only other creature who actually knew who she was.

It soon became apparent, however, that despite the valiant efforts of the tenant farmers, her estate was nowhere near as productive as it should have been. Nor did it take long for her to find out why either.

Her workforce was utterly demoralised.

At every farm she visited, she heard the same sorry tale—rents that were far too high; tithes that left the farmers and their families practically starving; labourers that worked the land being paid a fraction of what they should, none of which were conducive to productivity.

So Charlotte set about putting things to rights. She personally invited every tenant to attend a meeting at Thorpe Hall, and every tenant, without exception, had attended. At first, they had been angry and belligerent, thinking that now a new owner had taken up residence, things were only going to get even worse. But Charlotte had soon won them over by informing them of the sacking of Frederick Whitfield. The immediate reduction of annual rents to a more reasonable level and the promise to hire an honest manager to oversee the estate did no harm either. What finally clinched matters, however, was Charlotte's personal guarantee to financially support each and every one of them until such time as their farms could become profitable once more.

From dawn to dusk, Charlotte found her time wonderfully engaged, and it did not take her long to realise how much she had missed the day-to-day running of an estate, something which had occupied much of her time in Jamaica. In fact, life would have been idyllic for Charlotte if not for one thorn left in her side, one small yet significant matter that was really beginning to annoy her more than just a little.

Despite her protests and her orders, every time she took a ride, Samson insisted that he escort her, refusing point blank to let her ride alone. Even worse was the fact that each and every time she took a walk, Phoebe would be at her side.

It wasn't that she didn't enjoy their company, for, in truth, she loved them both dearly. And it wasn't that she did not understand their motives behind doing so. After all, the earl's residence was but a short ride away. It was just that every now and again, she felt like being alone, to have a little space to breathe, to think, especially when her thoughts turned to a certain man who would soon be coming to Thorpe Manor for a certain wedding.

So it was, one afternoon, with Samson away for a fitting of his wedding suit and Phoebe occupied with helping the cook plan the wedding breakfast, Charlotte took the opportunity to *escape*, practically running to the stables to find George sitting on a stone wall, peacefully puffing on an old clay pipe.

"George," she called, the urgency in her voice clear. "Would you be so kind as to saddle Holly for me and be quick about it, too."

For a second, George appeared confused and then looked more than a little worried as he stared back at her.

"I'm sorry, milady, but I wasn't to know you would be riding today. Holly is in the back paddock, with Hermes, and it will take me a while to get her in and tack her up."

"But I can get a saddle on Ivy for you if you wish, Lady Winters," another voice called out as a young man led another beautiful chestnut mare from the stable. "I was just getting her out of her stall."

"Good Lord, Billy," Charlotte said when she saw who the voice belonged to. "What on earth are you doing here?"

"I thought you knew, milady. Billy 'ere is my grandson, and we was . . . er . . .'oping that . . . maybe you might consider taking 'im on here, as a sort of apprentice maybe," George said with an optimistic gleam in his eyes.

"But I thought you worked at Haycock, Billy."

"I do. But I hates it there," Billy replied. "The earl is worse than ever and the bastard . . . er . . . master likes to use his whip on the beasts and men alike. The baron is no better, either, especially after he had to move back into the Abbey. Please, Lady Winters, I really don't want to go back there.

Besides, I would dearly love to learn 'ow Mr Samson did what he did to Satan, that is if you would be willin' to give me a chance, milady."

"Well, Billy, I don't know, I just don't know! Do you have a reference from your last employer? Can anyone vouch for your good character," she teased as she tried to keep a grin from her face.

"I'll work hard, Lady Winters. I'll be the best stable boy you have ever had, I promise," Billy pleaded.

"And I'll vouch for him, milady," George added. "The lad is already as good with the 'orses as I am and will do you credit."

For a moment Charlotte stared at them both, desperately trying to keep a straight face. "Well, do not think for one moment that your life will be any easier if you come to work here, young man, especially if you are to work with Mr Samson. But if you must, you may start today, not as stable boy, but as apprentice groom."

The boy flashed the biggest grin that Charlotte had ever seen, a look of adoration all over his face.

"So, shall I tack up Ivy for you, Lady Winters?" Billy asked. "Or would you like me to go and fetch Holly?"

"No, Ivy will be fine," Charlotte replied.

"Astride, milady?" Billy asked.

"Astride," Charlotte laughed.

A few minutes later, after Billy had tightened Ivy's cinch for the second time, Charlotte took hold of the horse's reins and led the mare over to the stone mounting steps. Without causing a fuss, she lifted her skirt a little, swung over her leg, and expertly settled herself into the saddle, her left hand firmly gripping her parasol as she did so.

"Beggin' your pardon mistress," George called out. "But I have orders from Mr Samson not to let you ride alone. 'E'll 'ave my 'ide if you goes out on your own. Can you wait a minute and I'll fetch another horse. Billy can go with you."

"No," Charlotte retorted. "There is no need, George. I will be perfectly fine on my own." Then, before he could say another word, she tapped her heels into Ivy's side, and her mount sprang forward in a clatter of hooves.

It was a beautiful morning, and Charlotte had it in mind to ride out to visit several of the tenant farms on her estate. Henry, it seemed, had made a complete mess of running things, and Charlotte instinctively knew that many bridges would have to be built if she was to get her workers completely on her side. She smiled to herself as she remembered the look on their faces when she had told them all that their rents were to be significantly reduced. It had been a start.

As soon as she reached the soft ground of the trail that ran through the woods to the south of the Manor, Charlotte urged Ivy into a gentle gallop, not yet daring to go full out, as she was not quite as familiar with the land as she had been as a boy. But Ivy was eager to please, and Charlotte grinned as she felt the horse stretch out her legs, laughing out loud as she gave Ivy her head. Faster and faster they went with Charlotte standing up in the stirrups, her cheeks flushed with excitement, the worries of the day entirely forgotten just for a few minutes of sheer joy.

****

Henry sat astride Satan, watching from the shadows provided by a copse of trees, as Lady Winters galloped madly towards him, knowing that his patience was finally about to pay off.

Each morning since the little bitch had taken up residence in *his* house, he had ridden out of Haycock Abbey along one of the more popular trails that ran through the woods adjoining the two properties. There he had waited, in the hope that he would catch the little bitch alone.

However, his plans for vengeance had always been thwarted, as whenever the woman rode out, she had been accompanied by that giant of a servant of hers—a servant that, in truth, scared the living daylights out of him.

Even Whitfield, who was a big bastard himself, had been no match for the man. When *Lady Muck* had fired him, Whitfield had made the mistake of saying some nasty things to the woman. Retribution had been swift, and even now, Whitfield still suffered from the beating he had received from that black bastard of hers.

But now, as chance would have it, the one person in the whole wide world that he wanted to meet alone in deserted woodland was riding hell-for-leather towards him, and for once, there was absolutely no sign of the nigger that normally accompanied her.

Excitement gripped him. He grinned as he checked the loaded pistol in the leather holster in front of his left knee, and the rapier that hung to his side. Then he viciously kicked his spurs into the sides of Satan.

****

Charlotte was about to ride through a gap in a dry-stone wall when she saw the other rider, instantly recognising his massive mount as Satan. For the briefest moment, she thought it to be Samson coming after her. But as the rider drew closer, she clearly recognised the man. Henry was also riding full tilt towards the gap in the wall, but from the opposite direction, seemingly heedless of the danger he was placing them both in. Abruptly, from fear of the two horses colliding, Charlotte had no choice but to pull up her horse, bringing Ivy to a full stop.

"You idiot, you could have killed us both," she yelled as Henry also pulled his mount to a stop.

"And good morning to you too, Lady bloody Winters," Henry snarled.

Immediately, every sense of danger that Charlotte possessed raised its ugly head, the tiny hairs on the back of her neck prickling as her heart began to beat fiercely. Her whole body became alert and tense as she instantly recognised the expression on Henry's face.

For she had seen that expression before!

She remembered, even though she did not want it to, the day when Charles had been but ten years old. Henry had cornered him in the nursery after their governess had gone down to the kitchen for tea. At twelve years of age, Henry had been so much bigger than Charles, and after dishing out a beating with his fists, Henry had dragged Charles up into the attic, where he had forced him into an empty trunk, callously locking him inside. Charles had nearly suffocated that day. Briefly, Charlotte found herself shivering with fear, for the expression now on Henry's face was the exact expression of triumph he had worn as he closed the lid of the chest.

And she had not been wrong to be fearful.

A wicked gleam appeared on Henry's face, and Charlotte quailed a little as he reached forward to slowly un-holster the pistol he carried on his horse, the ugly barrel coming up to point steadily at her chest. For a second, she held her breath, half expecting the agony of a ball tearing through her body. But Henry sat there and grinned manically, his finger not on the trigger, but on the trigger guard instead.

"What is the meaning of this, Henry?" she asked, her eyes once more fixed upon his.

"That is Lord Hamilton to you. Get off your horse," he demanded as he waved the gun at her.

"No," she replied as her whole body urged her to spur Ivy into a furious gallop.

Henry grinned as he gripped the stock more firmly, his

finger transferring onto the trigger of the gun in an exaggerated move.

"I said get off your horse!" he growled through clenched teeth. "Do it, or I will kill you where you sit."

His eyes told of the truth of his statement. With a calmness that surprised even Charlotte, her mind kicked into full speed as she instinctively assessed the situation, just as Samson had taught her. That Henry would kill her, she did not doubt, and he had the advantage of both gun and sword. But she, on the other hand, had her parasol!

She grinned to herself as she unhooked her foot from the stirrup and slipped from her horse, making it appear that she had given into to his demands. Yet she gripped her parasol, knowing that if she were to survive this ordeal, she would have to get closer to Henry — much, much closer.

"What is it you want, Henry?" she asked as she turned to see that he too had dismounted.

"This is all your bloody fault, Lady *bloody* Winters. All your bloody fault!"

His right hand waved the pistol towards her, the movement of its barrel punctuating every word as he transferred his riding crop firmly into his left hand. His face was now contorted into an ugly mask, the anger radiating from the man palpable, giving Charlotte every reason to suspect that the man was about to lose control.

"In what way, Henry?"

As she spoke, she calmly took a half step closer to him, knowing she had to get still closer if she was to have any chance of beating the threat of the pistol. Every movement she made was slow, calm and assured, and it was clear that Henry found her composure infuriating, for the man's reply poured out in a rant that reminded Charlotte of an unstoppable tempest crashing onto the shores of her beloved Jamaica.

"You stopped me from courting Lady Anne, and made me

look a fool in doing so," he hissed. "We should be married by now, that was the plan. That dowry of hers should be mine, as should Thorpe Hall. For God's sake, I no longer even have the money that my man, Whitfield, was screwing out of those idiot tenant farmers on the estate. Instead, I have to be content with the meagre pittance my father gives me. I have even had to quit London to move back in with my father here, for I can no longer afford to stay at my club. Do you realise how humiliating that is, Lady bloody Winters?"

Charlotte took another half step towards him, her eyes fixed upon his, even though the ugly hexagonal barrel of the flintlock pistol pointed directly at her heart. Henry was clearly agitated, and Charlotte knew, from bitter experience, what that could mean.

"And what would you like me to do about it, my lord?" she asked.

Slowly, so as to not draw suspicion, Charlotte shifted her grip on her parasol, firmly holding it just below the handle. Then she took yet another half step towards her stepbrother and deliberately allowed a flash of fear to pervade her eyes.

"Oh, you will see." Henry grinned. "A bitch like you needs putting in her place, needs teaching some manners. I am a baron, and you are nothing but some pretentious gutter trash from the slums of bloody Jamaica. My father agrees, too. It was even he who suggested I should teach you a lesson, and, if nothing else, we Hamilton's know how to do that. God, I am going to enjoy this. I am going to fuck you, Lady bloody Charlotte. I am going to fuck you and beat you like the bitch you are until you scream for bloody mercy, just like my father does to my mother. And then, my dear, I am going to put a ball through your tiny little brain before I take back what is mine."

In a feigned move, Charlotte cowered away from him, allowing an expression of total panic to show on her face. Yet her mind remained serenely calm. Yes, he had the advantage of pistol and riding cop. She, however, had the element of surprise, for Henry had absolutely no idea what was to come.

Henry once more gestured with his pistol, pointing the way towards a stand of trees that would hide them from the path. Charlotte froze on the spot.

"I said, in there, my lady," Henry growled.

Inwardly, Charlotte grinned for, in his ill-advised confidence, Henry took a step closer, ostensibly to grasp her by the arm, and the moment she had been waiting for arrived.

Samson would have been so proud, for Charlotte's first and second strikes were timed to perfection. She drove the point of her parasol violently into Henry's solar plexus, her follow-through striking him across the fist that held the pistol, a blow so hard that it clearly shattered bones in his hand. With a piercing girlish scream, the baron doubled over in pain, the pistol dropping harmlessly to the ground. Again, Charlotte swung her parasol, brandishing it as the fighting stick Samson had designed it to be. She danced to the side of the man and allowed the solid ivory shaft of the parasol to whip brutally across his shins. As he fell forward, his face met the open palm of her left hand in a perfect Dambe strike, his nose breaking in a gush of blood. Once more, the perfectly balanced parasol spun effortlessly in her hand, the solid silver finial making exactly the right contact with the back of his head, and she watched in abject satisfaction as Henry slumped unconscious to the ground.

"Now who" — she grinned, as her booted foot shot out to kick him in the ribs — "is fucking who, my lord?" She kicked out twice more for good measure.

It took every ounce of strength she possessed to drag her stepbrother's inert body towards a small tree and prop his unconscious form against the trunk, leaving only his legs stretched out before him. Then, taking the silk scarf from around her neck, she securely tied his hands behind the tree. Only then did she return to where the horses were now grazing peacefully to retrieve the pistol that he had so thoughtfully provided for her.

It did not take long for Henry to regain consciousness, and Charlotte watched on silently as he struggled against his bonds, his body and legs shaking in vain as he discovered how securely he was tied. Again and again, he pushed and pulled, his body convulsing as he fought against the bonds that were now cutting into his wrists, every foul word that was known to man pouring out of his mouth as he did so. Unfazed, she stood before him until eventually she lost patience and lashed out once more with her parasol, the silver head striking painfully on his kneecap, making him scream in pain.

"You fucking bitch!" he yelled once more as he struggled even harder.

"Well, well! That is no way to talk to a lady, Henry," she admonished.

Mistakenly, she leant her head slightly towards him, and unable to do anything else, Henry just hawked and spat at her, a big globule of bloody saliva landing squarely on the bodice of her riding habit.

"Now that really wasn't very pleasant, Henry, and if you do it again, I will be forced to tap you once more." She spun her parasol effortlessly in one hand to emphasise her expertise with her chosen weapon and watched as Henry tried once more to recoil from her.

"Bugger off, bitch," he mumbled.

"Oh no, my lord. I don't think so."

Smiling sweetly, Charlotte brought forward the pistol and watched as fear flickered across her brother's face. Very deliberately, so Henry could not misunderstand her intent, Charlotte raised the gun and pushed its barrel in front of his mouth, ignoring the man's groan.

"Do not make the mistake of thinking I have not the courage nor the skill to use this, my lord, for you will not be the first man I have had to kill," she warned with an unmistakably hard voice.

"Fuck off," he said.

Viciously, Charlotte slapped him across the face with the shaft of her parasol, the blow so hard that it whipped his head sideways as he let out another squeal of pain.

"Think not that you can bully me, Henry Hamilton, for you are in no position to do so. Besides, I think I have demonstrated, quite ably, that I am more than capable of protecting myself."

Charlotte hissed her anger as she once more stood and took a half step backwards, expertly cocking the hammer of the flintlock pistol with a resounding click that echoed through the woodland.

"I wonder what all of the *ton* will think when they find out that Baron Henry Hamilton tried to force himself on someone he thought to be a helpless woman and then threatened to put a bullet through her brain for good measure. And think what they will say when they find out that very same woman easily bested him, too."

Charlotte snarled, now putting on the act of a woman who had lost her senses. It was an act she revelled in, an act that was, she suddenly realised, not very far from the truth. Her whole body was suddenly aching to pull the trigger of her gun, to watch the ball enter the man's skull as his brains splashed out onto the tree trunk behind him. It would be so easy.

Slowly she closed her eyes and breathed deeply to calm herself as she decided upon her course of action.

"I once had occasion to warn you of the consequences of not behaving like a gentleman, Henry. 'Tis obvious that you did not heed that warning. So now I must decide what I am going to do about it—must decide what punishment to mete out. I suppose I could put a bullet through your black heart and blame your death on highwaymen. What is certain is that no one would possibly suspect a poor and weak woman such as myself of doing such a thing."

She paused then, and for effect, she giggled manically.

"But no, I think not that, for that punishment would be simply too swift. I know! I know just the thing! I think I am going to geld you, my lord. Yes, that is what I will do! I'm going to shoot off your balls, my lord."

Slowly and very deliberately, she lowered the pistol and pointed it towards his groin, her finger moving onto the trigger as she did so.

"What!" Henry shrieked. "No, you can't!" All the colour abruptly drained from his face, and in that instant, Charlotte knew she had won.

"Oh, but I can, Henry, and you are in no position to stop me. In Jamaica, when a *stallion* becomes too difficult to handle, we geld him, my lord. Makes the beast far more amenable, it does, once his balls have been removed."

Almost leisurely, she pointed her pistol at the point where both of his outstretched legs met at his hips, her finger now clearly moving onto the trigger.

"No!" Henry screamed. "No!"

"Oh yes, my lord," Charlotte snarled. "Say farewell to your manhood, my lord."

Charlotte watched in delight as Henry's face became ashen, his eyes nearly popping out in horror. She tightened her finger, and the hammer fell, a bright spark igniting the powder, a huge explosion echoing through the woodland as the ball ploughed into the earth between the baron's legs. It was then that she heard a slight hiss, and looking down, an acrid smell assaulted her nose as a wet stain appeared in the front of his breeches.

"Eew." Charlotte grinned. "How disgusting! You've pissed yourself, my lord."

She threw the pistol into the undergrowth, before once more leaning into the man's space.

"Now you listen and listen good, Henry Hamilton. I am now about to get on my horse and ride back to *my* home. Then I am going to find Samson, and after I tell him where to locate you, I am going to explain to him what has transpired here today. Please do not make the mistake of believing he will be as lenient as I have been, for I can assure you, he will not be. So, if I were you, if you can free yourself that is, I would run . . . run far, far away, for you have my word that Samson will be coming for you, and his wrath will be terrible to behold," Charlotte hissed.

CHAPTER SEVENTEEN

Charlotte, dressed only in her chemise and stays, grinned broadly at Phoebe's reflection in the mirror.

"Please, Lady Charlotte, you do not have to do this. I can have one of the maids dress my hair for me."

Phoebe sat before a mirror in Charlotte's bedroom, dressed in only in the purest of white stays, her beseeching dark brown eyes staring at the reflection of Charlotte.

"But to do so, my darling girl, will deprive me of the pleasure of serving you, as you have served me for all these years. After all, today is your wedding day, and what is more right and proper than for best friends to help each other dress for such an occasion? Now, how would you like me to do your hair?"

Charlotte picked up a silver backed hair brush from the dressing table and began to attack the mass of curls before her. Phoebe sighed theatrically, yet Charlotte saw her broad beautiful smile in the mirror before them both and she knew the argument had been won, even before it had started.

"In my tribe, it is customary for a bride to wear her hair in braids, so that is what I would like if you can manage it, my lady."

"Your wish is my command, and enough of the *my lady*, if you please. Today you are my friend. Today you are my equal, so Charlotte will do quite nicely."

"There, will that suffice? Charlotte asked. It had taken nearly an hour, but she had managed to create a unique style for her friend, one that suited her to perfection. But when Phoebe did not reply, Charlotte stood back and looked at her reflection in the mirror to see Phoebe fighting back the tears that were obviously brimming in her eyes. So Charlotte placed her arms around her friend's torso from behind and put her chin of Phoebe's shoulder so they were cheek to cheek.

"Now, now, we will have none of this," she whispered as she hugged her friend. "Come on, let us get you into your dress."

Charlotte had commissioned Phoebe's dress from a local modiste, insisting on something extravagant, until Phoebe had put her foot down and demanded a gown more in keeping with her station. In the end, together they had chosen a beautiful sky-blue silk, which not only complimented Phoebe's colouring but would be simply perfect for a summer wedding.

Taking Phoebe's hand, Charlotte led her to the bed where the beautiful dress had been laid out. Carefully, so as to not wrinkle the fabric, Charlotte picked up the dress and held it out to Phoebe. To her surprise, however, Phoebe merely stood and stared, with something of a pensive look on her face.

"I just hope that I can still get into it," Phoebe murmured coyly. "You see . . . I . . . er . . . seem to have gained a little weight . . . er . . . seemed to have increased a little over the past few weeks."

For a second, Charlotte froze upon the spot, her mind slow on the uptake, her face surely showing the confusion she felt. Then, as understanding came, Charlotte shrieked with joy and ran into her friend's arms, the tears of happiness flooding down her cheeks.

"Are you sure?" she squealed.

"Yes, I am certain. I am with child." Phoebe's smile was so huge that it practically cut her face in two. "I have already missed my woman's time twice, so about ten weeks, I think. Possibly from the first time we lay together after he spoke for me."

"Does he know? Does Samson know?" Charlotte demanded.

"No, and you must not tell him, Lady Charlotte, please, please do not tell him, for I wish it to be my wedding present to him," she begged.

"You have my word, my darling, but heaven knows how I am going to keep such a secret, for I am so happy for the three of you that I might die trying."

A little after one that afternoon, a procession of carriages left Thorpe Hall, the only absentees being Samson and James, who had been delighted when Samson had asked if he would stand up for him in church. In the first coach rode Charlotte, Phoebe, and the dowager duchess. She, Anne, and the duke had come down from London that very morning and would be staying at Thorpe Hall that night.

In the second were Olivia and Amelia, both of whom were dressed in pretty summer dresses and bonnets. They were accompanied by Lady Anne, who looked resplendent in a beautiful green dress, and both Lord William Holmes and Lord Peter Harvey, whom Charlotte, for *some reason*, had also insisted on inviting to the wedding.

The third carriage was more of an open cart than anything else and had been adorned with a profusion of flowers. Driven by no less than George Harris himself, it contained the entire household of Thorpe Hall, all of whom were excited to share in the day.

The tiny church was festooned with summer flowers, and it did not take long for the excited congregation to file into the church so they could take their seats, leaving Charlotte and Phoebe outside under the beautiful blue summer sky that provided a faultless backdrop for such an occasion.

It was the perfect opportunity for Charlotte to speak of the things she had on her mind.

"Phoebe" — she took hold of her friend's hands — "before you go into the church, there are some things I wish to say to you."

"Yes'm," Phoebe said with a hint of uncertainty.

"Do you remember when I was brought to David's home all those years ago, and I was given into your care?"

"Yes'm," Phoebe replied again. "Like it was yesterday."

"I was so scared, so bewildered. It was you, my darling, who changed all of that. For on that very day, and without question or condemnation, you simply became the friend I had always needed. When I was scared and alone, it was you that comforted me, and when I was full of joy, it was you rejoiced with me. I will never forget the day when David and I *married*. Whilst not a conventional ceremony, when David and I exchanged our vows, it was you that was there to hold my hand, just like it was you that was there to console me when he passed away. Now hear my promise, my darling girl, a promise that is but one of my wedding gifts to you." she declared as tears began to well.

"Like a sister, I love you, Phoebe, and like a sister, I will always be there for you, in the good times and in the bad. You have my word that, whatever happens, I will always provide for you and your family, just as you have my word that we will always be friends."

"Please, Charlotte, stop. For you will make me cry, and I do not wish to marry with red eyes."

Charlotte laughed and wiped away her own tears. "Do you realise, that is only the second time you have simply called me by my chosen name. Oh, I do hope it is not the last." She hugged her friend once more.

Charlotte entered the church first, and the parson indicated that the small congregation should stand. Slowly, she began to walk towards the altar knowing that Phoebe would be but a few steps behind. There she saw Samson, dressed in a suit of clothes that only a gentleman would wear, looking magnificently male, and his broad grin appeared as he caught his first glimpse of his beautiful bride.

As for Charlotte, she had eyes for only one man.

Standing next to Samson, James looked every inch the gentleman he was. Whilst nowhere near as tall as Samson, he too was an undeniably handsome and masculine man, dressed, as he was, in a perfect suit with a perfect necktie and perfect boots. As befitting the occasion, his face was sombre and serious, yet his eyes told a different story, eyes that were now firmly fixed upon her as she took her place to the left of the altar.

"Dearly beloved . . ." the parson began as Phoebe joined her man.

The entire formal garden and dining room at Thorpe Hall had been given over to the wedding breakfast, to which the whole village had been invited. Charlotte had also invited every single tenant on the estate to join in the celebrations, too, and as the afternoon progressed, carriage after carriage, cart after cart, arrived at the Hall. It was the perfect afternoon to celebrate, for the sun was shining so brightly that it appeared that God himself was smiling down upon the happy couple.

There was food enough for an army, and drink of every kind. A local butcher stood by a fire pit, basting an entire roast hog as his boy turned the spit. To add to the party atmosphere, woollen rugs, specially commissioned for the event, had also been set out on the formal lawn, turning the whole affair into a spectacular picnic.

A number of the villagers had also kindly agreed to bring

along their instruments and formed an impromptu band. As they started to play and before Charlotte could say *by your leave*, old George Harris, with a mischievous grin on his face and a twinkle in his eye, had bowed before her and then whisked her off as his partner in the gayest of country dances.

****

Olivia smiled to herself, hardly daring to believe how happy she felt. To her, everything seemed just perfect. The sun was shining, and without exception, each and every guest was having a wonderful time.

Of course, at the centre of the celebrations were the bride and groom, and Olivia could not help but rejoice for them, for their love for each other shone as brightly as the afternoon sun. Nor could she help but smile as she watched her friend, the Duke of Camberly, dance with a tiny little girl, the daughter of one of the tenant farmers. Her cheeks actually began to hurt as she saw the love in Lord William's eyes as he twirled Amelia around and around, the niceties of the *ton* forgotten for one wonderful afternoon.

But, for Olivia, the best thing of all was the conspicuous absence of both her husband and her stepson. George had understandably refused his invitation and had been furious when Olivia had gone against his wishes by attending. The thought of that worried her a little, but she had decided not to let the potential consequences stop her from enjoying herself.

As for Henry. Well, he seemed to have disappeared from the face of the earth. Not that she minded, for the son was almost as bad as the father.

It was then that the leader of their band announced a waltz for *thems that know 'ow*. Then, much to Olivia's amusement, old George Harris—who seemed to have appointed himself as Master of Ceremonies—began to clear the dance floor, leaving the duke bowing before Phoebe and Lady Charlotte curtsying before Samson.

It was almost comical when Samson respectfully took his mistress into his arms, for she looked diminutive when compared to him. Yet, in spite of his obvious nerves, he took her hand and waist in the manner of a gentleman. As for the duke, he too looked resplendent, his smile genuine as he respectfully took the hand of Phoebe.

Suddenly her thoughts were interrupted by a light yet masculine voice and, looking up, she saw someone she remembered so well from her past. Dr Reynolds, a man of similar age to her own, had been her physician whilst she had lived at Thorpe Hall and, during that time, he and his wife had become good friends to her and her first husband.

"Oh, Dr Reynolds, how wonderful to see you." She smiled as she looked up at the man.

"And you, too, Lady Hamilton." He smiled. "I could not help but notice that your husband, the earl, is not in attendance today. I was, therefore, wondering if you might do me the honour of this dance."

"But what of Mrs Reynolds, of Mary?" she asked. "Surely you should be dancing this waltz with her."

"Unfortunately, my Mary passed away some two years ago," he said in return.

"Oh. I had not heard. I am so sorry, Dr Reynolds. Please accept my condolences."

For a second, Olivia allowed pity to enter her eyes, for Mary had been a good friend and a loving wife. But in the doctor's expression, she saw nothing to elicit the pity she felt. Instead, all she saw was a handsome face with a steady smile—a kind face that, for some reason, sent her heart beating a little faster than it had been just moments before.

"Thank you. I mourn her loss every day, but life must go

on. So, I was wondering if you would do me the honour of this dance in her place?"

Olivia beamed as she took hold of his hand.

As the music started, the crowd whooped and hollered as the happy couple danced inexpertly but enthusiastically with James and with Lady Charlotte. Soon there were couples everywhere, dancing to the wonderful music. Some knew the steps and danced the waltz whilst others, with laughs and giggles, simply spun around and around, making the steps up as they went along.

But then, as she danced with her partner, Olivia saw something that made her heart soar even higher. From across the lawn, she watched Lady Charlotte artfully manoeuvre Samson over to his wife. Then after she had handed him to Phoebe, she had turned to take James by the hand, giving him little choice but to dance with her instead.

Within moments, the crowded dance floor had cleared to leave just the one couple as they effortlessly spun around and around in what could only be described an exhibition of the art of the waltz. Olivia felt herself grin inanely, for as they danced, James and Charlotte looked so perfect together, their bodies fitting like a hand in an expensive kid leather glove. Yet again, she began to wonder if there might be something developing between them, a tendre perhaps. Her mind thrilled at that idea, for whilst James was so much older than Charlotte, she could not think of a finer match.

****

It was as the dance finished that Charlotte called a halt to the proceedings, and with an enormous smile, took hold of Samson's hand and then Phoebe's, so that she was stood between them. Then, as George shushed the guests, she began to speak.

"My lords, ladies, and gentlemen," she said, her voice loud and clear. "I have always believed that actions are sometimes better than words. So now I would like my actions to speak."

With a teasing smile, she turned to George and held out her hand, a hand that was instantly filled with the two strips of silk she had given him earlier that day.

"What is this, Missy Charlotte?" Samson groaned.

"You will see, my darling man, you will see."

Taking one of the strips of silk, she lifted her hands to his head, pulling him down so that she could reach to tie the silk around his eyes. Then, when both Phoebe and Samson were blindfolded, Charlotte led her friends around to the side of the main house, where spread a small complex of buildings. And, with the buildings behind them, it was there she turned both of her friends to face the collection of expectant guests, before removing their blindfolds.

"Samson and Phoebe," Charlotte began once the guests were quiet. "I believe it is customary for the mistress of the house to bestow a gift upon the newlyweds. So if you would both be so kind as to turn around."

Charlotte grinned giddily as she watched Phoebe nervously take hold of Samson's hand. Then together they turned to look at what was behind them. For a second, with the crowd now absolutely silent, they stood and stared, until Samson turned back with confusion on his face.

"Missy Charlotte, what is this? That is the steward's house, is it not?"

"It is," Charlotte agreed. "As you know, when Lord Henry moved out, I discovered that the previous steward had been less than honest with his dealings amongst these good people. Consequently, I now find myself in need of a new steward for my estate, and can think of no one I would trust more than you, Samson. The house, along with the title of Steward, is to be yours and your family's for as long as you see fit."

"No, Missy Charlotte. It is too much," Samson said.

His deep voice was an emotional rumble, and as he stared incredulously at Phoebe, a single tear streaked down his face, the trail glistening in the afternoon sun for all to see.

Charlotte lifted her hand to his face, her finger wiping away the moisture upon his cheek. Then she turned and hugged Phoebe, and the tears began to flow in earnest between the three of them.

"No!" Charlotte cleared her throat, regaining her composure."If anything, it is not enough. There is no palace big enough in the whole world to repay you both for what you have done for me. So go, enjoy your honeymoon, for in seven days' time, there will be work to be done."

The whole crowd roared its approval as, with a huge howl of joy, Samson threw his arms under Phoebe and easily picked her up, her legs kicking in the air as she wrapped her arms joyfully around his neck. Then a few moments later, as he carried his bride over the threshold and the two of them entered the house together for the first time, there was yet another huge whoop of pure unadulterated pleasure came from deep within the building.

"I do believe"—Charlotte grinned as she linked her arm into that of Lady Olivia—"that Phoebe has just given Samson her very own wedding present."

It was only when the sun began to set that the party began to disperse. Of Samson and Phoebe, there had been no more sign. Not that anyone was expecting them to once more put in an appearance. Old George Harris was seen staggering a little as he walked happily back to his quarters in the stables, whilst parents began to ship off their sleepy children back to their beds in the village.

Practically the last to leave were Lord William and Lord Peter. Like the gentlemen they both were, before mounting their horses, they paid their respects to Charlotte, Lady Olivia, and of course the duke. For Charlotte, it was a truly comical moment, for neither could Amelia tear her gaze away from William, nor Anne away from Peter.

CHAPTER EIGHTEEN

James stood silently and watched the byplay unfold as the two young gentlemen said their goodbyes. In truth, he was not yet quite sure what he thought of Lord Peter. Oh, it wasn't that he disliked the man. Far from it. After all, in the time he had known him, he had seen many admirable qualities in the man. It was the fact that his baby girl seemed to be developing a fondness for him, and even though a match between them would be eminently satisfactory, James hated the thought of losing his only daughter.

Just like you hate the thought of losing Charlotte.

He groaned to himself with despondency.

For him, as the day had progressed, it had turned into something akin to a nightmare. It had been a truly marvellous occasion, one which he should have enjoyed immensely. Yet each time he had turned around, she had been there. Each time he had looked, she seemed to be staring back. She had even engineered a dance with him, too, a dance that had left him panting with lust, as once more she had fitted her body perfectly against his. Even now, as she was saying goodbye to Lady Olivia and Lady Amelia, she seemed to be looking at him, mocking him, taunting him with her lovely eyes.

"Blast it! You must stop this!" he groaned to himself as he turned on his heels, leaving Charlotte and his daughter standing there alone.

He heard Charlotte before he saw her, but intuitively he knew it was she that had followed him into the woodland to which he had retreated. His first instinct was to run all the way back to London, to the safety of his townhouse, his club, the House of bloody Lords. Anywhere but there.

But then he saw her, her auburn hair a golden nimbus as the last rays of the setting sun shone behind her, casting her slim body into silhouette. Once more he felt his heart threaten to stop as, spellbound, he found his feet moving all on their own accord — not away, but towards — until he stood before her, now knowing that he had but one choice.

"You followed me," he whispered as he took a step towards her.

"Of course I did," Charlotte murmured. "One of us had to do something about whatever this is between us."

"God's teeth, what have you done to me, you witch?"

Without further thought, he pulled Charlotte into his arms, only to feel her own snake around his neck as she returned his kiss with equal measure, her soft, plump lips a perfect match to his frantic embrace. He kissed her hard, crushing her into his body, not caring should anyone see him as he ravaged her lips. Gradually, however, ardent passion turned into a yielding and gentle embrace. James softened his lips and felt his woman melt into his body, a tiny groan slipping from her throat telling him that she too was exactly where she wanted to be. For an age they stood together, their mouths loving each other, until the disappearance of the sun turned day into night, the darkness wrapping them in a blanket of shade.

Suddenly, James pulled away, turning so that his back was to Charlotte, hanging his head in despair.

"This is madness. I . . . I cannot do this! We cannot do this! It is wrong!" he groaned.

He stood stock still, his mind nothing but uncertain in the growing darkness, only to sense her move closer. Then her hand upon his shoulder forced him to turn, forced him to look at her once more.

"What is wrong in two people wanting to make love to each other, James?" she whispered. "For that is what I want with you. When my David died, I thought I would never find another who would accept me for what I am, for who I am. But now there is you, and I find myself praying that it might be so once more. However, you must believe me when I say that I will understand if you choose it not to be, for the risks you would take to be with me are evident for us both to see. If you command it, I will walk away."

"But that is my dilemma," said James "Despite what my rational mind tells me, I cannot stop myself from thinking of you, from wanting you. I see you in every crowd, in every room, and each time I do, my body betrays my mind. Part of me wishes that I had never set eyes upon you once more, whilst another just wishes to hold you in my arms, to take you to my bed."

"Then why cannot that be? If we are careful and discreet, no one would ever need know."

"What!" James gasped.

"Did you see the door to the side of your bedroom?" she asked.

"Yes, but . . ."

"It is a connecting door to my own room, your grace" — Charlotte smiled coyly — "a connecting door which I would like you to use. However, the decision to do so has to be yours and yours alone. Come to me tonight if you will, for I desire nothing more. However, I warn you, James, that if you choose *not* to come to me, that will be the end of this matter, for I will not risk my heart any further."

And with that, Charlotte turned and walked away.

"Purgatory," James whispered to himself as he paced back and forth in his room, his eyes firmly fixed upon the oak-panelled door. "'Tis the only word for it."

The evening had been interminable, and it had taken an age for his family to finally retire to their respective rooms. On reaching his own, James had simply dismissed his valet and now strode his room alone as his ear listened for any sign of Lady Charlotte.

It was then there was a soft click of a key in a lock, a sound that, to James, was almost like the discharge of a loaded pistol. For a moment, his heart stopped, his mind hardly daring to believe what his body was about to do. Yet despite this, with a mouth as dry as a desert and a heart that refused to work, he still walked over to the connecting door to softly knock on the oak with a single bent finger.

The door opened, and Charlotte was standing there, her bottom lip caught nervously between her teeth, her hands clasped behind her back so that her small pert breasts seemed to be thrust towards him. She was still attired in the dress she had worn that day, but she had made time to let down her hair. A glorious mass of auburn curls now fell around her shoulders and back, little tendrils framing her beautiful face in a most becoming and feminine fashion

"So," she said, her voice practically a whisper.

"So," he replied as he took one stride into her room before turning once more to lock the door behind him.

"You have decided, then?"

"Yes, for I repeat myself when I say that you have me under your spell."

"I'm glad," Charlotte murmured.

His mind thrilled at her words as she slowly placed her arms around his neck and her body once more moulded into his solid chest. Tenderly this time, he kissed the woman in his arms, content to have her body pressed against his own. It was a soft and gentle and loving embrace, their tongues dancing lazily together as they took their time to explore.

Eventually, James sighed and pulled away a little so he

could rest his forehead lightly against hers, his gaze fixed on hers as he smoothed a lock of hair behind her ear.

"It would seem, my lady, that whilst you have no maid, I have no valet either. So perhaps it would be prudent if we helped each other prepare for bed," he whispered.

"It would be my pleasure, your grace," she whispered in return

James stood stoically as Charlotte began to undress him. No words were spoken as she slowly unbuttoned his shirt, each tiny strip of flesh that was exposed being caressed by the softest of lips. And, as she pulled away the shirt, her fingers and then her lips found their way through the hair on his chest to his nipples, lips that smiled when he growled with pleasure as she bit down on his flesh.

He kissed her fervently, sometimes hard, sometimes soft, but each caress leaving his lips tingling with added desire. Taking his turn, James twisted her around and began to unbutton her dress. As the fabric parted, he pulled it down to reveal her naked shoulders, planting a little kiss on the very spot where once an angel had kissed, before searching for that sweet spot where her neck met her shoulders as the gown slid to the floor.

His boots and trousers came next, as did the stays that Charlotte was wearing, their casual play becoming more urgent with each item of clothing that was discarded until, finally, each stood naked before each other, James's cock already standing proud before him.

"Charlotte, before, when we were together you . . . er . . . knelt before me," James stuttered. His cheeks were heated from what he was about to ask, but he was powerless to stop himself from making the request. "Would you . . . would you . . . er . . . would you, please . . . you know?"

"Would you like me to suck your cock, James? Is that it? Is that what you want?" With a grin as she sank gracefully to her knees before him.

"God, yes," he groaned.

"Then your wish is my command, your grace,"

She continued to smile as she took hold of his manhood lightly with one hand and pulled him towards her perfect mouth.

Breathless with anticipation, James closed his eyes. He felt first a kiss on the very end of his cock followed by the moist warmth of her mouth as she slowly enveloped him, her lips stretching to accommodate his girth as she slid further down his length."By God," he whispered, "that feels incredible."

For James, the sensations he felt as Charlotte made love to his cock with her mouth were unbelievable. But he also wanted to see her more clearly, so he gathered up her hair in his hand, and when she looked up at him with her big blue eyes, he rewarded her with a growl of animal lust that came with the pure unadulterated pleasure he felt. For him, the sensations she elicited were like nothing else on earth, and the sight of his cock slipping in and out of her plump red lips nearly had him spiralling out of control.

Perhaps Charlotte sensed this too, for she slipped him from her mouth and proceeded to lick and lap at his flesh instead. Then she reached down to gently take first one and then the other of his testicles into her mouth.

"I wonder," Charlotte mused. "Do you know, James, that it is said that one of the most sublime pleasures a man can experience is to shoot his seed into a willing woman's mouth." Once more she put out her tongue and licked him languishingly "So may I ask if you would you like to reach your peak in my mouth, your grace? You can if you wish, for I adore the taste of you." She returned her mouth to his cock as she continued to gaze up at him.

James could only groan and stare back at her. Never before had he seen or experienced anything more erotic than his cock slipping in and out of her painted lips. He had loved his late wife, but she had not wanted to experiment in the marital bed, and even the occasional mistress he had enjoyed since her passing had not offered him anything that could compare. Charlotte's moist warmth enveloped him, her hand moving up and down his shaft to match her lips, and James felt a sudden familiar surge, a sensation he knew would soon result in him reaching his peak.

"No, Charlotte, stop," he groaned as he pulled himself from her. "Not yet, my sweetheart, not yet."

Taking both of her hands, he helped her to stand. Then, almost dragging her behind him, he approached the large four-poster bed that dominated the centre of the room. Inelegantly, on her knees, Charlotte shuffled onto the bed and was about to turn when he moved his body behind her. He wanted to be in control this time, he wanted to explore, so he pushed his naked chest against her back and pressed his cock hard against her bottom.

He turned her head and kissed her deeply, and she shivered with pleasure as he caressed her body, his fingers taking their time to explore her curves. He cupped her breasts and then took hold of her engorged nipples to squeeze and tweak. He slid his hands slid down her sides, his fingers teasing and tickling her skin as he stroked her thighs. With one hand, he caressed the crease between the rounded mounds of her buttocks, searching for her little rosebud. His other hand reached around her body to rest between her legs, no longer worrying about what he would find there.

To his disappointment, James felt Charlotte flinch a little as he touched her there. She pulled away from him, perhaps thinking he would not be ready for what he would encounter between her legs. Instead, to his delight, she moved over to the side of the bed, reaching for her bottle of oil. Then she lay over the edge of the bed and pointed her rounded buttocks at him, smiling enticingly as she handed over the bottle.

Sliding from the bed, James stood behind her and grinned as he uncorked the bottle, pouring a few drops of the liquid onto her pert little bottom. Slowly his fingers massaged the oil into her flesh, and Charlotte shuddered as he played with her puckered rosebud, his finger turning in small circles around her opening. Then Charlotte took hold of one of his hand, her fingers holding one of his as she showed him exactly what she wanted. Pouring on a little more oil, James happily obliged, and very gently he slipped his finger inside her body.

Charlotte squealed as he penetrated her depths, the look of satisfaction on her face telling him his actions must be sending incredible pulses of pleasure throughout her body. He pushed his finger in more deeply and then pulled out. Then he pushed in once more, gently fucking her with his finger, opening her flesh to make her ready to receive him.

It was then a wicked thought entered his mind, and before she could stop him, he bent his head towards her exposed anus and used his tongue to slowly lick her opening, just as she had done to his cock but moments before. Her reaction almost made him laugh, for her whole body quivered beneath him as she involuntarily squealed out loud once more.

Knowing without any shadow of doubt that the moment was right, he took hold of the bottle once more. He quickly coated his cock with the slippery liquid and then, standing behind her, James positioned himself at her entrance.

"God, yes, James," Charlotte groaned.

Slowly James pushed his hips forward, hearing the hiss of discomfort that slipped from her lips as he parted her flesh. Then he groaned as he felt her body pull him in, her flesh gripping him as he pushed himself in up to the hilt.

"Heavens, you are big!" Charlotte panted. "Please, James, just give me a moment to become used to your size."

Smiling, James paused behind her, taking the opportunity

to look down to see how perfect her little rosebud looked now that it was wrapped around his cock. Her skin glistened as candlelight reflected from the olive oil that coated them both, and he revelled in the way his cock was buried deep within her body.

Almost leisurely, she moved a fraction away from him, sliding him a little from her body. Then she pushed back, and James moved to meet her. Knowing she was now ready for him, he pulled his hips back, sliding out almost all the way, before pushing once more to ease himself back in.

He wanted, no needed, to take things slowly, as he already felt the pleasure threatening to overwhelm him. So he fucked her with long, slow, steady strokes, his thighs slapping against her bottom each time he entered her fully. As he continued to thrust into his lover, the whole room filled with the animalistic sounds of two people enjoying their coupling, the bed beneath them squeaking in rhythm to their movements.

But then, for some reason, James unexpectedly felt detached — a lack of intimacy in this position becoming a problem for him. So he stopped and withdrew from her body. Hearing her moan with displeasure, he pulled her down onto the bed, and with a show of strength, he flipped her over so that she was on her back, her own little cock now standing proud and hard with the excitement she felt.

When they had first made love, her little cock had been just that, little and flaccid, so it had been easy for him to ignore it. But now, as he saw her hard little cock, he could only think it beautiful as it served to compliment her glorious body. So with his heart hammering, and before she could refuse him, he giddily leant his head down to her groin.

"God ... no ... stop, James. You don't have to," she moaned when she realised what he was about to do.

But James paid no heed, and she hissed as he took her little cock between his lips, tasting her flesh for the very first time as her body convulsed beneath him. What surprised James the most was that he felt no revulsion in this act and, as her hips arched to push herself deeper into his mouth, he licked and lapped and sucked at her flesh, his all-consuming emotion one of delight that she seemed to be enjoying this almost as much as he had, just moments before.

But soon Charlotte was pulling his mouth from her, her entrancing eyes now demanding more. She pulled on his shoulders, urging him up, as she opened her legs for him.

James, being the gentleman he was, obliged his lady, and settled his body on top of hers. Then he leant down to kiss her. As he did so, Charlotte reached between them to grasp him with her hands and pulled his cock towards her entrance, moving her hips, lifting her legs, so that she was in the perfect position to receive him. James did not hesitate, and in one smooth thrust, he entered her body once more.

Then he paused and pushed himself up onto his arms so he could look at the woman beneath him, a woman who was looking back at him with the most beautiful and wanton eyes. For what seemed like an eternity, he simply stared at her. Then a sudden clarity of thought soared through his very soul, almost as if God had slapped him around the back of the head. At the debutante's ball, he had almost convinced himself that Lady Charlotte was an imposter, that the person claiming to be his godson was, in fact, a real woman.

Well, now he knew for certain.

Whilst she might have been born a boy, this person, this woman with whom he was making love, was just that, a woman—a beautiful, funny, intelligent, gorgeous woman! Yes, she had always been and would always be just that . . . a woman. And, what was more, she was the woman with whom he wanted to share the rest of his life.

Leaning down, James kissed her deeply, a kiss that was returned in equal measure. Then he felt her hands on his bottom, pulling on his flesh, urging him on as she wrapped her long legs around his hips to draw him in hard. Needing no more encouragement, James began to move, his hips now beating a terrible rhythm as he firmly fucked his woman. Faster and faster he went, her movements matching his to perfection, her own little cock trapped wonderfully between them as their moans filled the room.

Charlotte slapped him hard on the buttocks, her hands greedily encouraging him still further, until with a shriek of release, she shattered beneath him, her whole body writhing and convulsing in release, as her seed spilt upon her belly. Then with one last thrust and a huge groan, James matched his lover. Every muscle in his body tensed as he reached his peak, his release more powerful than anything he had ever experienced before, as pulse after pulse of his seed shot deep into her body.

For what seemed like an eternity, James lay on top of Charlotte, basking in the sense of completion he felt whilst the intense pleasure they had shared ebbed gently away into contentment. He smiled as Charlotte wrapped her legs around his hips to trap him against her, almost as if she relished the feel of his weight on top of her. Her hands searched for his face so she could bring his lips to hers in a soft and gentle kiss.

"By God, that was good, James," she whispered as she caught his earlobe playfully between her teeth.

"Mmm, good is not a strong enough word, methinks." Gently he rolled to one side, pulling Charlotte with him so that her head rested upon his shoulder.

Then he laughed ironically.

"I still can't believe we have just done that again, when I had promised myself that our first night together would never be repeated. But, by God, I am glad we did. That was incredible."

"So does that mean we can we do it again?" She giggled as

she lifted her head in a mass of auburn curls, her hand reaching out to grasp his softening cock.

"My God, you near killed me the first time. I am not a young man, you know. I will need at least five minutes to recover," he joked as Charlotte lay her head back down and snuggled into his body.

"So you would like to take me again, would you? Does this mean we are officially lovers?"

"Yes, I suppose it does, but heaven help us if anyone finds out about you."

"We shall just have to be careful then, will we not?"

For a few lovely moments, the two of them lay together in silence as James stroked Charlotte's hair with his free hand. Outwardly he was calm and relaxed, yet his mind was in a frenzy, a mind that was finally ready to accept what was clearly becoming inevitable.

He loved Lady Charlotte Winters.

But the fact still remained that she was his godchild, that she had been born a boy. The fact still remained that should her identity ever be discovered, he and his family would be ruined.

And now, in his heart, he could see but one way out of this dilemma, just one way to protect both his family and his godchild. Silently, he moved his arm out from underneath her head and twisted so that he lay on the same pillow, his nose scant inches away from the woman he loved, his heart now beating as fast as it had been whilst making love.

"You know there is one way that we could be openly together and avoid suspicion at the same time."

"Oh, and what would that be?" Charlotte's sleepy words made him smile.

"Marry me." James replied casually. "Be my duchess."

James blanched a little as he heard Charlotte snort at his words, disbelief evident in her eyes. But he held her gaze with a serious expression, and only then did she sit up, staring at him intently.

"My God, you are serious, are you not?"

"Yes, I am. You have captivated me, bewitched me, and I find myself wanting more and more of you, more of this, despite the risk we take. Marry me, Charlotte. Be my duchess."

Her reply was automatic and unguarded. "Oh, don't be so ridiculous, James. How would it be possible? For despite my outward appearance and my most sincere wishes not to be so, I am in fact male, and as far as I know it, marriages between men are not exactly legal. Even my marriage to David was a fabrication of our own making, one which constantly threatened to come back and bite us in the leg like some rabid dog."

James merely grinned lazily as he flopped back down onto the bed.

"I'm sorry, Charlotte, but I no longer believe that you were ever a man. You are, in my mind, a woman, my woman, and I want us to marry. It is the perfect solution. Yes, I agree that there might be something not quite legal in this, but one of the advantages of being a duke is that you can get away with all manner of things. The Archbishop of Canterbury is a close friend of mine, as are several senior bishops. I doubt very much if I would have any difficulty in purchasing a special licence to enable the all-powerful James Beaufort, Eighth Duke of Camberly and the beautiful Lady Charlotte Winters to marry. Then no one would ever dare to doubt that you are anything, but the woman you are."

"No, James, no! The risk would be too great. Besides, I am beginning to love it here at Thorpe Hall and do not wish to live anywhere else. I have my businesses, my plantations, to think of, too, which may someday require my return to Jamaica. You have Wilton House and all your other estates, and your duties in the House of Lords. It would not work, James."

"You would not have to give up Thorpe Hall and could

visit as often as you like, and in truth, I love it here as well. Moreover, my son, Richard, will be returning home in a few weeks' time, and I know he is itching to become more involved in the running of the estates. That would give us more than time enough to please ourselves in which house to live."

Once more James pushed Charlotte down onto the bed, his hands capturing her cheeks as he did so. For a moment his eyes studied her face — her beautiful blue eyes staring back at him, her lips swollen from his kisses, all framed in a mass of auburn curls which lay on the pillow beneath her head. Then he smiled as he slowly leant forward and kissed her once more, a kiss that said *I love you so marry me,* even if he had not spoken the words. He growled with pleasure as he felt her body respond to his caress, her nipples once more becoming taught with lust. But then she pushed him away.

"Stop it, for I cannot think when you kiss me like that."

"Marry me," he repeated. "For in truth, I also lose my mind when you kiss me back."

Again, Charlotte pushed him away, once more sitting up as she pulled a sheet over her naked breasts to cover them modestly. He smiled again, for the look in her eyes told him everything he needed to know. There was no doubt in his mind that she wanted to be with him as much as he wanted to be with her.

But for James, there was only one way he could achieve that in a manner that would protect his family's reputation.

"Marry me," he demanded.

"No," she replied.

CHAPTER NINETEEN

It was mid-morning by the time Charlotte made it to the breakfast room, having earlier dressed without assistance for the first time in many a day. As before, James had left her bed in the middle of the night, and she had again awoken to the disappointment of being alone, of not having a solid body of a man to snuggle up against. Consequently, her mood was decidedly poor by the time she made it to the breakfast room, and she knew she would need a brisk ride after breaking her fast. For her, it was the best way of clearing her mind, giving her the opportunity to think on what had happened. Only then might she be able to face James for what she assumed would be the battle to come.

"Good morning, Charlotte," a voice called from the table as she entered the room, her mind in a haze.

A little startled to find anyone else there, Charlotte looked up to see the dowager duchess sitting at the table, a cup of tea in her hand, as she perused an out of date broadsheet she had found somewhere.

"Good morning, your grace." She forced herself to smile and then sat next to her.

The duchess, as usual, looked perfectly groomed and perfectly poised. She was dressed in a beautiful grey day dress that befitted her senior years to perfection, and her hair had been expertly styled. Yet it was the smile on her face and the twinkle in her eye that immediately caught Charlotte's attention.

"Now then, my dear, do tell me. Just what have you done

to my son to get him so befuddled?"

Charlotte gasped as the duchess fixed her with an all-knowing eye. Unable to help herself, she felt her cheeks heat at the directness of the dowager's words and for a moment she remained motionless, trying but not succeeding to look above suspicion.

"I'm sorry, your grace, I am not sure what you mean." She fidgeted in her seat, desperately trying to look innocent, just like a child who had been caught with her hand in the biscuit tub.

"What I mean, my gal, is that James left some thirty minutes hence, to return to London, on some pretext of an important division in the House of Lords. Hogwash!"

"Oh." Charlotte was powerless to stop herself from gasping again, unable to hide the intense disappointment she felt. Her heart sank into the pit of her stomach on hearing James was gone, that her duke had once more run away.

"And that was after the two of you spent the night together." The duchess grinned. "No . . . please don't deny that you spent the night with him . . . for in truth, I got little sleep last night, as my bedroom was directly next to your own."

"Oh dear," said Charlotte as her face heated with humiliation.

"Do not feel embarrassed, Charlotte, as I, for one, could not be happier that he has found someone like you. So what happened? Why, after all that, has he run from you? Was he that bad in bed?"

"God! No! He was . . . well . . . wonderful."

"So what is the problem then?"

For the longest moment, Charlotte sat before the breakfast table wringing her hands together in her lap, refusing to look at the duchess. It was a tactic that did not work.

"Well?" the duchess demanded.

Charlotte winced, for the duchess's tone of voice left little doubt that she was expecting an answer and would be relentless in achieving that.

"After we . . . well . . . erm . . . well . . . he . . . he asked me to marry him, to be his duchess," Charlotte blurted.

"Ah, now I see. He asked you to marry him, and you turned him down, didn't you?"

"Yes."

"But heavens, why? Why turn him down? Is it that you don't love him? For it is as plain as the pimple on the end of my nose that he loves you."

"He loves me?" gasped Charlotte.

That James cared for her was indisputable. Nor could the fact that James found her physically attractive be denied. But when he asked Charlotte to marry him, she had instantly concluded he had done so out of a sense of duty, out of a desire to protect everyone involved from any danger of scandal.

Nothing had been said about love!

"Ah, finally we get to the truth of the matter. He didn't tell you that, did he? Oh, the stupid boy!"

"No, but it would have mattered little, even if he had done so, for my answer would have been the same. I cannot marry him, your grace."

"And why the heavens not? Do you not love him back?"

Inwardly, Charlotte groaned, her heart knowing precisely how she wanted to respond, yet her brain knowing all the words that could never be spoken. Oh, how she wanted to shout to the heavens, to rail on the gods, for giving her the body they had, for denying her a chance of the true happiness that being a woman would bring.

"Yes, I do. But . . . oh, Lord . . . it is so complicated. I simply cannot marry him, your grace. I cannot."

"What is it? Is it your difference in age, or is it that you are still married or betrothed to someone else? For if it is this, I will never forgive you for leading him on so."

Shamefaced, Charlotte looked down at her lap as her mind worked furiously to fabricate some sort of story that would placate the duchess. After all, she could hardly tell James's mother that the sole reason she had not agreed to marry her son was that fact that she was, indeed, a man herself.

"No, please believe me. It is nothing like that at all. I am, in truth, free to be with whomsoever I choose. It's just I have no desire to marry anyone, no desire to be a duchess. Besides, there are people here who depend on me. I couldn't leave, not now, especially as I have only recently regained . . . er . . . bought Thorpe Hall."

"Well, that I can believe, as I, for one, can attest to the stresses and strains of marriage to such an office. But I beg you to think on it, Charlotte, for it has been a long time since I have seen such happiness and then such disappointment on James's face. Could I not prevail on you to reconsider?"

"I don't know. I honestly don't know," she whispered as she fled from the room, tears threatening to fall.

Her ride forgotten, Charlotte retreated to the room she had made her own, the study she used to run her estate. It was the perfect place for her to hide, for her to think, her mind working furiously as she digested everything that had been said. According to the duchess, *he loved her*. Why had he not said so? For she also loved him. But would it have made any difference to her decision had he declared himself? That thought scared her the most, for part of her, a very large part, knew that, had he told her how he truly felt, she might have, would possibly, would probably have, would maybe have said perhaps.

Charlotte was still ensconced in her study when, later that morning, a loud, urgent knock sounded on the door. Without being summoned, a maid entered with a very grave look on her face.

235

"Lady Winters, the Countess of Weybridge is here, with her maid," the girl squeaked. "And I think you had better come right away."

The moment that Charlotte entered the vestibule, she realised that there was something seriously amiss. Standing there, supported by her own maid, was Lady Olivia. Her face was deathly white, the pain that she was so obviously experiencing causing her to wince with even the slightest movement. It took Charlotte but moments to sum up the situation, then she ran to her mother's side in a flurry of skirts.

Instantly summing up the situation, she turned to the maid. "Jane, go and fetch Samson and Phoebe from the steward's house, and tell Phoebe to bring her medicine bag. Go!"

"Yes'm" the girl replied as she dashed away.

Her mother shuffled like an old woman as Charlotte guided her through the vestibule towards the sitting room, almost as if it were too painful to lift her feet even an inch from the ground. Each step came with a whimper, each lurch forward with a whine, each little sound of anguish causing anger to flare in Charlotte's chest.

"Oh L . . . L . . . Lotte," Olivia whispered as tears poured down her face "I did not know who else to turn to. I think . . . I think I might need some more of Phoebe's medicine."

Then the countess fainted, dead to the ground.

Samson picked the countess up as if she weighed nought but a feather and carried her upstairs into Charlotte's bedroom. There, Charlotte and Phoebe stripped Olivia out of her dress and her loosely tied stays, staring open-mouthed at what they found.

Pure anger coursed through Charlotte, for someone — the earl, they both presumed — had beaten her mercilessly. Her back and buttocks were like pieces of raw meat, crisscrossed with angry welts and weals that could only have been caused by the vigorous application some sort of whip or riding crop. Only once before had Charlotte seen the like. On that occasion an overseer had nearly flogged a worker to death with his whip, cutting deep gashes into his back, his only crime having been to raise his eyes to his *master*. David had been so angry he had fired the overseer on the spot, but not before planting his fist in the man's face.

The moment Phoebe had seen the countess's injuries, she had instantly reverted to the healer she had been trained to be. Within moments she had administered a light dose of laudanum to kill the pain and had quickly moved onto smoothing a salve on Olivia's back, a salve of her own making which she had once used to treat the backs of slaves.

"How did this happen, Olivia?" Charlotte demanded, trying to keep the harshness from her voice.

For a moment, a silence hung in the room that Charlotte thought would last forever. So she sat on the edge of the bed, stroking her mother's hair in the most comforting of ways as she fought back her own tears.

"Please, Olivia," Charlotte spoke softly as if she were talking to a child. "Please tell me. What happened?"

At first, Charlotte thought her mother too frightened to say anything. But then Olivia gave out a sob and began to speak.

"My husband is not an easy man. When he is in his cups, as he was last night, he likes to force his attentions on me, and causing me pain seems to heighten his enjoyment. Oh God . . . his . . . his . . . er . . . favoured method is to have me on my hands and knees so he can mount me like a prize stallion whilst, at the same time, using his riding crop to punish me for whatever misdemeanour he deems fit to find."

"Oh, the bastard," Charlotte muttered.

"This is not the first time this has happened, as you might have guessed Last night, though, was particularly bad. I have never seen the man so angry. At first, he just raved like a lunatic, saying all sorts of vile things, mainly about you, Lotte. Amelia was so distraught and frightened that she locked herself into her bedroom. But then he forced his way into my bedroom. Oh God, he forced me and did this to me, Charlotte!" She moaned again as a spasm pain once more rippled through her body.

"But what brought this on? What could you possibly have done to deserve this?" Charlotte spluttered.

"I went against his will and attended the wedding. Then I was seen, Charlotte. I was seen dancing with an old friend at the wedding breakfast," she whispered. "He blamed me for taking you to the Manor, too." Olivia groaned. "Blamed me for you wanting to buy Thorpe Hall in the first place."

Charlotte sat open-mouthed as the reality of Olivia's words hit her like the hoof of a bucking horse. How could she have been so stupid as to not see this coming? Thorpe Hall and its estates were the reason the earl had ordered Charles killed in the first place, and now, after all that, he had still lost the land. She should have realised that a bastard such as he would vent his anger on someone. Just the look on his face as he had left the law offices should have been enough to warn her.

"Oh, God, I'm so sorry, Olivia. This is all my fault, isn't it? I'm the reason he did this to you." She stood and turned away, now unable to look at her mother.

"No, it is not," Olivia whispered as her tears now began to soak into the pillow. "It is mine. I should never have married the man in the first place. He is a vile, evil creature. I have even, many times, thought of taking my own life. But I have no choice. I have to endure, for Amelia's sake. I have to protect her . . . until . . . until she is safely married. She has said that . . . that I can go . . . go and live with her once she is married. But . . . but until then . . . Oh, God . . . I . . . will have to go . . . go back to him, for I have no money of my own, nowhere else to go."

Now tears were pouring down Charlotte's face, too, tears she tried, in vain, to wipe away with the back of her hands. That was her mother lying there with her back ripped to shreds, and it was her fault it had happened. Anger suddenly rippled through her, anger that was directed solely at herself. She should have realised that this could happen, especially after the last time Olivia had needed Phoebe's medicines. She should have stopped it from happening again.

Well, she was damn well going to stop it from happening again. Once more she sobbed and then took a deep breath to try and regain some form of composure before turning back to her mother.

"Lady Olivia, I simply refuse to let you go back to that monster. You will always have somewhere else you can go, for you can stay with me, for as long as you want."

"But I cannot," she whimpered. "For Amelia's sake. She is his daughter, after all, and I could not endure it should he ban me from seeing her, as would be his right. Besides, what prospects would she ever have if I left him? Think of the scandal. Lord William's father would never consent to the marriage if that happened. Please Charlotte, for Amelia's sake, you must let me go. 'Tis only until she marries."

In a panic, Olivia tried to turn onto her back, her hands grabbing at one of the bed sheets to modestly cover herself, her eyes registering the pain she felt despite the effects of Phoebe's ministrations.

"But . . ." Charlotte spluttered. "No, you must stay here with me, at least until your back is better."

"I cannot. Please, Lotte. Just give me some more of Phoebe's medicine to see me through this, and then let me go. It will only go worse for me if he realises I have gone. Please, Charlotte, please," she begged.

Charlotte felt more than a little impotent as Olivia swung her legs painfully over the edge of the bed. More than anything in the world, she wanted to fold her mother into her arms, to hold her, to comfort her, to tell her everything was going to be all right. More than anything in the world, she wanted to tell her mother the truth, the whole truth. Perhaps if she knew who she was, her mother would accept her help. After all, she had enough money — enough money a hundred times over.

But, in her heart, she knew her mother was right. What hope would there be for Amelia should the countess leave the earl, even if it meant risking her own life to stay? Amelia would be ostracised by the *ton* for her mother's *indiscretions* and would never be able to marry William. What was even worse, the poor girl would probably end up being married off by the earl in some sordid business deal.

No! This could not happen! This would never happen.

And Charlotte knew exactly how she was going to prevent it.

"Very well, Lady Olivia. Whilst it is against my better judgement, I will let you go. For Amelia's sake, you must do what you think is right." she acquiesced.

As will I, as will I!

Chapter Twenty

"Are you sure you want to go through with this, Missy Charlotte?" Samson asked. For such a big man, his words were so softly spoken that they practically disappeared into the cold night breeze, and Charlotte had to strain to hear what he was saying.

"There is no other way, Samson. Had the earl not beaten my mother half to death, I might have been content with his financial ruin. But now this has to be done, for I will not risk further the lives of my mother and my sister at his hands. And it has to be done tonight, for I am reliably informed that the earl intends to return to London on the morrow."

Samson nodded and then grinned, his teeth showing starkly against the blackness of the night. "Very well, mistress, shall we be about it, then?"

The night sky was covered in clouds that obscured the moon and the stars, and the shadows in the garden outside Haycock Abbey were dark and deep. Charlotte was dressed entirely in black, as was Samson, her trousers and jerkin more appropriate for a man than a woman. Around her head, she had wrapped a strip of black silk in a fashion that covered her entire head except for her eyes, and in the depths of the shadows, she appeared almost invisible.

Samson led, and Charlotte followed, the soft leather shoes she wore hardly making a sound as they ran towards the house, making their way to the steps that led down to the servants' entrance at the back of the Abbey. Charlotte had intended to have Samson pick the lock to some door, but much to her surprise and delight, a small window had been left slightly ajar, a window too small for Samson but not for her.

Silently, she motioned to Samson, who stood with his back to the wall before cupping his hands. As if she was mounting a horse, Charlotte stepped into the *stirrup,* and he effortlessly lifted her to the window. From a sheath at her side, Charlotte pulled a wicked looking dagger and used it to raise the latch of the window. After an extra boost from Samson, she then wriggled inside, into what seemed like a poorly stocked pantry. She stood still for a moment, her ear against the wooden door. When she was satisfied she could not detect a single sound, she firmly locked the window behind her and then slipped out of the pantry and into the kitchen, one she remembered so well from when she had lived there as a child.

The room was warm, lit by the faint glow of an oven that gave off just enough light to see that the outside kitchen door was not fasted by a lock but by bolts on the inside. She scurried across the floor, and within moments, Samson was standing next to her inside the kitchen.

Smiling, but not saying a word, Charlotte gestured to Samson with an unmistakable *this way* and then cautiously let herself out of the kitchen. Samson followed, the long coil of rope he had brought with him in one hand, and a fighting stick ready in the other.

The house was dark and seemingly deserted, the family and meagre staff that the earl kept all having retired to bed for the night. Slowly and silently, keeping to the edge of each step lest the wood beneath creak under their weight, Charlotte and Samson climbed the stairs towards the main bedrooms of the house.

Even now, so many years after she had lived there, she remembered the layout of the house well, and it took but a matter of moments for her to find the door she wanted, the door to the earl's private chamber. The earl, she knew, occupied the

biggest and most private wing in the house for the sole purpose of behaving as he liked without the knowledge of wife
or servants. But for once, this served her purpose, for it would
be unlikely they would be disturbed during their endeavour.

As they reached the bedroom door, Charlotte once more
paused so she could listen for any sign that they might have
been discovered. Yet all she could hear was the raucous snore
of a man fast asleep in the chamber beyond. This time it was
Samson who took the lead. Holding his fighting stick close to
his body, he pushed down on the handle with his free hand
and opened the door a fraction so he could peer into the room.
When satisfied that the earl was fast asleep, they slipped inside and closed the door behind them, Samson silently pushing across a bolt he found on the inside of the door to ensure
that they would not accidentally be interrupted.

The room was lit by a solitary candle, which had almost
burned down to a stub, and by its light, Charlotte could
clearly see the four-poster bed that dominated the room. Next
to the bed was a small table on which was a single glass and
a half-empty brandy decanter, and Charlotte grinned again at
the sight.

Her feet silent against the floor coverings, Charlotte
walked over to the bed. For a moment she stood and stared
down at the prostrate figure lying there, smelling the faint
odour of stale brandy on his breath, suggesting that, yet
again, the man had been in his cups before retiring that night.

Then she stood motionless, knowing exactly what it was
that she wanted to do next. With a hand so steady that it belied her mounting nerves, Charlotte carefully reached into her
pocket and pulled out a small vial containing a colourless liquid. With infinite care she uncorked the bottle. Being mindful
not to spill a single drop on her hand, she poured the entire
contents into the earl's brandy glass. Taking the stopper from
the decanter, she then poured a generous amount of brandy

into the glass, swirling it a little to make sure all evidence of the liquid was dissolved in the spirit.

Throughout all of this, Samson stood silently on the other side of the bed, waiting for her command. He watched as she completed her task and then, after placing his rope and his fighting stick in a place where he could easily reach them, he very gently sat on the edge of the bed, the mattress dipping beneath his weight.

The movement of the mattress made the earl stir. Instantly, he tried to sit up, his eyes opening wide, his mouth flapping in surprise as if to shout out. But Samson was too quick for him. One massive arm wrapped around the earl's neck whilst another hand slapped across the man's mouth, and despite a violent flapping of arms and kicking of legs, Samson held the man, his grip so tight that the man could hardly breathe.

"Be still, my lord," Samson hissed, his deep husky voice breaking the silence, "or I will not hesitate to break your neck."

The man's eyes widened even further. He nodded and stilled his body, and Charlotte moved to stand before them both. Slowly, and quite deliberately, she lifted her hands and untied the knot that held the silk around her head. Then she stared at the earl as she slowly unwrapped the covering, delighting in the surprise that washed over his face as he saw precisely who was standing before him.

"Samson is going to remove his hand from your mouth now, my lord, but if you once try and cry out for help, he will snap your neck like a dry twig. Do you understand, my lord?" she asked.

The earl nodded, and Samson removed the hand covering his mouth, only to place it against his temple as he continued to hold the man around the neck. Firmly he pushed against the side of the earl's head. The man winced as pressure began to mount against his neck, leaving no doubt as to Samson's ability to do as had been threatened.

"What do you want of me, you bitch," the earl croaked.

"I am here to tell you a little story, my lord, but before I begin, I suggest you take a drink to fortify yourself." She picked up the brandy glass and held it out to him.

"Bugger off," the earl growled.

"Now, now, that is no way to speak to a lady. Samson, if you please."

Gleefully, Samson pulled back the earl's head almost as far as it would go without snapping his neck. Charlotte, in turn, stepped forward and with one hand, she clamped shut the earl's nose, waiting for him to open his mouth to breath. It did not take long, and as he gasped for air, his mouth looking a little like a carp in a pond, she poured the whole tot of brandy into his mouth, only to have Samson clamp his hand over both mouth and nose once more. The earl had no choice but to swallow, his throat gagging and spluttering as the fiery liquid seeped down his throat, almost causing him to wretch.

"Good," Charlotte said as Samson resumed his grip. "Now, to my story, I think. *Once upon a time*, for all such stories should begin with once upon a time, there lived a good and bold knight of the realm. His name was Sir Oliver Royce."

Inwardly, Charlotte giggled as she saw the earl's eyes widen even further.

"Ah, I see you recognise the name from the expression of surprise upon your ugly face, my lord. Well one day, the brave Sir Oliver met and fell madly in love with the beautiful Lady Olivia, and together they made a wonderful life, living in his ancestral home, Thorpe Hall. Then they were blessed with a child, Charles, a son and heir, and as the child grew, the family prospered and were as happy as any in all England.

"But then tragedy struck. Sir Oliver was riding with the local hunt one day, alongside a man he thought to be his friend . . . you, my lord . . . when a terrible *accident* occurred.

Despite being an expert horseman, Sir Oliver was thrown from his horse and was killed, the only witness to this tragedy being *you*, my lord.

"How, you may ask yourself, do I know of your involvement in this matter? I had a very good friend of mine, one Mr Silas Green, pay the landlord of the Dog and Duck a visit. As you can imagine, Mr Jones, the ex-constable who investigated the *accident*, was most forthcoming with the details of the day, especially when Mr Green threatened to put a musket ball through the man's kneecap. Mr Jones was quite happy to recount how he had always suspected foul play, and how you had bribed him to remain quiet."

For a moment, Charlotte paused, watching as the blood drained from the earl's face, leaving him deathly pale, this being all the evidence she needed. Now she knew, without any shadow of doubt, that the earl had somehow been responsible for the death of her father.

"And your motive for this monstrous crime? Perhaps it was that you coveted Lady Olivia. For, in her day, she was considered to be a very beautiful woman. Perhaps it was that you coveted the Thorpe estate, which, at the time, was one of the most productive and profitable in all England. I think, perhaps, it was both.

"As you well know, my lord, Lady Olivia was completely distraught with her husband's death, and for a time, she lost her mind to melancholy. The estate suffered from its lack of management, whilst Sir Oliver's son, bereft of both his parent's love, became a sad and lonely boy. What a surprise then, when exactly a month after Lady Olivia came out of mourning, she found you standing on her doorstep, a bunch of flowers in your hand. Despite her son's protests and those of her friends, in her disturbed mind, you became her saviour. You were someone who could manage the estate on her behalf and someone who could be a father figure for her son. I would imagine that you also used the lure of being a countess to persuade her to marry you as well. After just a few short months you were wed, and Charles was forced to move from the only home he had known, even being required, by you, to leave behind his beloved pony.

"Move forward a few years to the day that Charles was due to go off to Eton. By this time, it had become known to you that the Thorpe estate had been left in trust to him, and you could not have that, could you? So, during his journey to school, you arranged to have Charles kidnapped, did you not? And when the kidnapper delivered him to you, did you not then order Charles' death? What was it you said? Ah, yes. *Find a quiet stretch of woodland before putting a bullet in his head and burying him deep.* I think those were your words.

"Yes, my lord, I do know that you were the one that ordered this." Charlotte heard the earl gasp. "For unbeknown to you, Charles was not unconscious in the back of the cart, as you had surmised, and heard every word of the conversation you had with your man."

"This complete and utter fabrication. Charles was taken by the press and was killed whilst serving in the Royal Navy," the earl snarled.

"No, he was not, my lord," Charlotte growled. "You ordered him killed and have always thought it done. How wrong you were. For instead of killing the boy, the ruffian you hired took Charles to Liverpool and sold him to the captain of a slave ship. The captain was a truly evil man, who throughout their journey to Jamaica used the boy as his personal sex slave, repeatedly raping him whenever he had the whim to do so."

"How come you by this tale of fantasy? Like I said, my stepson, Charles, was tragically taken by the press all those years ago. Died serving his country, he did."

"Only in *your* fantasy, my lord." Charlotte's voice dripped with sarcasm. "But the truth of the matter is that I know for a fact that what I say is true, my lord, for *I* was there when Charles was kidnapped, my lord, and it was *I* that endured the whole terrible and sordid narrative, *my lord*."

"What? What the hell are you talking about?"

"Oh, my dear earl." Charlotte sighed theatrically. "So slow on the uptake as always. Shall I spell it out for you? The plain truth of the matter is that Charles survived his ordeal, and thanks to the intervention of a wonderful man, he, or should I say she, is now standing before you!"

For dramatic effect, Charlotte paused at this point in her narrative, waiting for the penny to drop, waiting for the moment in which the earl would realise exactly who she was. Then, much to her amusement, the earl's mouth fell open wide in abject horror.

"Yes, my lord, that is the truth of the matter. For you see, I *am*, or should I say I *was* once, the boy you knew as Charles,"

"No, it can't be possible," he whispered. "You are a woman. You can't be Charles, you can't be!"

"Oh, but I am, I assure you."

"You can't be. I . . . I . . . I . . . ." he blustered.

"Ah yes, you twice tried to make me your mistress, if memory serves. That would have made interesting reading in the society columns, would it not."

"No, I refuse to believe what you are saying. This is all complete rubbish, the product of a delusional mind," he sneered.

"Is that so my lord? Was I delusional when, as a boy, I walked in on you and Elizabeth, the thirteen-year-old downstairs maid? If I remember rightly, you had your trousers down around your ankles and were forcing her to suck your cock."

"No . . . it . . . it . . . can't be possible. It can't be."

"But it is. Before you, see the boy you once ordered killed, the boy that is now the woman. Before you, also see the son of a murdered father."

"Prove it," the earl demanded.

"I do not need to prove it, my lord, for I already know the truth."

"So what is it you want from me?"

Charlotte paused, then stared directly into the eyes, her jaw clenched fierce and hard. "Revenge, my lord, nothing short of complete and utter revenge.

"When I came back from Jamaica as Lady Charlotte Winters, I had but two goals. The first was to use my money to financially destroy you whilst at the same time recovering what was legally mine, Thorpe Hall. The second was to reconnect with my mother, and to come to know my halfsister as well, a young woman of such admirable quality, despite the father that sired her.

"Much of this I have, by now, achieved. I count both Lady Olivia and Lady Amelia amongst my closest friends. In addition, I am well on the way to financially ruining both you and that bastard son of yours. As you know, I now own Thorpe Hall, something I took great pleasure in arranging. I also own the mortgage you have on Haycock Abbey, having purchased it from a very grateful Bearings Bank. Oh, and by the way, it was I who was responsible for the beating you received at the hands of Silas Green, and it was I who was *personally* responsible for the beating Henry received a few days ago, after your son tried to assault me on your orders, my lord. In fact, I quite enjoyed myself when doing that, especially when the coward pissed himself."

"Oh, you bitch," the earl growled.

"That may be so, my lord, but you, in your turn, are an evil, merciless bastard. You are a man who thinks that he can do whatsoever he likes to get what he wants, just because an accident of birth has made him an earl. You are also a sadistic bastard who delights in regularly beating his wife so badly with a riding crop that she will probably be scarred for the rest of her life."

Hamilton sneered. "So now we come to the crux of the matter. Well, what happens between a man and his wife is his own business, not yours. I can do what I like with my own wife, and there is nothing you can do about it. For that matter, I will do what I like with my own daughter too, marry her off to whoever I like. Not that popinjay, Jameson, that is for certain. I am an earl, a senior peer of the realm, and I can do what I bloody well like," he ranted.

"And therein lies the problem I face, for you are most probably right in what you say. No, let me amend that statement. You *would* be right, but only if *I* deem to allow it . . . which I certainly do not."

"And what do you think you can do to stop me?"

"Oh, more than you could possibly know. Perhaps I could continue to ruin you financially, but where would the fun be in that? Alternatively, I could have you hauled before the House of Lords, to stand trial for the murder of my father. Sadly, that is a process that would probably exonerate you, thanks to an irrational need for the Lords to protect their own and a lack of physical evidence to support my claims.

"So, instead, I have but one choice open to me if I am to protect both my mother and my sister from you. Instead of taking you before a magistrate or before the House of Lords, I hereby appoint myself as judge and jury to hear your case in their stead."

"What . . . what . . ." the earl moaned. "No. You can't. I am an earl. You can't."

"Oh, but I can . . . and I have. George Hamilton, Earl of Weybridge, I accuse you of the murder of my father, Sir Oliver Royce. I also accuse you of the attempted murder of Charles Royce, of myself that is, and I accuse you of the sadistic and systematic abuse of your wife, the Countess of

Weybridge. What say you, Samson?" she asked.

"Guilty, my lady," Samson growled from behind the earl.

"Guilty," she agreed. "A unanimous verdict, I'm afraid. And the sentence, Samson?"

"Death," Samson rumbled.

"Death it is." Charlotte replied in a voice so soft that it was nearly swallowed by the night.

For a second, the earl stared incredulously as if he could not believe what he was hearing. But then he laughed, a noise that was little more than a superior, smug snort, yet still a laugh.

"This is a farce," he sneered. "You would not dare harm me. I am an earl, a peer of the realm. You murder me, and every constable in England will come looking for you. My son will not rest until he discovers who it was that ended my life."

"Oh, I think you overestimate Lord Henry's ability to do anything, *stepfather*, especially as he is currently in hiding, running for his life like the coward he is. Besides, once you are gone, and if I deem him worthy, he will be far too busy playing at earl and desperately trying to save himself from the bankruptcy that I may choose to impose. But none of this actually matters to you, for whether you realise it or not, the sentence has already been served, my lord."

"What? No! No, please, do not do this? Please, stop this madness," the earl begged.

"Is that how my mother begged you to stop, my lord, when you were turning her back into strips of raw meat. And did my father beg for mercy when you tipped him from his horse and brained him with a rock? It is certainly how I begged for the rape to stop, when I was but a boy! At least your death will be painless. Perhaps you can already feel the poison that was in your brandy. My companion, Phoebe, is quite adept when it comes to these sorts of things. Soon your heart will begin to slow, my lord, as will your breathing. Slower and slower your heart will beat until, finally, it is going to stop altogether. And no one will ever suspect foul play. A seizure of the heart, the doctors will say, too much stress, too much consumption of brandy brought on by worry over the debts you have, over the disappearance of your son, they will say. Then your body will be laid to rest, and my mother and I will rejoice at the passing of an evil man." She hissed as she took a step back.

"No, please, you can't," the earl groaned.

"Oh, but I can . . . and I have! Samson, if you please," Charlotte commanded. "I do not wish to hear another word from this filth."

It took another thirty minutes for the earl to die. For the whole of that time, Samson kept hold of the man, his hand firmly over his mouth so that he could not cry out, so he could not beg for forgiveness. Charlotte, for her part, stood and stared, never for a second taking her cold, hard gaze from his eyes — eyes that pleaded with her until the very end.

Only at the finish did the earl's body begin to convulse, as he desperately fought for life, but gradually his rasping breaths slowed until glassy eyes stared unseeing up at the canopy of his bed.

"So, it is done," Samson said as he stood and collected his fighting stick and rope, the only evidence that could possibly incriminate them. "Now, Missy Charlotte, may I please get back to my bride, for I am sorely missing the warmth of her bed!"

"Yes." Charlotte chuckled with a note of amusement. "Come, let us be away."

Carefully, Samson uncoiled the rope he had brought and looped it around one leg of the large four-poster bed. He then pushed open the bedroom window and threw both ends of the rope down to the ground, before turning back to

Charlotte.

She smiled. "You first, just in case your great bulk moves the bed."

Silently, after tucking his fighting stick into his belt, Samson clambered through the open window, and whilst Charlotte once more covered her face with silk, he swiftly descended to the ground. Now alone, Charlotte posed the body within its bed, making sure to leave it in a natural position beneath the bedclothes. Then she paused to look around, checking that no evidence was left behind. The kitchen door was bolted from the inside as was the pantry window, leaving no indication that anyone had affected an entry to the house. She slipped silently over to the bedroom door, now that there was no fear of the earl calling out, and pulled back the bolts to make it appear as normal in the morning. Then, after one last pitying look at the earl's body, she too climbed from the room, partially closing the window behind her to make it look as if it had been opened from the inside against the heat of the night. As she reached the ground, Samson pulled on one end of the rope, the other slipping easily through the gap in the window, before the two of them faded noiselessly back into the night.

Chapter Twenty-One

It was a little after midday when Charlotte heard the carriage as it came hurtling up the driveway towards the house, her heart knowing exactly who it would be. Phoebe sat with her in the parlour, blooming in the early stages of pregnancy, and the two of them shared a knowing glance as, moments later, Lady Olivia came tearing into the room unannounced, a look of pure joy fixed to her face.

Just for a moment, the two of them stood facing each other in silence. Then, with a whoop of joy, Olivia was in her arms, hugging her fiercely as a flood of happy tears poured down her face.

"He's dead, Charlotte, George is dead. The man is dead, Charlotte."

"What!

"George is dead. His valet found him this morning. He's dead, Charlotte. They found him in his bedchamber, stiff as a board, they did. Oh, Lotte, I am finally free of the man. I'm free!"

Charlotte tried very hard to stand dispassionately, her heart pounding violently. After all, there was still a remote chance that something might have been found amiss. Yet she played her part to perfection as she stood before Lady Olivia.

"Tell me. What has happened? Slowly now," she demanded.

"When George's valet brought him his breakfast this morning, he found George in his bed, as dead as a doormat. Dr Hall was called for and he diagnosed a failure of the heart. There

254

could be no mistake, Charlotte. George is dead. I am free of him, Charlotte, free," she gushed.

"That is wonderful," Charlotte murmured as she hugged her mother back.

"My goodness, look at me," Olivia sniffed. "I will be going straight to hell for this. My husband is dead, and I can only think of rejoicing."

"So you should," Charlotte said. "For he was an evil man who caused you great pain."

"And I doubt anyone is going to mourn his passing. Oh, God. I will have to go into mourning. Amelia will have to go into mourning, too. Oh, my poor girl! She will not be able to marry until she is out of mourning."

"A fair exchange, if you ask me, especially as I believe he would not have allowed the marriage," Charlotte said. "She is still young, as is Lord William. If he loves her, he will wait."

"Oh . . . but what of Henry? He is now earl. What if he refuses to give Amelia permission to marry?"

"I think that he will not give any trouble on that score." Charlotte smiled softly. "I just hope he has enough money to pay her dowry."

"What? What do you mean? What has transpired between you and him that might make you think that?" Olivia demanded

Charlotte stood, her heart now pounding in her chest, as she glanced briefly at Phoebe. Phoebe, in turn, simply glanced back, her smile reassuring as she too stood and walked over to the parlour door.

"You are free of the earl as well, Lady Charlotte," Phoebe said. "You know it is now time, time to tell all. If you will excuse me, I will go and arrange for tea and give you both a chance to talk."

Once more, Charlotte sat, this time next to her mother. She took her hand between her own and then looked the woman square in the eyes, her heart hammering violently as she did so. For she knew Phoebe was right, and now that the earl was dead, it was time to tell all. Well, nearly all.

"What is it, Charlotte! What is this all about?" Olivia demanded once more, staring intently back at her.

Charlotte breathed deeply, her small breasts heaving beneath the bodice of her dress as she sucked steadying air into her lungs. She continued to stare at her mother while she carefully composed in her mind what she was about to reveal.

"There is something I need to tell you, but please, Olivia, promise me you won't hate me. It would break my heart if you hated me," she whispered.

"I could never hate you, Charlotte, but I have to say that you are scaring me with your words. What is it? What is it you have to tell me?"

Charlotte sighed deeply, and then took a deep breath to steady her nerves. "It is about your son, Charles."

For the next twenty minutes, Charlotte told the entire story to her mother, only leaving out the part where she and Samson had affected the earl's death. She explained how and why she had been abducted, and of the terrible treatment she had received at the hands of Captain Thaddeus Jones. She told her mother of how she had been sold into a brothel in Kingston, and of how she had first settled upon her true gender. Then she struggled to put into words the joy she had felt as, thanks to Phoebe's medicines, her body had gradually changed into that of a woman. The love she had experienced when she had married her beloved David, however, had been easy to describe. She told her mother of the everlasting sadness that she would feel at his passing, too. She explained how she had returned to England and had confessed everything to James so that she could once more become close to her mother, to her sister, without exposing her true identity to the earl, and she told of how she had engineered the purchase of Thorpe Hall to regain her birthright.

Finally, she shared with her mother her unending desire to forever remain Lady Charlotte Winters, the woman she was and had always dreamed of becoming.

Throughout the entire story, Charlotte regarded her mother as she sat in silence, knowing her mind must be struggling to believe, her mouth dropping wider and wider and wider as Charlotte's tale unfolded. When her narrative ended, Charlotte simply turned her back to her mother and slipped her shoulder from her dress, revealing, once more, the birthmark that she sported upon her skin.

"There, Mama, do you remember my angel's kiss?" she croaked.

When, a few moments later, Phoebe came back into the room, Charlotte was hugging her mother once more, this time so hard that it was difficult to tell where one woman started and the other finished. Silent tears were pouring down both of their faces as they shared the moment, their bodies shaking with emotion. Phoebe, ever considerate, merely put down her tray and slipped back out of the room.

Minutes later, the two women found themselves staring at each other in silence, until Olivia lifted her hands to Charlotte's face to wipe away the tears that stained Charlotte's cheek. It was a wonderfully tender moment, and Charlotte closed her eyes, a childhood memory of when her mother had done this before almost causing her to break down once more.

"This is simply incredible . . . is simply wonderful." Olivia said softly.

Never before in her entire one and thirty years had Charlotte heard anything more perfect. With those few words, her mother, her wonderful, beautiful, incredible mother, had given her hope that she could accept Charlotte as the woman she was. She couldn't help herself as once more tears of joy poured down her cheeks. She threw herself into her mother's arms again, her head resting against her ample breasts, as Charles had done when he was a little boy.

"You . . . you d-don't m-mind," she hiccupped. "Y-you don't t-think . . . think of me as . . . as . . . an abomination, as . . . s-some . . . some sort of monster?"

"No, my darling, although I must say the thought of you will take some getting used to. Yes, part of me knows I should feel disgust, should feel abhorrence, for it simply is not natural for a man to want to be a woman. But you are my child, and I never once stopped hoping that one day you would find your way home to me. Now that God has seen fit to return you to me, nothing has changed. You are still my child, a child that I will always love unconditionally, irrespective of the guise you wear."

For a moment, Olivia was quiet as she stroked Charlotte's hair, her own tears silently dripping down her face once more. Unexpectedly, she then suddenly and excitedly gasped aloud and pulled Charlotte up to gain her attention, acceptance washing over her expression like a tidal wave.

"No, it is not a guise you wear, is it? Even as a child you had a gentle, almost feminine soul. Perhaps even the soul of a woman. That is it, isn't it! You are a woman, are you not? A woman in every respect, a beautiful vibrant woman, a Lady! And you always have been, haven't you, my darling?" she asked.

"Yes! God, yes!" Charlotte cried, her heart overflowing.

"Then, as far as I am concerned, it is my daughter that is sitting here in my arms, not my son. Oh, my! I have another daughter!" she rejoiced.

"Do you remember, Mama, that day when you showed me my father's will and explained to me how Thorpe Hall had been left in trust for me?" Charlotte asked a few minutes later, as she once more wiped away her tears.

"Yes, my darling, like it was yesterday," Olivia whispered.

"That day, I promised that, when I grew up, you and I would live happily ever after in Thorpe Hall."

"Yes," she croaked.

Suddenly, Charlotte laughed and sniffed, all at the same time, a snort and a giggle coming from her as she pointed to her breasts."Well, as you can see, mama, I am all grown up. So how would you and Amelia like to come and live with me here?"

For a second, Olivia gave Charlotte a sceptical look. Then she grinned, a grin that almost immediately disappeared as yet another thought obviously occurred to her.

"But what about Henry? I'm sure he will have something to say about that. After all, Amelia and I are now financially dependent upon him, and I am certain he will try and assert his authority over his sister."

Charlotte chortled as she thought back to the moment when Henry had pissed himself and then once more glanced at her mother's eyes glistening in the afternoon sun that was streaming into the parlour.

"One thing you are not, mama, is financially dependent upon Henry, for I have enough money to last three lifetimes. Besides, I do not think that we will have to worry about him, for in truth, and in so many ways, I own the man! He will be of no bother, I can promise you that."

Her words made Olivia grin once more.

"Oh . . . Oh," Olivia gasped. "I have just realised something. It was you that paid for Amelia's coming out gowns, wasn't it?"

"Guilty as charged," laughed Charlotte. "And I will pay her dowry, too, if I have to."

"I don't think that will be necessary, for William has already told me that he intends to marry Amelia, even if it means their elopement to Gretna Green! But what *are* we going to tell her about you?"

"Nothing," Charlotte insisted. "And you must promise me, Mama, that you will never speak of this with her. Promise me, Mama."

"Yes, of course. But why? Surely she has a right to know. After all, you are her brother . . . er . . . sister."

"No," Charlotte insisted. "Before today there were but three people who knew of my true identity — Phoebe, Samson, and the Duke of Camberly. Now there are four, and I would like to keep it that way so that I can maintain my position in society as Lady Charlotte Winters. To Amelia, I will be . . . be like the aunt she never had."

"But what will I tell her, what excuse will I use to explain why we will now be living here?"

"Does that mean that you will, Mama?"

"I would love nothing more, my darling."

"Then we will tell her that we have agreed to be companions to each other . . . or some such. I would imagine it will be of great comfort to her to know that, once she is married to William, you will be well looked after. I refuse to risk you living in Haycock Abbey once Henry has taken up the earldom. So, if I have to, until you are both out of mourning, I will even rent you a house in London and provide you with funds. Then once Amelia is safely married to William, you can live with her, or come and live here with me! Or even both!"

Olivia once more gasped aloud, apparently another thought crossing her mind. Judging by the look on her face, it was a very serious one, too.

"But what of the duke, what of James? I thought that you and he . . . Oh! Oh, my!"

Olivia's voice trailed off as she covered her mouth with a hand, as her cheeks suddenly flamed red. Yet her supposition was clear, and Charlotte could do nought but to tell her mother the truth.

"Ah yes, James. As you have rightly surmised, he and I have shared a bedchamber on more than one occasion, and he is perhaps now the greatest reason why my secret must remain just that—a secret."

"Oh, my."

"But what you don't know is that, after the wedding, he even asked me to be his duchess," she admitted.

"Oh my!" Olivia declared once more. "But . . . but . . ." she spluttered.

"But I turned him down," Charlotte confessed.

"That was not what I was going to ask, my darling daughter," Olivia whispered. "I was going to ask if you love him! So tell me, daughter. Do you? Do you love James?"

"Yes."

"And does he love you?"

"Yes, I think so, although he has not directly declared himself."

"And do you want to be his wife, his duchess?" she asked.

Chapter Twenty-Two

Like the milksop he was turning out to be, James was in hiding, having retreated to his study whilst all around the house was complete pandemonium.

Ten days before, Lord Peter Harvey, son and heir to his great friend, the Marquess of Blandford, had formally asked for Anne's hand in marriage, and as Anne had already gleefully accepted his offer, James had been only too pleased to agree to the match. Now preparations were underway for a ball to be held that evening at his London home, a ball at which he would formally announce his daughter's betrothal, a ball that would also be the very last of the season.

So, like the sensible fellow he was, James had discreetly withdrawn from battle and was steadfastly ignoring Anne and her grandmother, who were marshalling their troops with the authority and skill of James of Wellington, no less. Even his son, Richard, who had returned from his travels especially for his sister's betrothal, had made himself scarce, whilst preparations for the most spectacular of evenings were completed.

There was, in fact, only one drawback James could think of to hiding away. It had, once more, given him time to think on the problem that was Lady Charlotte Winters.

By all accounts, the funeral of the Earl of Weybridge had been short and sweet and attended by few. Olivia and Amelia had been there, of course, as had Henry, who had come out of hiding to readily assume the condescending mantle of earl that his father had so diligently trained him to be. He had been invited, of course, as had Anne, but *pressing duties* in the House of Lords had kept him away—away from Lady Charlotte Winters, who had been at her mother's side throughout.

Now, despite being in mourning, Olivia and Amelia had moved into their own residence in London, leaving Henry behind at Haycock. Lady Charlotte had also returned to London and had resumed her occupancy of Conway House, much to Anne's great delight. In fact, the only characters missing from this Comedy of Errors were Phoebe, whose belly was increasing by the day, and Samson, who was taking his duties as Steward of the Thorpe estate extremely seriously whilst, James assumed, keeping a very close eye on Henry.

When James had ridden away from Thorpe Hall on the morning after the wedding, he had desperately tried to convince himself that it was for the best. After all, Lady Charlotte was no lady. Lady Charlotte was a man. Lady Charlotte was more than twenty years his junior. Lady Charlotte was his godchild. Yet, the moment he had arrived back in London, every fibre of his being had wanted to turn around and gallop back, mindless of how tired his horse might be, mindless of the facts of the situation.

But he had resisted, for the plain fact of the matter was, no matter how much it had hurt his pride and his heart, Charlotte had turned him down.

The plain fact of the matter was that Charlotte had also been *right* to turn him down, for a union between them would have been nothing short of madness.

His mother, ignorant of the true facts, had been furious with him. Somehow, she had learned of his proposal and had assumed that Charlotte's refusal had been entirely his fault. The way she had berated him had even made him feel but seven years of age once more. Yet, in her own way, she had been right. For the night he had proposed to Charlotte, he had not told her how he truly felt, that for only the second time in his life he had lost his heart. So perhaps, after all, it *was* his fault that he had been rejected.

"God," he groaned to himself, "You are nought but a coward. You ran away, for mercy's sake!"

Ever since their return to London, Charlotte, Amelia, and Olivia had been regular visitors to Anne and the dowager duchess. Time and time again, he had been given the opportunity to speak to her, to set things to rights. Yet he had steadfastly and stubbornly avoided her, choosing instead to spend far too much time at his club or at the House, lest he run across Lady Charlotte once more.

But now he could no longer be the coward, for Lady Charlotte was to be one of the guests of honour at Anne's ball.

The duke groaned, only to silence himself once more when there was a knock on the study door, followed by the handsome face of Richard Beaufort, Viscount Addington . . . his son.

James forced a smile as Richard entered the room. At three and twenty, he had matured into a wonderful, kind-hearted young man, with the easy smile of his mother that endeared him to everyone. The fact that he was tall, intelligent, extremely handsome, and had shoulders the width of the White Cliffs of Dover, did little to harm his charm either.

James waved him in. "Richard, come in. What can I do for you, my lad?"

"Erm, Grandmama has sent me on a mission to prise you out of your lair, Father. Time for you to change and all that," he grinned.

By nine that evening, festivities were in full swing, with carriage after carriage depositing their guests upon the steps of the house. Inside, James observed, all was perfect. A sumptuous assortment of food was laid out in the dining room for supper, immaculately presented footmen with silver trays laden with glasses of wine freely circulated amongst the guests, and a twelve-piece orchestra sat ready to play the music for the first reel.

The dowager duchess was in her element as hostess for the evening, and she stood at the head of the receiving line as more and more guests joined the crush. Next to her stood Anne and Richard—Anne with the broadest of smiles, Richard with his ever-present boyish grin.

James also stood in the receiving line, although he sorely wished he could be anywhere else but there. Inwardly, he was more nervous than he could remember having been for a very long time, for soon would herald the arrival of the one person he wanted to avoid—the one person he so desperately wanted to see. However, to hide his apprehension, he affixed a benign smile on his face and politely greeted his guests, for if nothing else, he was not going to let his daughter down.

And then his heart suddenly lurched as he saw first Lady Amelia and then Lady Olivia ascend the stairs, accompanied by Amelia's betrothed, Lord William. Both ladies wore fashionable black gowns, as both remained in mourning. Yet each had embellished their gowns, Lady Amelia with silver and Lady Olivia with gold—something that was sure to set tongues wagging for their lack of propriety.

Yet it was neither of these ladies that caused James to groan. For there, standing a few steps behind them all, was Lady Charlotte Winters. She wore a gown of the purest white silk trimmed lavishly with gold, a gown that softly caressed every feminine curve she possessed. Her thick auburn hair was beautifully styled and was topped off with a circlet of gold that matched the golden necklace and eardrops she wore. As was her style, her face was delicately painted, her eyes subtly highlighted with kohl and a shimmering golden powder, and her lips a luscious ruby red.

In short, she was simply stunning.

First she stopped before the duchess, and James watched as she exchanged a kiss of the cheeks with his mother. Then she greeted Anne in a similar fashion before stopping to introduce herself to Richard with what could only be described as a flirtatious curtsy, one that was rewarded with a somewhat flustered bow from the boy. Only then did she stop in front of him, her eyes cast down demurely as she curtsied deeply before him.

"Good evening, your grace," she practically whispered.

She then lifted her head, only to capture his eyes with her own. For James, her gaze was like a punch to the stomach, all the air in the room seemingly sucked out into nothingness. He could not help himself, and like the schoolboy he had once more become, he felt his cheeks redden as his whole body threatened to embarrass itself. For she was truly beautiful, no diamond in the rough, but a brilliantly polished stone that shone brightly amongst all those around her. And, by God, how he loved her!

"Good evening, Lady Charlotte," he stammered. "And . . . and might I say . . . how wonderful you look this evening."

"Thank you, your grace. May I, in return, thank you for my invitation this evening, for I was not certain as to whether you would make me welcome."

She spoke the words softly, almost shyly, and for some reason, James suddenly felt somewhat embarrassed that Lady Charlotte should ever feel unwelcome in his home, no matter what had happened between them.

"No, no," he mumbled. "Nothing could be further from the truth. Anne would never have forgiven either of us if you had not attended. Besides, whatever has passed between us, you know you will always be welcome here."

"Thank you, your grace. That means a lot to me," she whispered as she moved gracefully away to allow yet another guest take her place in front of James.

****

As Charlotte moved into the ballroom, she took in a gasp of air. Oh, how her heart had been pounding, and even now she wondered how she had managed to retain the contents of her stomach. The duke, dressed in tightly fitting buckskin breeches and a richly embroidered waistcoat with tailcoat and cravat, had looked so devilishly handsome that it had taken every ounce of her will power to stop from throwing herself into his arms in front of every member of the *ton*.

"Well, that went well," Olivia whispered as Charlotte joined her in the ballroom. "I thought I had seen him looking flustered at the first ball you attended, but that was something else."

"Oh, God, Olivia. I can hardly breathe." Charlotte gasped again as she turned to face her mother.

"I know, my darling. Just stick to the plan, however, and I guarantee success," she whispered before grinning triumphantly.

As befitted the occasion, the mood in the ballroom was light and gay, and Charlotte played her part to perfection. With her mother to accompany her, she worked the room with a grace and poise that set even the most senior doyens of the *ton* to talking. Each lady was met with a confident word, each gentleman greeted with a coy and flirtatious smile, her fan never far from her face as she giggled behind its delicate lace.

Right from the start, Charlotte had been inundated with offers to dance and, demurely, she allowed her dance card to fill. She promenaded with an ancient earl and endured a cotillion with an uninspiring count. She even laughed and giggled with Amelia and Lord William throughout the lively

Scottish reel that they shared with a very young and nervous Lord Braithwaite.

Yet, much to Charlotte's chagrin, James steadfastly refused to take the bait. She knew that he was watching her, for she could feel his gaze on her like the heat of a roaring fire. Nevertheless, each time she glanced in his direction, he averted his eyes, his temper so obviously becoming more and more sour with every passing minute.

The plan had been so simple. Charlotte would be the epitome of style and grace. She would be the perfect *lady* and James would be unable to resist. But now, had it not been for the fact that his own daughter was guest of honour at this debacle, Charlotte was certain he might have damned the world and stormed out to drown his sorrows in the bottom of a brandy decanter.

That was until the Master of Ceremonies announced the first waltz of the evening, the one and only dance she had deliberately kept free of a name.

Knowing that this was her last throw of the dice, Charlotte determinedly threaded her way through the crush, her eyes firmly fixed upon her quarry, until she found herself standing nervously in front of the man she loved. Her heart was pounding, her mouth so dry that it felt like sand, yet still she found the courage to look him in the eye and found the audacity to speak.

"Your . . . your grace, I was wondering . . . wondering if . . . if you would do me the honour of this dance?" she stammered.

Suddenly the whole room seemed to go silent as James stared back at her in amazement. Charlotte knew that this just wasn't done, for a lady of breeding would never ask a gentleman to dance, just like she knew that the duke's first instinct would be to give her the cut, to turn away and run far, far away from her.

But then she met his gaze, with hope in her heart and love in her eyes.

"Please, your grace . . . my love," she asked once more, unable to keep the tremble from her voice, oblivious of anyone who might hear her words of affection.

Then her heart soared to the heavens as he simply held out his hand.

Without speaking, he led her onto the dance floor just in time for the music to start, and for the third time in their short acquaintance, their bodies came together in perfect harmony. Soon they were fluently spinning and turning in time to the music, Charlotte's feet practically floating across the dance floor. The two of them barely noticed when the crush parted, as if Moses had ordered it, to allow them the space they needed to dance together in effortless grace and synchronisation.

For Charlotte, it was as if she were in a wonderful dream. With each turn and spin, the respectful distance between them closed, and mindless of anyone else in the room, Charlotte daringly allowed her body to meld with his, her small breasts pressing delightfully against his chest. As the music washed over them, her breathing quickened with excitement. Her heart began to race as she suddenly became acutely aware of his deep dark eyes staring at her, and even if she had wanted too, she could not have looked away, for the love in his gaze held her more securely captive than any other cage in the world.

It became a perfect moment.

So lost were they in each other that even when the music ceased, they danced on, only realising that the waltz had ended as the sound of polite applause brought them to a stop.

Slowly James stepped back and bowed politely as Charlotte, in turn, curtsied to her partner, her eyes never leaving his for a moment. And then, before she knew what was happening, James had grabbed her by the hand and was dragging her bodily through the crush, out through the open terrace doors, and into the darkness of the night.

Obviously not caring what others might think, the moment it appeared they might be alone, James took her into his arms and kissed her once more, a kiss she returned with every ounce of love she could muster, a kiss that melted her heart and told her everything she needed to know. His mouth was so warm, the caress of his lips softer and more loving than she could possibly have imagined, and for the briefest of moments, it was as if their very souls were one.

"Ask me again, my love," she whispered through the kiss. "Ask me again," she demanded as a happy tear dripped down her face.

The duke grinned. "Lady Charlotte Winters," he began formally, "despite the obstacles we face, I find myself loving you with every fibre of my being. Marry me, my darling. Be my duchess and make my world complete."

"Yes," was her simple reply.

****

As Charlotte and James finally stepped back into the ballroom to face their friends, two more figures stepped nervously out of the shadows beside them.

"Well, well, well." Lord Richard chuckled softly as he turned to his companion. "Who would have thought that the old man had it in him, and with Lady Charlotte, no less."

Lady Jane Chalmers stood before him, her gaze fixed upon his, eyes that glowed silver in the moonlight and Richard cursed himself, yet again, for being such a fool as to go on his *Grand Tour* without first proposing to her. Oh, he had had his reasons, for at the time they had both seemed so young, so innocent, so naive. Richard had known, in his heart, that they both needed time to mature before making any sort of commitment. However, as he toured Europe and had inevitably met many beautiful and available women, it had become painfully clear that, for him, there was no one to compare to his sister's best friend.

But one problem had remained. During his time abroad, Jane had completed her first season, and he had convinced himself that she would, by now, be betrothed or even married. To his unending delight, however, she had not made such a commitment to anyone, and the moment they had once more found themselves in each other's company on his return to London, her beauty and charm and grace had once more taken his breath away. Now she was here, with him, daring the wrath of the *ton* by being alone with a man, and his heart swelled with love as he stroked her face gently with the back of his fingers.

Jane shivered at his touch and slowly closed her eyes. All those weeks ago, Lady Charlotte had guessed that there was someone special in her life, someone she desperately loved and desperately wanted to share a life with. At the time, Richard had been so far away, so far removed from England, from her, that she had not dared to hope. All season, she had born witness to the blossoming romance of her friends, Amelia and Anne, and all season her heart had grown more and more depressed. But Richard had returned home, had come back to her, and now there was but one thing that would make her own happiness complete.

Daring to hope, Jane reached up with her lips and kissed her love. It was a soft, slow, tender kiss, her first kiss, a kiss that was full of gentle naivety. She couldn't believe that she had been so bold as to do so, but as she felt Richard return her embrace with passion and love, her heart simply soared.

"Jane," Richard murmured as he leant his forehead lightly against hers. "A year ago, I made the biggest mistake of my life, and that was to leave you in London without first speaking my heart. But now I have returned, I find myself still loving you with every fibre of my being. Marry me, my darling. Be my duchess *in waiting* and make my world complete," he asked, his words echoing those of his father.

"Yes," came the simple reply.

The End

YOU MAY ALSO ENJOY THE FOLLOWING FROM EXTASY BOOKS INC:

The Sands of Time
Renee Matthews

Excerpt

"Tomorrow, we will once again take to the sands and bathe in the blood of our enemies. The Gods shine down upon us as Agron leads you all toward more honors for the House of Korba." The roar of the gladiators seemed to shake the villa itself. All of their eyes glowed with the desire to win, fight, kill, and prove they were more than the slaves everyone thought they were. Each of them held the desire to die or leave the arena as men with their own wills and desires.

"Look at them all. Built like wild boars," Melantha purred into Atticus' ear. He tried to hold back his laughter. The daughter of Tobias Korba has always tried to play off her desire to be with a man of the sand but Atticus was not blind as the girl might think.

"They are trained to kill like Death itself." Atticus smiled as Melantha leaned away from him as if his violent words were going to harm her.

He watched as the man trained with their wooden weapons. Every single one of them, Atticus protected in the arena.

All of them lived to fight on no matter the level of injury that they might have received. To outsiders, the House of Korba was truly blessed by the Gods of Olympus.

The sea of built, dirty, and scarred bodies made Atticus long to remain where he was. To watch those below him and spend time with them at the end of the night before the challenge tomorrow, he knew there was no way. The burning of the R scar on his wrist had become almost unbearable. That meant whichever Ricker was here, they were very close.

If a Riker was in his world, it could only be for something that was going to cause him problems. No one in his family ever visited because they missed seeing his face and just wanted to catch up. No, if a Riker was here then it was going to end in a fight of some kind. Always did.

Atticus glanced over the gladiators and over to the slaves who waited on the Lady and Master of the House. They were all dear to him. Each of them knew what he could do and felt protected while he was here. Once he left, that was when fear filled them whether they would admit it or not. For a moment, Atticus wondered if he didn't return what would happen to them and if they would truly be all right without him.

"Where have you journeyed off to this time, Atticus," the sharp voice of the Lady of the House, Helena, snapped Atticus away from his thoughts.

The red haired devil of a woman bothered every fiber of his being. More than once, her sudden death had been an idea that flowed into his head. "It would seem that I must be leaving." Atticus stood quickly, not letting her have a chance to grab onto him in protest.

"Leaving," Helena's shout had to have bounced off every inch of the villa. There was no chance the gladiators below had not heard her.

Four sets of eyes quickly glanced over and locked on Atticus' brown eyes. Each of them seemed to search his eyes looking for some answer to their unasked question. After a moment, they seemed to have found it and went back to the person in front of them as if nothing happened.

Atticus looked at the two women staring at him as if waiting to know all of his plans. "I'll be back," he muttered as he walked off the balcony. Not looking at the worried glances thrown his way, Atticus tried to focus on the burning pain and let it fill him. It had been a long time since he had dealt with other Rikers.

He had been a fool. Allowed himself to get comfortable with this life. After all these years, he should have been waiting for this. They too came and fucked with his life and tried to destroy all that he held dear. "If they come near Zacheus or the others, I'll kill them until it sticks." Atticus bit into his lip as rage filled his being. He needed to get out of here before he ripped the world apart with a storm unlike anything they had seen before.

Once the terrible heat slammed into him, his eyes turned bright blue allowing every inch of him too quick to the same. "They are near the old arena," Atticus smirked to himself. No one went there anymore so there should be no witnesses, if, or when a fight broke out. The scar burned as he reached out to see what other Riker had appeared.

An old feeling filled his soul. It was a childish feeling. That same feeling of joy that comes with the first snow, the confusion of a first kiss or the hope of a dream. No one in his family held onto those feelings for long. It had to be the younger ones.

ABOUT THE AUTHOR

Charlotte Johnson is an English author with an obsession for writing romantic transgender fiction. Lady Charlotte's Revenge is her first full length novel, which combines her passion for all things Jane Austin with an absolute belief that transgender people throughout the world have an unconditional right to respect and to love.

Charlotte, who lives with her family near London, has also penned, to some critical acclaim, over 50 other short stories.